VIOLENT DEMAND

BLACKROSE BROTHERHOOD

BOOK THREE

ARIANA NASH

Violent Demand, Blackrose Brotherhood #23

Ariana Nash - *Dark Fantasy Author*

Subscribe to Ariana's mailing list & get the exclusive story 'Sealed with a Kiss' free.

Join the Ariana Nash Facebook group for all the news, as it happens.

Version 1 - Nov 2023

www.ariananashbooks.com

ARIANA NASH

VIOLENT
Demand

BLACKROSE BROTHERHOOD #3

Octavius

Saint

JAYDEN

BLURB

Cast out and hunted by the Brotherhood, **Octavius** is on borrowed time. He has one chance to prove his innocence, one chance to put things right, before Mikalis hunts him down and executes him.

He must find Saint.

But the Brotherhood member-turned-nyk whom they all seem to fear, is unlikely to make it easy. Still, Octavius has nothing left to lose. He will recapture Saint, or die trying.

*

Saint has seen it all. He doesn't care why or how he was freed from the Brotherhood's captivity. He just wants to gorge and f*ck his way toward the impending apocalypse. Is that too much to ask?

The Brotherhood member that's following him? The quick, vicious, but curiously alluring one with a shock of white hair? He doesn't matter to Saint. If he gets too close, Saint will finish him. Because the last thing Saint wants or needs is to get dragged back behind bars. If that happens, this time, with everything he knows about their fearless leader, Mikalis, Saint will tear the Brotherhood apart.

Octavius needs to stay away for his own good, because if Saint catches him, he just might teach him what it truly means to be nyktelios. And how the Brotherhood has been lied to for millennia.

Besides, what does it matter, when none of them have long left to live...

CHAPTER 1

And the primordial goddess Nyx rose up with her undying warriors beside her and banished Erebus, her brother, her lover, to the depths of chaos for all eternity.

- Partially recovered carving from an unknown city beneath Knossos, destroyed 7000BC.

ctavius

OCTAVIUS KEPT his head down and his hood up as he passed a gang of men lurking in a streetlight's illumination.

St. Louis, Missouri. The murder capital of the US, and the perfect hunting ground for nyks. In the past, Mikalis had sent teams to clear the city's north side, but the nyks always came back.

Octavius was here, so maybe there was something to that rumor. Although, he wasn't a nyk, but he was hunting one. Possibly the most dangerous nyk of all.

Traffic hummed in the distance. Sirens wailed and faded. He kept on walking, the same as he'd been doing for the past few nights. Walking, surveying, *tracking.* You didn't have to look very deep to see how the north side's residents struggled. Drug paraphernalia littered the alleys, gunshots were a nightly occurrence. The Brotherhood kept the nyks out, but as for the rest of the city's troubles, they weren't for the Brotherhood to solve.

Causation or correlation, Raiden would ask. Did nyks cause the crime rate to skyrocket, or did they come to St. Louis to hide among the human-made chaos?

Shit, he needed to stop thinking about Raiden and his stupid smile, or the blinkered scientific way he had of analyzing the world around him, and how sometimes a glimpse of Raiden's easygoing and casually handsome looks was enough to stop Octavius's heart.

He cursed under his breath. It had been months since he'd fled the Brotherhood. Raiden probably despised him just like the rest of them did. *Traitor.* At this very moment, Mikalis was personally hunting Octavius down like a dog. If he caught him, he'd put him down like one too.

Octavius couldn't stay in St. Louis much longer. The Brotherhood would catch up to him.

One more night, perhaps two. The nyk was here. He *felt* it. It made sense. Where better to hide out? And this nyk was smart, ruthless, and savage, although likely mad too, like most of them. Outside of Octavius, the nyk he hunted was at the top of Mikalis's hitlist:

Saint.

The one and only Brotherhood member who had flipped back to being nyk. Killing indiscriminately, envenoming his human victims, turning them into blood slaves, causing chaos in his wake.

A cat yowled at the end of the alley. A bottle rattled into the gutter. The clatter drew Octavius's eye.

An intoxicated male stumbled from behind a dumpster. "What the fuck you lookin' at, man?"

Octavius held up a hand. "Nothing, man." *You didn't see me.* He pushed the demand into the man's mind, mentally injecting it, and the drunk human veered away, mumbling about losing his keys. He wouldn't remember seeing Octavius. Nobody did. Octavius moved like a ghost through this world, leaving no memory of his passing, just the way he liked it. There was nothing out here for him anyway.

He'd lived for the Brotherhood, lived for Mikalis, and they'd turned on him at a snap of Mikalis's fingers.

Fuck 'em.

He'd prove them wrong. All of them. Make them eat their accusations. Even Raiden. *Especially* Raiden. Octavius had tried to talk to him, to explain he wasn't a traitor, but the light had faded from Raiden's eyes and hundreds of years of friendship had evaporated in seconds. He had proof, Raiden had said. And then he'd told Octavius to run.

Octavius would show them how wrong they all were.

He'd find Saint, track him down, recapture him, and he'd damn well get the truth about what had happened when the Brotherhood headquarters fell. Saint had to know something. Why else would the real saboteur release him moments before Atlas imploded?

It was a slim lead, but it was the only hope Octavius had.

Six months he'd been on the run. Six months ghosting through the US, scanning news reports for suspicious spikes in murder rates, trying to find Saint, but everywhere he looked, stupid humans killed each other, skewing the murder rates. No wonder the nyk population was increasing. Humanity was a mess, and nobody gave a shit. But finding Saint wasn't easy. All his records—when Atlas had been operational—had been sealed so damn tight, even Octavius hadn't been able to hack into them. And he'd tried. None of the Brotherhood ever talked about Saint, but they were all curious. He had to be monstrous if Mikalis kept him hidden away. But any clues to his whereabouts were few and far between.

3

Saint was the key to all this. Octavius was sure of it.

He just had to find him and stay alive long enough to question him.

At the very least, if Octavius caught Saint, it might buy him some breathing space with Mikalis. Because he was going to need a miracle to survive the Brotherhood leader's wrath.

Another siren howled a few streets away. Octavius glanced down a narrow side alley between two rows of boarded-up buildings, expecting to find another cat or vagrant rummaging through trash. Instead, he caught the blur of something *other*, and stopped. He took a step back and peered deeper into the dark.

A light drizzle fogged the glow from the nearby streetlights. Strips of plastic stuck in a fence fluttered, but nothing else moved.

The distant sirens stopped. Not faded away. *Stopped.* And the flapping plastic froze.

The small hairs on the back of Octavius's neck lifted. Someone was watching. Someone who could stop time in a bubble of reality, with a snap of his fingers.

Mikalis.

Shit.

He wasn't ready.

Even if Octavius wanted nothing more than to look him in the eyes and stand his ground, Mikalis would gut him where he stood.

He quickened his pace and crossed the street. Mikalis could be anywhere. They'd all seen how he stepped from his self-made shadows, as though he controlled darkness itself. But he hadn't emerged yet, which meant he was watching.

Octavius was being hunted.

Fear rarely touched him. A long life riddled with torture had numbed him. But he felt it now, like ice-cold fingers skimming down his spine. *Memento Mori*, remember you must die. But he never, ever expected his death to come via the hands of the one man he'd devoted his life to, the only soul on this earth Octavius had relied on. The betrayal stung again, scorching acid in his mouth.

Lane signals blinked over an intersection ahead, where time continued as normal. Late-night traffic rumbled through. If he could just reach the busier road, he might have a chance of losing Mikalis among the mortals. He didn't like to cause unnecessary damage, as it might draw attention to the existence of the Brotherhood.

Octavius broke into a run. The busier street came up fast. Just a few more strides, and he'd dash across the intersection, then use a mental demand to hijack a human in their car. Get the hell out of St. Louis.

The sideswipe hit him like a truck, snatching him clean off his feet. Briefly weightless, he had less than a second to react, then slammed into a wall. Cold fingers clamped around his neck. Brick dust and blood burned his tongue. His fangs dropped on reflex, but as he bared them, it was already too late.

Mikalis's eyes burned red in the dark. "Your last words had better be begging for forgiveness, *traitor*."

Octavius slammed his forehead against Mikalis's with enough force to kill a man. Mikalis flinched, then lifted his gaze and peered through black lashes with a growl.

Release me! Octavius pushed the desperate demand into Mikalis's mind. But it slid right off, as though there was no normal mind there to influence.

"I know you *did not* try and influence me. You are not that foolish," Mikalis snarled. His fingers tightened. He lifted Octavius into the air, holding him aloft like a prize trophy.

This was it. Octavius's last moments on this earth. He kicked and tried to claw Mikalis's fingers off. Octavius had seen the rise and fall of the Roman empire. He'd seen wars decimate populations, seen humans evolve and fuck up over and over, and now he'd never see how it ended. Even after all this time, all the pain, all the centuries, he didn't want to die.

He grasped at Mikalis's arm, rendered weak by his impossible strength. Ripples of unseen energy rolled off the Brotherhood leader, warping space and time, hiding their fight from the real world. Octavius would die here, and nobody would know it, but worse? Nobody would care.

I... did not... betray you... He pushed that thought at Mikalis, desperate to be heard. But Mikalis wasn't listening. He opened his mouth, making room for the twin pairs of savage fangs that would plunge into Octavius's neck in the next few seconds.

Headlights swept over them. A truck engine roared, and its horn blasted.

Mikalis turned his head, squinting into the high beam.

A moment's distraction, that was all Octavius needed. He bucked, thrust his leg out, and by some miracle, wedged his boot between them. He kicked, dislodging Mikalis's hold, and dropped to a knee on the sidewalk. Mikalis reeled. The semi honked again. Octavius lifted his head. If he lunged, he could tackle Mikalis into the path of that truck—

A liquid black blur shot from down the street, slammed into Mikalis, picked him up, and flew with him into the path of the truck. Brakes screeched, the semitrailer unit jackknifed, and the big rig's monster front grille slammed into Mikalis, exploding the inky black liquid blur. Glass shattered, metal screamed, and the entire truck buckled around Mikalis and the *thing* that had thrown him into its path.

The fuel tank ruptured. Fire boiled, and the explosion came next, blasting over Octavius, driving him backward against the cracked wall. He turned his face away from the heat and noise, weathering the blast, and dared look at the wreck still unfolding in front of him. Ripples of orange flame boiled skyward, dousing the street in firelight.

As quickly as it happened, it was over. Mangled bits of metal rained onto the street and the twisted wreck groaned. Could Mikalis survive that? He'd probably survived worse, but he wouldn't be happy about it.

Whatever had knocked Mikalis into that semi's path clearly had a death wish. Octavius wasn't hanging around to wait for Mikalis to wake up and wipe the entire block off the map.

He turned away, seeking the cool shadows, but movement among the flames caught his eye. A man walked from the fire, or he seemed to be male. But he couldn't be human. Embers zigzagged like fireflies across his black suit and the fire he'd started reflected in silver nyk eyes. He adjusted his shirt cuffs, as though he wasn't half ablaze, then flicked his eyes up.

Saint.

The name burst into Octavius's head.

Octavius bared his fangs.

This was his chance. If he stopped Saint now, Mikalis would have to listen. But also, *fuck*. Saint had just thrown Mikalis into the path of a truck, then set the Brotherhood leader on fire, while Saint himself didn't appear to have a scratch on him.

"*Stop.*" Octavius flung the demand at Saint, unleashing it like a right hook.

Saint rocked back a step. He gave his head a shake, fixed his glare on Octavius again, smiled, and continued forward. That smile was a wicked, curious thing. Full of hunger, and knowing, and a thousand ways to kill Octavius.

Saint had resisted the demand. Just how ancient was he?!

Saint blurred, turning to a liquid shadow, and rushed Octavius in a wave. The shadow swallowed all the light from the fire, or had it swallowed Octavius? He tried to push it off, to fight back, but whatever Saint was, it wasn't solid. Firm arms crushed Octavius close, the shadow coalescing once more into something solid and real. Saint opened his mouth, fangs gleaming, venom dripping.

"No!" Octavius bucked, but Saint's arms crushed tighter. He couldn't breathe, couldn't fight. "*Stop!*"

The mental demand sank its teeth in, and Saint stopped. A puzzled expression softened his face. Octavius wheezed around the crushing pressure of Saint's arms. All right, so he just needed a moment to catch his breath, to figure out how to control Saint.

Mikalis suddenly loomed behind Saint. He swung a metal bar, striking the back of Saint's head, and Octavius dropped to the sidewalk a second time. He scrabbled backward, out of their radius.

Saint spin-kicked Mikalis back toward the flames. Mikalis's clothes had all burned away, leaving just rags behind. His skin was scorched, melted off in places.

They traded blows quicker than Octavius could track, two titans fighting for their lives. This was no longer Octavius's fight.

Whoever won, they both wanted him dead. He couldn't intervene.

Sirens wailed, coming closer.

It was time to get away.

Octavius hurried out of the fire's glow, broke into a run, veered down a side street, and vaulted over a fence. If he could get some space between him and those two behemoths, he'd buy a few hours to put some distance between himself and the winner. He was going to need more time to think this through. Saint's strength had been on par with Mikalis's. And his shadow form? How was Octavius supposed to capture that?

Once out of their orbit, and away from St. Louis, he'd adjust his plan to make sure when he approached Saint, Mikalis was not nearby. And now he knew he could use mental demands on Saint, he'd be able to make him listen.

Octavius ducked under a chain-link fence, entering a train yard. He hurried over slick tracks and ducked behind an old diesel locomotive. Pausing, cloaked in darkness, he slumped against the train's engine, surrounded by the heady smell of diesel and wet metal. Octavius was no easy target, but battling Mikalis and then Saint... They'd made him feel weak. He'd vowed never to feel helpless again. He hated it, hated the uneasy sickness churning in his gut. He'd made sure to be the most powerful creature in the room, always better, always smarter, always stronger. He couldn't be weak. He couldn't stand it.

He breathed too fast. He couldn't lose it now. He had to get out of the city, had to think, and he'd come back harder.

Something crunched in the railroad gravel.

He knew—even before he looked up—who was there.

Black trousers, white shirt, and a black jacket, still smoking at its edges. His smile said he'd won. He'd beaten Mikalis. And now he'd come for Octavius. There was a moment, a second, in which he could have demanded Saint stop, forced him back, but Octavius froze, weak with fear.

Saint slammed Octavius's head against the train carriage, batting his consciousness away.

CHAPTER 2

ctavius

HE WOKE to distant sounds of lapping water, the hiss of wind through trees, and a thumping headache. No sirens, no traffic, no background noise at all. The bedroom around him was basic, but comfortable. He sat up and fingered the bruise on the back of his head, wincing as the still-healing fracture warned him not to touch.

Someone had brought him here, put him on the bed. But where was he?

He recalled seeing Saint and Mikalis fight. After that, little else. Train tracks, perhaps? He remembered the smell of diesel. The more he tried to remember, the more his head pounded.

He threw off the blanket—at least he was dressed still—and got to his feet. The blinds were closed, but he sensed it was past sundown. Daylight weighed heavier on his bones.

Had Mikalis brought him here? No, if Mikalis had gotten to him, he wouldn't have woken at all. Saint then? That also seemed unlikely. Saint had tried to kill him too.

The clatter of cutlery and pans sounded from somewhere in the house. He wasn't alone.

Whoever had kidnapped him had taken the time to remove his boots and place them neatly by the door. They'd also laid him on a bed, not dumped him on the floor. That suggested someone cared.

He glanced at the view from the window, between the blinds. Tall pines and old oaks dappled a gentle slope leading down to a lakeside and a small boathouse. This was a ways from St. Louis. Somewhere in the Ozarks?

Octavius opened the door, careful not to make a sound, and moved silently down an inner hallway. Cooking smells wafted his way, and freshly brewed coffee. Sizzling bacon helped hide any hint of his approach. As he rounded a corner, a vast double-height kitchen and lounge area opened up, complete with exposed oak beams and huge windows overlooking the lake. And there was a man in the kitchen area, dressed in ass-hugging shorts and a loose button-down shirt, untucked and loose around his waist. Sunshine-blond hair and an all-body tan suggested the stranger was from the west coast, California probably. He hummed to music pumped into his ears by two earbuds.

Octavius approached behind him. All he had to do was grab his head and jerk it to the side, and the man would drop like a stone. Strange, his scent was woody, like warm cinnamon, and Octavius knew it, suggesting he knew him, but he couldn't place from where.

The Californian let out an off-tune rendition of "Natural" by Imagine Dragons. Octavius only recognized it because Zaine had insisted on singing the same song every time he beat Kazimir at pool back at the Atlas compound.

The Californian spun. His blue eyes widened. Freckles flushed. He screamed and swung a pan like a bat.

The stupid mortal didn't stand a chance.

Octavius sidestepped around the sloppy attempt at an attack, encircled the fool from behind, trapping him in his embrace, and breathed him in. The fool struggled like a rabbit in a snare. Human, definitely. But also something else. Something worse. He smelled of blood, of cinnamon, of Saint.

Snarling, Octavius shoved the idiot away. "Feeder," he growled.

The man stumbled against the edge of the kitchen counter. "Asshole," he snarled back, baring tiny human teeth.

Octavius snatched the pan from the idiot's hand and tossed it into the sink. "You have ten seconds to tell me where I am or I will kill you."

"Kill me?" The feeder dared scrunch up his face, as though disgusted. He straightened and dragged his blue-eyed glare over Octavius from head to toe. "You won't. Not if you want to live past those ten seconds."

Was this idiot threatening him? He stood there almost naked apart from the tiny shorts, like a nyktelios chew toy, and thought he could threaten Octavius? Did he not know the danger he was in?

"I am Brotherhood," Octavius said. "And now you only have five seconds to live."

He snorted again, ran a hand through his floppy golden hair, and shoved past Octavius. "I'm making coffee. You want some?"

Was he mad? Driven insane by venom perhaps? "You clearly don't understand the danger you're in, so I'll grant you a few more—"

"I'm not the one who is in danger." The feeder glanced over his shoulder and dared a smirk.

A growl bubbled from the back of Octavius's throat. He snatched the feeder by the back of the neck, bent him over the countertop, and pinned him there. *Now* he knew fear. Yes, Octavius could smell it on him. Finally, the feeder understood who he was dealing with. Now Octavius would get the respect due to him.

The punch to his back struck low, over his kidneys, and the bolt of pain that surged through him like lightning dropped Octavius to his knees. Fingers twisted in his hair, yanked his hand to the side. Cool breath fluttered over his neck. A nyk, he knew that much. The feeder's master. And he was strong. Too strong. Saint.

Fear iced Octavius heart, but anger too.

"Touch my feeder again and I will tear your throat out, *Brotherhood*," a smooth male voice purred with no hint of anger, just fact. That ripple of fear and something tight, something sharp, spilled down Octavius's spine. In the next heartbeat, the grip on him vanished. Octavius shot to his feet, teeth bared, and spun, searching for the nyk. But the kitchen was empty, except for the feeder, who was now pouring coffee as though nothing had happened.

What the fuck was this? Some game Saint was playing? He had to be here—

Then he saw him, reclined on the sofa, one arm resting along the back of the cushions suggesting he'd been there all along and hadn't just had Octavius on his knees.

Saint arched an eyebrow. "Do we have an understanding?"

He wore a white shirt and the black pants from the night before, looking as if he'd just returned from a shift at an office job. He didn't look like the kind of monster who deserved to be locked in the bowels of the Brotherhood for centuries, but the oldest nyks were masters of disguise, and the most dangerous. Mikalis didn't look like the ancient killer he was either. He walked among humans as though he had every right to be there, and so did Saint.

With his pride having taken a beating, Octavius hung back and tried to reevaluate the situation. The feeder was Saint's. Saint was a nyktelios—he had been Brotherhood, but then for whatever reason, he'd flipped back to being the enemy—and Octavius was in his lake house, brought here by him after the fight with Mikalis.

Saint was powerful. That much was obvious.

And Octavius needed him, either to answer questions about why he'd been released before Atlas had imploded or to keep him here long enough to give up his location to Mikalis and buy Octavius some one-to-one time with the Brotherhood leader, during which he'd plead his innocence.

"He's a little prick," the feeder said, handing Saint a mug of hot coffee.

The smallest of smiles tugged at Saint's lips. "Leave us, Jayden."

The feeder huffed. "But he's hot, like a vicious little wolf cub."

"Fuck you." Octavius bared his teeth at the foul corruption of a man and watched him saunter from the room. He'd hoped, perhaps naively, that Saint would still be Brotherhood, that it had all been a mistake and he could reason with him, but clearly Saint was nyktelios, which made him the enemy. And the feeder, Jayden, was already dead, envenomed and enslaved; the fool just didn't realize it. Saint's venom kept him compliant. Long ago, Octavius might have cared for Jayden's fate. He'd have probably tried to help him. But feeders weren't worth fighting for, and all nyks had to die. That was the way of things to keep nyks from ruining this world.

"Why was Mikalis trying to kill you?" Saint asked. He leaned forward, cradling his coffee in both hands. He moved smooth, and slow, like a snake knowing it was the apex predator in its territory.

Octavius clenched his jaw and gazed out the windows, at the serene moonlit lake. "A misunderstanding."

Saint laughed, and that laugh touched the same part of Octavius his words in Octavius's ear had touched earlier, slithering beneath Octavius's defenses. He could not let his guard down around Saint. He'd seen him shove Mikalis into a truck. Nobody did that and survived. Yet, here was Saint, acting as if nothing had happened. Of course, he had his feeder to quicken his healing, but even so. He'd recovered fast from the beating Mikalis had given him.

"I'm familiar with his misunderstandings," Saint said, "as I'm sure, as *Brotherhood*, you're well aware." He sneered the word Brotherhood, as though he'd tasted something bitter.

"The fact you're a nyk is no misunderstanding. It's different for me. Mikalis has been lied to. He believes I... He has been led to believe I betrayed him. I didn't."

Hungry delight sparkled in Saint's silver nyk eyes. "There's a lot of history in those statements, more than you're aware of. Mikalis does not suffer betrayers. He will hunt such enemies to the ends of the earth." Saint smirked and leaned back on the couch. "The irony."

There didn't appear to be any immediate threat from Saint or his feeder. Octavius made a conscious effort to relax and leaned back against the kitchen counter. If he could keep Saint talking, he might reveal information Octavius needed. "He'll come for you."

"Oh, I know."

"You should hand yourself in."

Something ancient and sly sparkled in Saint's nyk-eyes. "Should I? You know nothing of me, yet you know what I should do? Jayden is right, you're a little prick, full of your own Brotherhood self-importance."

This was ridiculous. Octavius wasn't playing games with a nyk and his feeder. He was here for a reason. He needed answers. "Why were you let out?"

Saint's smile faded. "'Let out'? Ah, back at the compound."

"Someone let you out moments before Atlas was destroyed. Why?"

"I assume this *someone*, whomever they are, wanted me alive. No?"

He must know more. "Why?"

Saint narrowed his eyes. "Why do *you* want to know, Little Wolf?"

"My name is Octavius."

"I know who you are." Saint stood and approached the kitchen, bringing his coffee with him. He sipped it, occasionally eyeing Octavius, calculating, reading, assessing, and making no attempt to hide the fact. "I know more than all of you combined. It's why Mikalis fears me."

"Mikalis is not afraid of anything."

Saint's smile was back, like a lash of a whip. "Oh, you're wrong, he's afraid of a great many things."

Would Mikalis have locked up Saint to keep those fears from being exposed? No, he'd locked him up because Saint had gone rogue and tried to destroy the Brotherhood from the inside out. Exactly what Octavius had been accused of. Looking into Saint's eyes was like looking into Octavius's future. But Octavius would rather die than turn nyk. He had to save himself from that fate.

Saint finished his coffee and rinsed the mug in the sink.

Octavius knew of Saint, in a way that many of the older Brotherhood members were aware of each other. In the past, the Brotherhood hadn't been grouped together, like they were today. Years would pass between seeing another member face-to-face. Sometimes, Octavius had gone decades without seeing Mikalis. Saint had been one of them, but hidden away. They'd all orbited the same mass—Mikalis—but rarely met. Saint had been there thousands of years ago. His name had been uttered among the Brotherhood long before Mikalis had recruited Octavius.

But how far back did their relationship go, and what had gone so very wrong that Saint had turned from Brotherhood back into nyk?

It would have been a lie to say he wasn't intrigued by Saint. Saint was almost a myth among legends. And here he stood, washing out a mug just a few strides from Octavius, so... normal. He almost didn't seem real.

"It seems you and I might be the same, Little Wolf."

"Don't call me that."

Saint straightened, and while he wasn't physically imposing like Storm or tall like Kazimir, he had *something*. The same something Mikalis had. As though, inside Saint, there was an ancient, coiled creature, waiting to strike. "Let's be clear. I've spent so many hundreds of years in Mikalis's chains that if you think to take me back in a misguided attempt to appease him, know that I will kill you and you will not see the blow coming. I intend to live out our final days free and unincumbered by the Brotherhood. If you're smart, like I think you are, you'll do the same, Little Wolf."

He rested a hand on Octavius's shoulder, in a gesture that was likely meant to suggest comradery. Octavius shook him off and snarled at Saint's back as he headed out of the living room area and toward the back rooms, probably to feed and fuck his pet human.

"It's Octavius!" he called after him.

This was absurd. Saint wasn't going to give him any answers. Like all nyks, he was just interested in feeding and fucking. It was almost a tragedy, how far he had fallen. Saint would have been a mighty Brotherhood member long ago.

No wonder Mikalis had locked him up. He was powerful and dangerous.

But why hadn't Mikalis *killed* him, like he did all the other nyks they encountered?

It didn't matter.

Octavius would put that mistake right and kill Saint now. If he did nothing else for the Brotherhood, at least he would have ridden the world of a powerful nyktelios and his stupid feeder.

He turned the oven's burners on so they each hissed out noxious gas and then stepped back from the stovetop. Saint's death would have to be enough for Mikalis to grant him a chance to defend himself. There was no other way.

CHAPTER 3

 aint

IT WAS REMARKABLE THAT, after thousands of years, the Brotherhood still spewed the same lies. He'd hoped the white-haired one who had been tracking him for months—Octavius—would have been different.

Mikalis had definitely been trying to kill Octavius, suggesting Octavius might at least be reasonable. But no. The Brotherhood was destined to make the same mistakes over and over, just as they always had.

Saint closed the bedroom door behind him and slumped against it. Weariness tugged on his bones. He dropped his head back, thumped the door, and closed his eyes. He'd been alive too long for this bullshit. All he wanted to do was gorge and fuck his way through the apocalypse. Was that too much to ask?

"Hm," Jayden purred. His warm, soft hand eased into Saint's, then the rest of him pressed close. Saint kept his eyes closed and breathed in the smell of human, blood, and sweetness. "Still tired?" Jayden asked, walking his fingers up Saint's chest. "Let me fix that."

He *was* tired and had tried to hide it from Octavius. The little wolf whined like a child, but he was powerful. They *all* were. And the fight with Mikalis had left Saint wrecked, in more ways than one.

He was a fool to hope Mikalis might change. Hope? No, not that. His hope had died millennia ago.

Jayden's warm lips skimmed Saint's neck in the ghost of a kiss, and Saint's fangs throbbed, seeking the pressure of warm flesh. The urge to bite beat through him. Not yet. He liked this, this quiet, having Jayden's hands on him, his body close, his heart beating a rhythm between them.

"I like him," Jayden murmured between fluttering kisses.

Saint snorted and opened his eyes to find Jayden's freckle-dashed face peering back at him. By the damned, he was gorgeous. "Jay, he tried to kill you."

"And I almost hit him with a pan. I think it's love."

Saint laughed again and eased Jayden aside. Jayden saw the best in everyone, even Saint. But Octavius didn't seem the sort to have a heart. The viciousness with which he'd attacked Jayden had surprised even Saint. There were those who believed the Brotherhood lies, and those who *lived* them. Octavius was one who lived them.

The cult of Mikalis.

Saint unbuttoned his shirt and crossed the room, heading toward the bed. "It's definitely not *love*." He turned, sat on the edge of the mattress, and pulled off the shirt. Jay's gaze roamed his chest, sizzling heat where it landed. "Come here."

Jay hesitated long enough so they both knew this was happening, then sauntered over. He wore tight shorts and one of Saint's shirts, clothes he'd thrown on after a day of fucking and feeding. Saint had already taken blood, leaving Jay somewhat weakened. He'd need a few days to recover, but that didn't mean Saint couldn't indulge in other pleasures. Intimacy wasn't always about blood. And he'd been locked up for so long, fed blood through bags, starved of physical touch, that he'd probably never sate his lust for the little pleasures.

Saint spread his knees and Jay slotted between them. "Be careful, Jay. The Brotherhood are all killers." Saint ran his hands up Jay's naked thighs and clutched his ass. His cock, hard in his shorts, happened to be at Saint's eye level.

"So are you."

"Hm." Saint mouthed his dick through his thin shorts, and when Jay stuttered a gasp, Saint looked up the length of him. He'd dropped his head back. So easy to please. So responsive. Almost too eager.

It hadn't taken long to find the perfect feeder. Saint had seem him the third night in St. Louis. The laughing man with the golden hair. But when Jay had thought nobody watched him, when he'd been alone, his smile had died. A heavy sadness clung to him even now. The kind of sadness he'd sought to drown in meaningless hookups or at the bottom of a bottle or banish at the end of a needle. When Jay had taken a wrong turn on leaving a bar, Saint had followed.

Jay would have died that night if Saint hadn't stepped in. The three men who'd attacked Jay for the twenty bucks in his pocket were discovered the next day. Another three murders in the murder capital of the US. Another statistic.

Jay made a fine feeder. He was young, strong, and waiting to be saved.

His fingers dove into Saint's hair, and his hips rocked, his body trying to chase the high Saint's mouth would deliver. Saint's fangs dropped; venom leaked, bitter on his tongue. Instinct demanded he bite and own and fuck so Jay fell deeper into his thrall. But from there, there would be no escape. Jay was Saint's. Nyktelios and feeder, as it had been since the beginning of time. As it was meant to be.

"Wait, something is wrong," Jay said, falling still.

Saint lifted his head, thoughts fogged by weariness, hunger, and desire.

Jay sniffed. "You smell that?"

Saint breathed in, and beneath the musky smell of male and sex, he smelled it too. Cooking gas. *Octavius.* With a growl, Saint stood, grasped Jay by the arms, and spun him around. "Stay here. Do not come out."

"Wait—"

Saint's senses prickled with a warning too late, and the rest of Jay's words vanished beneath a thunderous blast of debris and heat. Time slowed. Noise broiled, heat scorched the air. *Protect Jay.* Saint turned his back on the blast and freed the reins on his true form. Wings burst from his flesh. Fire scorched clothes from his skin. He lunged, threw his arms around Jay, and folded his wings in. Agony lashed up his back, burning like a hundred whip lashes. Jagged debris rained—metal, wood, and glass. It clanged and thumped and pounded, trying to crush Saint under its weight. He had Jay, could hear his strong heartbeat, feel him trembling in his arms. *Protect him,* that was all that mattered.

The blast came and went in moments, leaving a ringing in Saint's ears. He couldn't hear, but that would pass. He heaved, pushing his back up through the mound of rubble, and thrust out his shredded wings, flinging bits of building back.

Jay.

Saint dragged Jay's immobile body through the smoldering wreckage—*get him away*—into cold night air, then stumbled to his knees as weakness washed over him. He was hurt too, hurt bad. Instincts roared and lashed, trying to tear out his control, but if that happened, he'd kill Jay for his blood. No, Saint had control. His wounds would heal. They always did. But Jay's wounds...

"Jay?" He laid Jay down near the edge of the lake, away from the burning house. Why wasn't he moving? Saint's heart stuttered. Jay's head lolled to the side, eyes closed. Blood painted his golden hair.

"No." What was wrong, where was he hurt? Saint eased back and stared, struck silent by the jagged piece of rebar jutting from

Jay's chest. If Saint removed that bar, he'd bleed out in seconds. If he left it in, he'd die in minutes. Death was here, stalking them, in the rattle of Jay's breathing and his ragged heartbeat.

"No, no, no..." Saint could save him, but Jay had already consumed too much of Saint's blood from frivolous sex. If he let him take more now, it risked turning him, and then Saint would lose his bright, brilliant, fun-loving feeder to the curse. Jay would be nyktelios.

Better that than dead. Or was it? He'd lose him as a feeder, might lose him as a person too. But he couldn't sit back and watch Jay die.

There had to be another way.

Octavius.

The vicious fiend who had done this. His blood, not Saint's, might fix Jay. It could work.

Saint glanced back at the wreckage of the lake house. The building looked as though a huge beast had bitten half of it away. Smoke billowed from the smoldering rubble. Some of the nearby trees smoked too. Sparks sizzled. Saint didn't care about any of that. He narrowed his eyes, searching for movement in the woods.

There. The Brotherhood vampire was fleeing the scene, fast.

Octavius was about to pay for this with his gods-damned life if Jay died.

CHAPTER 4

ctavius

HE RAN.

He'd get far enough away, watch the dust settle, and then go back in for the kill, while Saint was weak. The blast *must* have weakened him. This was Octavius's moment to prove he was still Brotherhood. He'd kill Saint, and Mikalis would have to listen to him.

A rustle in the trees to his right was all the warning he had. A shadow rushed from the dark, a shadow even Octavius's night-attuned eyes struggled to see. Something hard slammed into his middle and hauled him into the air. Branches tore at him, cutting his face and hands as he was dragged backward. He twisted, bucked, tried to kick away from the hold, but he couldn't even see the creature he fought. Just smoke and a warp in reality, like a heat haze on a desert road.

The shadowy haze stopped and Octavius slammed into the ground so hard, bones in his chest snapped like twigs. He roared, but a hand clamped around his throat, *crushing*, cutting off his voice.

"I will snap your neck, Brotherhood." It wasn't even a voice, more a collection of growls and snarls resembling words.

The rippling weaves in reality coalesced into solid form, and while the face belonged to Saint, the flesh was burned from bone, most of his clothes were gone—burned, some torn—and behind him, enormous shredded wings arched so high and wide, they seemed to blot out the world.

Octavius bucked and clawed at the hand on his neck, but with every moment he struggled, the more the grip tightened, crushing his windpipe. Muscles and bone creaked and fractured.

"If that man dies, so do you." Brilliant silver eyes blazed.

Man? What man?

"Your blood. Give it to him. *Now.*"

Saint dumped Octavius onto the ground beside the feeder. A section of metal bar protruded from his chest, and his heartbeat stuttered, each beat potentially his last.

"No," Octavius wheezed. His throat was wrecked, but he spluttered out that word.

A thunderous growl rumbled from Saint. "Do it."

"...not... saving... your... feeder!"

Saint reared up and roared so loud it would have been a miracle if it wasn't heard in St. Louis. Birds started from the forest, and the sound of that roar rolled like a wave across the lake and hills.

He grabbed Octavius's right arm and snapped it backward.

White-hot pain tore through Octavius. He clamped his teeth, venom dripping, and stared back at the monstrous nyktelios. "I'd... rather... die..."

"Die a betrayer?" Saint asked. "Is that truly what you want? Then they will never learn your truth. "

Octavius cradled his broken arm against his chest and glared at Saint. He was right. If Octavius died here, he's always be guilty. And if Octavius didn't betray Mikalis, who did? But he couldn't give a feeder his blood. It went against everything

Octavius believed in. Assuming Saint had already shared blood, then Jayden might turn if he took in more of Saint's blood while in this state. It was better to let the man die and end his suffering.

"Do it, or I will rip out your heart and eat it in front of you." Saint's eyes blazed.

Octavius swallowed through his healing throat. If the man died, Saint would kill him. He'd do more than that—he'd rip Octavius apart. That much was clear. And he wouldn't stop there. Rabid like he was, he'd go on killing. He'd slaughter anyone he came across and might even get as far as St. Louis. He'd create more feeders. Mikalis had failed to kill him once. What if he kept on failing? What if Saint was *stronger* than Mikalis? He might create an army of nyks.

But if Octavius saved Jayden, none of that would happen. At least, not yet.

"Too slow!" Saint grabbed Octavius's good wrist, the one not yet broken, and bared his fangs.

"No, wait!"

Saint struck. His teeth plunged into Octavius's wrist. If his fangs injected venom, it would ravage Octavius's body, killing him. But Saint needed him alive; he wouldn't inject venom. This was just about blood. Saint tore at the wound, opening it wide so the blood flowed. He yanked Octavius onto his side and knelt over Jayden, hauling Octavius's arm with him.

"Wait, I can—"

Saint slammed Octavius's bleeding wrist against Jayden's lips and held it there with one hand as he used the other to yank the rebar from the man's chest.

Fuck, fuck, fuck. This was a nightmare. "Stop, wait!" But nobody was listening. "Please," Octavius begged, and hated himself for it.

"Saving him costs you nothing," Saint growled.

It did. It would cost him everything! "Mikalis will think... I'm working with you."

If Mikalis learned he'd fed a feeder, he'd never take Octavius back. Not on top of everything else. This was wrong. *"Stop!"*

Saint roared, shaking off the attempt to control him. "Get the fuck out of my head, Little Wolf. Why do you care what Mikalis thinks? He does not care for you."

Strange, how hearing it now, on his side, hurting in all ways, beaten and abused by a powerful nyk, was perhaps the first time he understood what that meant. Mikalis did not care. Saint's words hit him like a slap to the face. Octavius had served Mikalis for millennia. One accusation, that was all it took, and Mikalis had turned on him.

"Jay?" Saint said, his voice much softer. So soft, in fact, that Octavius studied the monster who knelt over his feeder. The madness in his eyes was not madness after all, but terror. He *cared* that Jay lived.

But that wasn't possible. Nyks didn't care. They killed and fed and fucked like a plague. Saint was nyktelios. But he'd been Brotherhood. Did that mean something?

Octavius looked at the young man dying beside him. This wasn't going to work. If Jay didn't swallow, Octavius's blood wouldn't find its way into his veins. He'd die here, and Saint's rampage would be legendary, and Octavius could have stopped it.

"Let me help him," Octavius croaked out.

Saint bared his fangs. "If he dies, you will beg me for death after I am done torturing you, Brotherhood."

Octavius nodded. "He won't die." Saint let his arm up, and Octavius removed his bloody wrist from Jay's mouth. He gestured for Saint to move off the man, and after Saint crawled aside, Octavius straddled Jay's legs. Octavius righted his own broken arm with a savage crack and winced around the thumping pain, then raised his right wrist, biting into it again to reopen the wound.

Leaning over, he clutched Jayden's jaw, forcing it open while tilting the feeder's head back. The blood had to run down his throat. Hopefully, his reflexes would kick in, forcing him to swallow.

Jayden's chest wound didn't look encouraging. But Octavius wasn't paying attention to that. It would heal, if Jayden consumed enough blood. Octavius gripped his jaw in his left hand, flexed the fingers of his right hand, and pressed his wrist to Jayden's open mouth. He might choke and drown, but he was dead regardless. They were out of options.

Saint loomed in Octavius's peripheral vision, hard to ignore. If this failed, Octavius would have to try to flee again, then call the Brotherhood before Saint did too much damage. He risked his own capture, but he'd do it, because it was the right thing.

Come on, Jayden.

Jay's heartbeat flickered, dying like a candle flame spluttering out.

Octavius closed his eyes and pushed his will into the dying man's mind. *"Drink."*

Blood dribbled from the corners of his open mouth.

"Drink, damn you."

Jayden's chest heaved. His throat moved, swallowing.

"Again," Octavius demanded, forcing the demand into him, leaving him no choice.

He swallowed again. Then again. His lips sealed onto Octavius's wrist and his tongue swept. A sudden, blinding rush of desire tore through Octavius. He winced around it and tried to push it back, but his body knew exactly what he wanted, and it happened to be the man lying prone beneath him, sucking on his veins. Jayden's eyes fluttered open, then his hand came up and caught Octavius arm, holding him in place. Tiny human teeth pinched Octavius's skin, and a needful moan escaped Octavius's best efforts to contain it.

No, he couldn't succumb. This was how losing control began. With need and desire. But then Jayden's glare locked on to his and made it clear he wanted this.

A hundred different urges poured into Octavius's mind. His fangs throbbed with need. His cock was full and eager. A human sucked from his veins, and the most natural thing in the world would be to hold him down and bite and fuck him—both at once.

He couldn't do this. He couldn't become the very creature he hated. He was better than this. Better than a nyk. He was Brotherhood.

Breathing hard, he straightened and tried to tug his wrist from Jayden's hold, but the feeder was strong. A second yank, and he pulled free. Jayden gasped and threw his gaze toward the sky. Blood stained his chin and cheek. Rivulets ran down his neck. Octavius watched his pulse throb at his neck.

Just a bite, just one; feed from the vein, feed the hunger.

No, he had to resist!

He scrambled to his feet and staggered away, stumbling against a nearby tree. Dropping his shoulder against it, he licked his wrist clean of blood, tasting Jayden, and watched the skin stich itself back together. Desire burned him up. He was so damned hard, he only had to think about taking him and he'd come. Instead, he gritted his teeth and worked through all the reasons why this was wrong.

He still had control, he was not nyktelios, he would not surrender to the desperate needs of the creature within him.

Saint hadn't moved, as though he feared if he did, Jayden's recovery might not be real. Then Jayden gave a soft cough and tried to prop himself upright. "Oh, I ruined your shirt."

Seeing a feeder gaze big doe eyes at the nyktelios that was slowly poisoning him might have been the most disgusting thing Octavius had ever seen. He snarled at them both, as well as at himself for being a part of it.

"You!" Saint pointed at Octavius, then in a blur of liquid shadow, he filled Octavius's personal space. "If you so much as think about destroying us again, you're dust in the wind. Understand?"

Octavius peered up at the nyk's ancient silver eyes. "You're welcome."

Saint lunged, slamming Octavius against the tree. *"This is your doing.*" He snapped his teeth close to Octavius's throat. "I should kill you now."

Octavius didn't fight, not this time. He still burned from hunger and desire, still fought his personal demons. Remnants of that lust simmered back to life, and as he peered at an ancient nyktelios in his full monstrous glory,—eyes ablaze, mouth full of fangs, and wings arching from his back—Octavius's cock hardened with want all over again.

He let his eyes flutter closed, and for the smallest of seconds he wanted Saint to bite him, to sink his teeth in. He might just come if he did.

Saint breathed him in, let out a low rumbling warning growl, and brought his head down. Even with his eyes closed, Octavius sensed Saint's hot mouth hovering over his. Saint might kill him, and even that thought dialed his desire higher. What would it be like to fight and fuck and bite and feed like Saint did, to give in to the powerful urges seeking to undermine thousands of years of control?

No! It was nyk madness!

Octavius thrust out both hands, shoving Saint away. "You're weak. I smell it on you. Get out of my face, nyktelios."

Saint chuckled and turned his back. As he approached Jayden, he gave his shoulders a shake and his monstrous form blurred away, leaving just a man in burned and bloody clothes.

Octavius sighed his relief. Somehow, he'd survive this mess.

Saint reached down, hauled Jayden to his feet, and tucked the feeder against his side. "You're coming with us, Octavius," he called back as the pair hobbled toward the car parked on the driveway.

Octavius shivered out the last tremors of desire. He could run, but Saint would stalk him through the shadows. He'd never make it.

He was a prisoner, he realized. Saint's prisoner.

The plan hadn't changed. He'd just need to be more careful with the killing blow and take Saint out decisively. No more mistakes.

He'd still kill Saint, if it was the last act for the Brotherhood he ever performed.

CHAPTER 5

aint

ON THE ONE HAND, Octavius deserved to die a long, slow, painful death for attempting to kill them. On the other hand, he'd saved Jay's life. This was a dilemma, and after multiple millennia, not much surprised Saint anymore. Except Octavius. The Brotherhood member was a baffling and alluring tangle of contradictions. He seemed to be devoted to the Brotherhood, yet he'd just broken one of their cardinal rules.

He stewed in silence in the passenger seat, while Jay lay sprawled along the back seat, sleeping off the trauma.

Someone would have seen and heard the explosion, even in as remote a place as the Missouri forests. Saint needed to get some space between them and suspicious human authorities, but also get away from St. Louis, where he'd left Mikalis scraping himself off the road.

Not a pleasant memory. Not something he wanted to dwell on.

They had a few hours until dawn. He'd have to find somewhere before then to wait out the day.

He pulled the car to the edge of the mountain road.

"Why are you stopping?" Octavius asked, his voice tight with accusation. He talked like that a lot, as though every moment he spent in Saint's presence was a disgusting stain on his perfect life. But a few softer moments peeked through, such as when he'd told Saint that Jay would live. Damnit, Saint wanted to hate him, and everything he stood for, but couldn't; he'd been the one to save Jay.

"Changing my clothes."

"At the side of the road?"

"Where else?" Saint opened the car door, climbed out, and hurried to the trunk. He always packed an emergency bag for moments such as these.

He grabbed a blanket from the trunk, opened the rear door, and tucked it over Jay. He stirred but didn't wake. His hair had melted in places, glued together, and Saint was struck again by how close he'd come to losing him.

Saint looked up and caught Octavius watching in the mirror. Saint bared his teeth in warning.

"I'm not going to touch your feeder, Jesus," Octavius grumbled.

After returning to the trunk, Saint stripped off his shredded clothing. That was one of the many good reasons to always wear a suit. The shirt or pants were easily replaceable. "You should know, I predate Jesus by several thousand years."

Octavius snorted and muttered, "Don't we all?"

He was a sassy one, this little wolf. A lot of bark, and a vicious bite. Perhaps Saint might relish seeing more of that bite as soon as they were safely sheltered from the sun. And Octavius had no idea just how old Saint was. Which was probably a good thing. People behaved differently around him once they knew the truth.

Cool mountain air swirled around his naked legs. He reached into the trunk for the pants and caught Octavius watching in the side mirror. Saint tugged his pants up his legs, making sure to give him a fine view of his bare ass, and then he fastened the zipper.

When he glanced back, Octavius had turned his face away.

The little wolf had been aroused when feeding Jay, and after, when Saint had warned him. None of that was unusual behavior. Feeding was intimate. What had been unusual was his fear of it, of losing control. That was the Brotherhood's doing. Octavius and the rest were as brainwashed as Nyxians, except the Brotherhood worshipped Mikalis, not Nyx.

None of it mattered anyway.

All of it would be gone soon. The Brotherhood, the people, all of it.

He slammed the trunk, buttoned his shirt, and climbed back behind the wheel.

"Where are we going?" Octavius asked.

Saint pulled the car back onto the road. "Somewhere safe before dawn. How long have you been with Mikalis?"

"With the Brotherhood? A few thousand years."

Impressive that he'd been devoted for so long. "And just like that, Mikalis turns on you. That's how he rewards devotion."

"He's been betrayed before." Octavius glared pointedly. "One of the Brotherhood ripped it all apart from the inside. Sound familiar?"

Hm, so that was the version of events Mikalis had told them. It wasn't untrue. "I didn't betray him. Although, he likely doesn't see it like that. You and I appear to have much in common."

"We have *nothing* in common. I am Brotherhood. I do not enslave feeders, I do not run around doing whatever I please, causing chaos because I can, and I do not make more nyktelios. You are everything I despise and have spent the majority of my long life trying to erase from this existence. So tell me again how we're fucking alike." He panted, waiting, after ordering Saint to answer.

Saint pinched his lips together, trapping the smirk. "So fiery." All that angst and devotion wrapped up and tied down by thousands of years of lies, in a firm little body wired so tightly he might combust if he ever let himself go.

"Fuck you."

35

Saint chuckled. Jay was right. There was something charming about Octavius's viciousness. He'd make an enjoyable distraction as the end of the world approached. Perhaps Saint could convince Octavius to join them. He'd clearly enjoy it, once he got over his mountain of Brotherhood hang-ups. "So you believe Mikalis is going to reward you when you kill me or when you hand me over in chains?"

Octavius kept his gaze on the road ahead and opted for silence. Although the tic in his cheek answered for him. Subtle, he was not. Of course Octavius was hoping Saint was his answer to regaining his place among the Brotherhood. Why else would he still be with them? "Such devotion. What did he do to earn your love, Octavius?"

"It's not love," the little wolf snarled.

"He claims none of you are permitted to love, yet he demands you love him unconditionally."

"It's nothing like that. It's..." He paused, searching for the right words. "Mutual respect."

Saint laughed. "I was Brotherhood. I know exactly what it's like, and trust me, it's *not* mutual."

Octavius twisted in his seat and angled toward Saint, as though he might lunge and try to take the wheel. If he did that, they'd plow off the road into the trees and end up fighting again, which would lead to Jay bleeding, Saint threatening to kill Octavius, and another suit ruined. Octavius was smarter than this, Saint was sure of it, beneath all the neurosis. "Why did you turn on him?"

"I didn't turn on him," Saint explained. "I told him the truth, and he didn't much like it. Mikalis has a complicated relationship with the truth."

"You're deluded. You're just another blood-sucking nyk. I don't know why I'm wasting my breath speaking with you."

He had passion, although misguided. "Except, I'm not like the other nyks you've encountered, am I? I have the silver eyes, and I fuck a feeder, and apparently I don't give a shit about anything besides my own needs, so that makes you and I enemies? Do you not see how shortsighted and absurd your beliefs are?"

"They're not beliefs, they're facts. Absurd is me listening to a nyk's bullshit."

"You're listening because under all that Brotherhood neurosis you know I'm worth listening to. I'm the oldest nyk you'll ever meet, Little Wolf, and right now, I'm all that stands between you and certain death. Memento fuckin' mori, Octavius."

Octavius laughed, but it sounded hollow. "Your pathetic attempts to turn me against Mikalis and the Brotherhood are ridiculously transparent. I'm embarrassed for you. An ancient and mighty nyktelios, reduced to fucking an addicted twink and hiding in the woods. Bravo, you must be so proud of yourself."

Saint gripped the wheel until it creaked under his knuckles. He could slam Octavius into the hillside and dust him. He had that irritating ability to get inside Saint's head, but Saint was physically stronger. He certainly sounded as though he wanted Saint to kill him. But the little wolf might be useful should Mikalis track him down again.

The little wolf just might earn Saint one last chance to speak with Mikalis.

One last attempt to say he was sorry.

CHAPTER 6

ctavius

THE SLEEPY LION Motel sign had a few neon letters missing, which was probably an indication of the quality accommodation Saint had brought them to. Three other cars were parked out front in the lot, and there wasn't another building in sight.

Saint pulled his car to a stop and eyed the lobby door. "You and I are going to go in there, and you'll do your little persuasion trick on the staff to get us two rooms."

Octavius frowned. He wasn't Saint's pet to order around. That was Jayden's role. "No."

Saint huffed a sigh. "Fine, I'm ravenous anyway. I'll go in, kill whoever is at the front desk, then anyone else spending the night, and we'll have the entire place to ourselves. How does that sound?"

"What, no, don't—"

Saint left the car and strode toward the lobby area, all swagger and confidence. *Fuck.* Would he kill everyone here? No, he wouldn't do it. It didn't make any sense. Why draw that much attention to himself?

Swearing, Octavius tossed a glance at Jayden, checking he was still asleep, and then hurried after Saint.

Saint threw him an infuriating know-it-all grin and opened the lobby door.

A little bell tinkled. Saint looked up. "Quaint." He flashed a smile at the woman behind the front desk. "Hello, there," he said, in a very non-American accent. English? South African? Australian? Octavius struggled to place it. "My friend and I were wondering if you had a couple of rooms in this fine establishment?"

Janice, her name badge said. Octavius hung back, unsure if he was about to witness Janice's last few minutes alive—not that he cared. But Janice's death would bring more humans snooping around, then the cops, and all that furor might catch Mikalis's eye. Better to slide in under the radar, especially as he needed more time to figure out his next move.

Janice eyed Saint and then skipped her gaze to Octavius. Granted, they were a lot to take in. Saint was dressed as though he'd just left a wedding party, and Octavius still wore the same stained hooded top and black pants he'd had on when he'd tousled with Mikalis and Saint in the street. He likely smelled like wood smoke, blood, diesel, and a whole array of other potent scents. And then there was the hair. Men with platinum blond hair were... rare.

He and Saint made an odd pair.

"Oh, and my other friend, in the car back there." Saint chuckled. "He's er... Well, he had too much to drink."

It wasn't just the accent. Saint's body language had changed too, like a chameleon blending in with its environment, except the accent was way off if he was trying to blend in with the Missouri locals. Perhaps that was the point—disarm Janice with too many unusual variables so she didn't think to ask questions.

"Welcome to the Sleepy Lion," she drawled, unimpressed. "I've got two adjoining doubles. I just need your names, addresses, and phone numbers on this form. It's seventy bucks a night."

"Right, yes, names..." Saint grabbed the form. "Octavius, would you like to step in?"

"No." He folded his arms and leaned a hip against the desk. Frankly, he wanted to see how this was going to play out.

"Really?" Saint lifted his gaze. "You're just going to watch?"

Janice glanced at them both, sensing the tone had changed but not yet understanding why her instincts were beginning to ring alarm bells.

"Fine then. Although your way is far more discreet." Saint leaped over the desk, grabbed Janice, and shoved her down into her chair.

It shouldn't have mattered. Octavius shouldn't have cared. And he didn't, not about Janice. He cared that Saint did not win this, that his nyktelios ways were wrong and there was a different way. *"Stop,"* he pushed into Saint's mind.

The ancient nyk flung his head around and growled. "Not me, use it on *her.*"

"Oh, really? I'm so sorry. I misunderstood," he drawled, heavy on the sarcasm.

Octavius spied the camera above the door. He reached up and yanked the power cable out, then joined Janice and Saint behind the desk. From how wide Janice's pupils had blown, she was surely already second-guessing her life choices, now that she was pinned under Saint's hands.

Octavius glanced at the map of the motel on her desk, spotted two adjoining rooms, and turned to Janice. He gripped the back of her chair and leaned down. His shoulder brushed Saint's, igniting a blast of tight little shivers that made his insides flutter in inexplicable ways.

He peered into Janice's watery eyes. *"Rooms 102 and 103 are occupied. You don't know by who, and you do not care. When you finish your shift, you will explain this to whoever takes over. You'll forget this conversation ever happened. Do this, and you will be safe."* He turned his head and found Saint so close he could see silver facets in his eyes. "Nobody is going to hurt you," he said aloud, so Saint heard too.

41

Octavius straightened. "You can let her go. She won't stop us."

Saint stepped back and watched as Janice blinked a few times, then relaxed in her chair and stared though them, as though they did not exist.

Octavius typed a few commands into the computer and scanned two keycards. He gave one to Saint, who stared at him, his face deliberately blank. Octavius's skill with manipulating minds typically earned him that look. Once people learned he could manipulate them, few trusted him.

"That's an impressive talent," Saint said, reverting back to his typical American accent as they left the lobby.

"It once got me burned at the stake."

Saint's steps faltered.

Octavius smiled over his shoulder. "As a witch." He faced ahead again and sauntered under the motel's long wraparound porch to Room 103. The surprise on Saint's face had been real, and satisfying. If Octavius could surprise an ancient nyk, then he could outwit one too.

But first, he needed to shower.

AFTER SHOWERING HIMSELF CLEAN, Octavius washed his clothes under the showerhead as best as he could, thinking over his options. The lobby had a phone out of earshot from Saint. He could call the Brotherhood and alert them to Saint's whereabouts. He *should*. But blood was going to become an issue soon, and if he was going to risk clashing with the Brotherhood, he needed to be at full strength. Jayden had taken more out of him than he cared to admit. As had the previous night's fight.

He'd survived these last six months without feeding from the vein like a nyk by breaking into hospitals and using his persuasion to manipulate the staff into bringing him blood bags. But there were no hospitals out here, and no convenient blood delivery without alerting the Brotherhood to his exact location.

He couldn't drink from the vein. He couldn't break more rules.

And it would be dawn soon anyway. He just had to ignore the gnawing hunger.

With a towel tucked around his waist, he padded into the main bedroom area and drew the drapes closed. The rooms, although small, were equipped with the basics. This might have been one of the better places he'd stayed in since running from the Brotherhood.

Octavius flopped back onto the bed.

If any of them found out he'd helped save a feeder, any bridges he'd had left would be burned. But it was all for the mission, and the mission was to bring in Saint.

The nyktelios was not what Octavius had expected, Saint was right about that. But he *was* ancient, and that meant he was clever, sly, and manipulative. It just appeared as though he was reasonable, when in fact, he was more a monster than any nyk Octavius had faced before. One thing was clear. He couldn't bring Saint in alone. Despite his own strength, it wasn't enough. He needed help.

But who to call? Kazimir rarely interacted with Octavius, too busy with his social life and sauntering around Atlas like a cockerel in a hen house. Zaine was out of the question, as Octavius had threatened his feeder Eric. Storm was Mikalis's puppet. Octavius didn't know how to get in touch with Aiko, and the stoic knife-thrower was usually in Europe anyway.

There was one person he could call, the same man who had told him to run.

Raiden.

Damn, he missed his friend.

Raiden had been the only one who understood him, understood *them*. They'd been close, closer than friends. Not sexually close. It wasn't like that. Raiden listened, and he knew when to stay quiet too, when to give Octavius space; whenever the past had crept up on Octavius and tried to swallow him, Raiden had been there.

Sometimes, the world became too loud, too much, too cruel, and Octavius withdrew inward. The last time it had happened, a few hundred years ago, Raiden had been there to help pull him out of it.

And now, Raiden had given him a chance, told him to run, deliberately going against Mikalis's orders. He might listen.

Octavius needed to get to a phone without Saint knowing. Once he made contact though, the clock would be ticking. If they were still in the Ozarks, then they were approximately a day's drive away from New York, or a few hours by chopper. Mikalis didn't even need a plane or helicopter to get where he needed to go. Like Saint, he shadow-walked. How far could he travel like that? He regularly bounced around cities in hours, but Octavius didn't believe he could jump continents.

If Octavius reached out to Raiden, told him where Saint was in exchange for a truce with Mikalis, they'd have a few hours before Mikalis arrived, either by chopper or other means.

Voices rumbled from the adjacent room. Saint and Jayden. Jayden was awake then. Octavius closed his eyes and sighed, strangely calm. More calm than he'd been in days. Warm and sleepy too...

He opened his eyes. These weren't his feelings. He sensed the feeder, as though Jayden were the other part of a magnet, pulling on Octavius. Damnit. The link would fade, just so long as they didn't share blood again. Saint's hold on the feeder would likely overpower any tenuous connection Octavius had.

The voices faded, and Octavius closed his eyes again, resting, mulling over what to do.

A warmth grew low down, a different kind of pull. It didn't feel right, almost like nerves, but he rarely experienced anxiety. Was there something wrong with him? Then the feeling shifted and rolled down his back like warm hands. A sudden rush of lust awakened his cock and stole a gasp from his lips.

He snapped open his eyes.

Shit, he knew what this was.

He twisted on the bed and thumped the wall.

Jayden's muffled voice sailed through from the other side, the mumbles garbled.

Octavius bowed his head. "*I feel you,*" he sent to Jayden. And then wished he hadn't as a sharper thrust of lust lit him on fire and hardened him still. Damn them. Were they doing this on purpose? He couldn't stand having his body hijacked because they wanted to fuck. Couldn't they keep their hands off each other for a few days?

The interconnecting door floor open and Saint charged in. "Get out of Jay's head..." He trailed off as his gaze traveled all the way down Octavius's chest, over his abs, and hung up on how his cock tented the towel around his waist.

Octavius gave the nyk a droll look. "It's not by choice I'm in his head."

Saint swallowed. His gaze flicked up. "I'm fucking him, so you can stay here and get busy with your hand, join us, or leave."

There was a whole lot of wrong with those suggestions. All of them in fact. Octavius spluttered and gave a shrill laugh. "You really must be insane to think I'd stoop so low as to join you." He scrambled off the bed, tore off the towel, flung it down, and tugged on his damp pants. There had been a few moments in between losing the towel and thrusting on his pants that he'd felt Saint's eyes on him—all over him, in fact—and that had made this alien lust *worse*. As though he wanted Saint's gaze on his naked skin.

"Stoop for me, Little Wolf, and I'll gladly fuck you—"

Octavius flew at him and must have caught him unawares because he managed to slam Saint to the wall. Saint spread his hands, playing at surrender, when they both knew he could throw Octavius around like a doll.

They stayed like that, Octavius holding Saint pinned. He wanted to say something lashing, something sharp, but the words wouldn't come. Probably because he was still fucking hard, and now he had Saint up close, Saint couldn't fail to feel how hard he was, since Octavius's dick was pressed between them.

Saint's lips drew into a devilish smirk and Octavius despised him even more than he had before. Despised him and *wanted* him. That had to be the bloodlust, the hunger, and that vicious, ancient part of him he kept under control because Octavius would *never* willingly desire a nyk.

"I'm leaving," Octavius snapped. He pushed off and stormed from the room, but not before hearing Jayden ask if the *little wolf* was joining them.

Oh, Octavius would be joining them later. Right after he'd made a phone call.

CHAPTER 7

ctavius

JANICE DIDN'T BAT an eye as he burst into the motel lobby and grabbed the phone. Thanks to his earlier intervention, she wouldn't remember he was here, or anything he'd say on the call. He dialed Raiden's cell.

Damn it, his cock was still half hard and the rest of him flustered. He wasn't in any fit state to call Raiden.

He slammed the receiver down.

He couldn't call him while he was worked up. Damn Saint!

And Jayden was back there with him, the both of them probably fucking like rabbits. He slumped against the desk and thrust his hands into his damp hair. What was it about the pair of them that got into his head? None of this should be this difficult. He just had to kill or capture Saint. And he needed help to do that. Those were the facts of the mission.

Gods, he was ravenous.

Hunger, that's why this mission had become challenging. He

needed blood or all of the urges he was keeping shut away would begin to escape.

Janice pulled her wheeled chair to the desk and tapped away on her computer. Octavius peered over her shoulder. She was replying to a post on Facebook, something about cats and tuxedos. Her perfume wafted, that and the smell of humans—a musky odor, sweet yet salty. He turned his head and there was the pulse thumping in her neck, calling to him like a siren song. She wouldn't even know if he took a bite. Nobody would know.

He'd know.

The fact he was even contemplating it revealed how far he'd fallen, and being around Saint was making that primal part of him hungrier, more dominant.

Like Saint was dominant.

"Fuck." He had to get the nyk and his stupid feeder out of his head, but while he was hungry, those desires were only going to get worse. If he was going to call the Brotherhood, call in help, he needed to feed. He needed to get his shit together. He couldn't feed from Jayden, not with Saint there; the two of them fucked with his head too much.

That left Janice.

He studied her face. She wasn't all that old, in human years. He could make it good for her, make it so she dreamed good things and woke up as though she'd had the best sex in her entire life.

It was still wrong. Drinking from the vein was off-limits, but the others had—Zaine had, Kazimir had—all in the name of the mission.

This was for the greater good. He had to do this, to stop Saint. This was Saint's fault.

Octavius's fangs extended. Two pairs, one pair to open the vein, one to deliver venom. Once his venom hit her heart, she'd be lost to his thrall. One bite wouldn't turn her into a permanently addicted feeder. One bite was nothing.

Just a sample. Just enough to keep him going.

One bite was all he needed.

CHAPTER 8

 aint

As MUCH AS he'd have loved to spend the day feeding and fucking
Jay, he couldn't. Jay was still weak. He needed time to recover. Saint
had been thinking about finding a temporary feeder, but then Jay
had his hands on Saint, and on his cock. He wasn't going to deny Jay
his fun. Then Octavius had thumped on the wall and Jay's eyes had
glazed over, as though he were somewhere far away.

Octavius, the bastard, had been in Jay's head, doing that witchy
thing he did.

He hadn't expected to find the Brotherhood member near
naked, his cock so hard it had tented his damp towel. Then he'd had
Saint against the wall and had looked as though he might try and
kill him again, at which point Octavius's undeniable erection had
dug into Saint's hip, and it had been amusing.

Better yet, when he'd dropped the towel, Saint had gotten an
eyeful of Octavius's lean, pale body, and he'd have fucked him right
there, if he'd asked. Octavius was a vicious thing, but seeing him

hard, his body on fire with rage and lust, his fangs out, and his blue eyes flashing their hatred... It had shocked Saint *and* aroused him, painfully.

Then the little wolf had dressed and left in an angry huff.

"Is he joining us?" Jay asked in a sleepy voice.

"No." And that was a damn shame. All that passion with no outlet? Octavius would soon burn out, or snap.

Jay lay on the bed, eyes fluttering closed, unable to stay awake, but he still had the energy to pout. "He's not as angry in my head. Just kinda... scared."

Saint was about to ask what he meant, but Jay's eyes stayed closed and his breathing slowed. Saint tucked him into the bed instead, watched him sleep a while, then left the room to search for Octavius, expecting to have to hunt Octavius down. But he sat, resting on the trunk of the car under a starlit sky, arms crossed, staring across the parking lot toward the woods.

He could have fled. Saint hadn't yet decided whether he'd bother tracking him down. He figured he'd wait and see what his mood was when it inevitably happened. But Octavius had stayed. Probably because he feared Mikalis more than Saint. The Brotherhood leader had an unyielding grip on them all.

Saint made his steps heavy, so as not to startle Octavius, and propped his ass on the trunk next to him. The sunrise was threatening the ridgeline, bleeding a thin red line behind the swathes of trees. The nights here were truly quiet, apart from the hum of the air conditioning. But close enough.

"You know, the endless days and nights I spent in confinement cut me out of the world. I no longer felt things, heard things. Living became tedious. And I'd have given anything to have someone end it."

Octavius glanced over and arched a pale eyebrow.

"To realize there's no end coming and time is endless, it is true torture. I lost myself in that cell beneath Atlas, and the one before it, the one before that... So many bars. I became hollow. Then the one called Kazimir visited. He didn't say much, not in the early days. He looked me over, studied me, said nothing, and so I asked him to kill me. I think those words resonated with him, as though he knew my pain. After a while, he brought books, then CDs, then digital songs on tiny devices, and a television so I could see how the world had changed while I'd been removed from it."

"Nobody was supposed to go into Room Three B. And nobody talked about you. Ever. Kazimir broke the rules."

"Rules Mikalis made."

"Yes, because you're a nyk who tried to destroy the Brother-hood. You deserved to be punished."

"Because he told you I'm the big bad wolf." Octavius still didn't see it, even though the truth was looking him right in the eyes.

"Yes. Exactly."

"You witnessed it, you saw what happened between me and him?" Saint asked.

"No," he admitted. "It was before my time."

Saint nodded and stared at the fading stars as the sun's red glow grew brighter. "Every other Brotherhood member received word of my great betrayal. I turned nyk and tried to burn it all down. That's what he told them. But nobody witnessed it, and nobody ques-tioned his truth. I was gone, with no way of speaking up. So his version of events became true. History is written by the winners."

Why would any of them question Mikalis? Octavius remained quiet for a little while. A lone car rumbled by the motel. Its taillights blinked red in the dark.

"What happened then, in this version of yours?" Octavius asked quietly.

"There are things I know about Mikalis, about the Brother-hood, that *will* destroy it all if set free into the world. You love him and your Brotherhood. I see that. They all do, and they all have reasons for that love. I have no wish to take that from you. Or them."

He narrowed his eyes on Saint and Saint saw that brilliant mind working. It was in there, like diamond found in coal. He just liked to bury it beneath blind devotion. "Am I being too reasonable for you again? Should I go rip some heads off hikers, eat a few babies? Would that better suit your picture of Saint, the mad nyk kept in the Brotherhood basement?"

Octavius's grin flashed across his lips, there and gone again like a firefly at dawn. "For all I know, you do exactly that."

"He's told you the world is black and white. Nyks are bad, the Brotherhood is less bad, all wrapped up in a convenient bow." Saint smiled. "Octavius, you know. You don't need me to tell you. You *all* know Mikalis is lying."

"If he is, then it's for a good reason. You must see how the nyktelios are a plague on the human race. They must be stopped. That is a fact."

And he'd been so close to looking a little deeper, to finding the truth. Saint couldn't tell him. He'd never believe it unless he discovered the truth for himself. Saint was always going to be the nyk they should all fear. Mikalis had made that the truth, so it *became* true. How could he tell him that Mikalis found the broken ones, the ones so desperate that, when he offered them his hand—when he saved them—he knew they'd devote their lives to him.

Mikalis manipulated every single Brotherhood member.

"All right, I'll make a deal with you, Octavius." Saint offered his hand. "I will help prove your innocence to Mikalis. We'll find whoever betrayed him. You certainly can't clear your name alone, not with the entire Brotherhood against you."

"It wasn't me. I'd never betray him, or them." He eyed Saint's hand as though it might bite him. "What do you get out of this?"

"One last chance to prove I'm not the big bad wolf you all believe me to be."

The sun had almost risen, and its endless drain began to sap the strength from Saint's veins. Octavius would be feeling it too. They'd both have to go inside to avoid the worst of its effects.

Octavius took Saint's hand. His grip was firm, warm, and confident, even though his hand seemed slight, his fingers lithe. "All right, nyk," he said. "But if *you* betray *me*, I'll make sure the full weight of the Brotherhood comes down on you, even if it costs my life."

"Oh, I do not doubt it, Little Wolf." Saint let the handshake linger, enjoying the touch more than he'd expected to, until Octavius grew impatient and shook him off with an almost-growl.

"You have delicate hands."

The little wolf's growl turned threatening. With a laugh, Saint left him there, sitting on the trunk. He'd come back inside and out of the sun soon.

"Saint?" he called.

Saint turned and raised his hand, shielding his eyes from the sun.

"Why would I believe your version?"

There was only one easy way to answer that. Saint turned his back on Octavius and stepped onto the porch. "Mikalis is my sire."

MIKALIS IS MY SIRE. Those four words could be enough to create ripples that would undo Mikalis. Saint wanted that—as vengeance, out of spite—but also... he didn't. Vengeance and spite were not how he'd planned to enjoy his last few weeks of freedom before things got *messy.*

He closed the blinds and paced the room while Jay slept.

If he were the nyk Octavius thought him to be, everything would be so much easier. He wouldn't *care.* Do not care, do not drink from the vein, do not reproduce.

As though any of them could choose not to care. The members of the Brotherhood were hypocrites, all of them. Or more accurately, Mikalis was, and he shaped his devoted little puppets to be better versions of himself.

Maybe Saint should have told Octavius *everything.* No. It didn't work like that; he had to discover it on his own. And now they had an opportunity. Octavius would get Saint inside the Brotherhood.

He'd have to, to root out the real traitor among them, the traitor who had released Saint before all of Atlas had imploded.

Why release him?

Octavius had asked that very question.

Saint sat on the edge of the chair beside the window and listened to the noises of the motel waking up. Doors slamming, footfalls on the timber porch, cars pulling up or leaving. Octavius would be next door, probably resting. He'd need it too. They'd pointlessly torn into each other as enemies just because Mikalis had made it so.

So why release Saint? Why not just keep him locked up while Atlas collapsed around him? What would a traitor gain by keeping Saint alive?

Perhaps the nameless figure working against Mikalis sought to create maximum damage and had assumed freeing Saint would do that. Or, they wanted Mikalis distracted. Both options amounted to the same outcome. Had they thought Saint would try to kill Mikalis?

Nobody else would be allowed to hunt Saint. Mikalis wouldn't trust anyone, not even his closest ally, Storm. *Definitely* not Storm—Mikalis knew Storm and Saint had a history. Mikalis wouldn't want *any* of them knowing his secrets.

It was likely the real traitor wanted Mikalis focused elsewhere while they put other plans into motion. Plans that had potentially been in motion for a long time, if Mikalis had been caught unawares. Plans that would tip the scales in the favor of the nyktelios?

Saint could feel it, had felt it for months now. A pressure at the back of his mind, building to critical mass. Sometimes it was a thumping in his head, like a banging drum, calling to him. The nyks, as the Brotherhood called them, were winning.

Mikalis no doubt felt it too, could sense the impending disaster, yet he still hunted Saint.

Because he knew Saint had the weapons to ruin him.

But Saint wouldn't. Like he'd said to Octavius, he had no wish to ruin the Brotherhood. He never had.

"Saint?" Jay, on the bed, propped his head up on a hand. "Are you all right?"

"No." He really wasn't. He couldn't say any more. There was too much to explain anyway. Jay wouldn't understand it. He knew what Saint was, knew him as *vampire*, like the human myths, but those myths did little more than scratch the surface of the truth.

Jay shuffled backward on the bed and threw off the sheet, exposing half a space on the double bed beside him and inviting Saint over. He wore only a fresh shirt, and his handsome body had regained its golden sunbaked glow. Saint crossed the room and lay next to him, fully clothed. At times like these, just being with someone kept him grounded, kept him from spiraling out of control.

Jay wrapped a leg around his and tucked his arm under Saint's, then hugged him to his chest. He shuffled down, pulling Saint close. "We can fuck if you want."

"No," he said again. He needed to think, and as pleasurable as Jay's body was, he'd too readily lose himself in sex.

Jay's fingers stroked over Saint's heart, through his shirt, until he fell asleep once more.

The day Saint had escaped Atlas, the electronics had failed, opening his cell door. Perhaps it had just been a fluke he'd survived. He'd fled, mindless and elated, but also racked with grief. In all the months, years, centuries that he'd been hidden, he'd hoped Mikalis would come to him. Mikalis never had. Not once.

Nobody betrayed Mikalis and lived. Even those who loved him.

CHAPTER 9

ctavius

Octavius paced.

Mikalis sired Saint? The revelation was almost too significant to comprehend.

It explained why Saint was so powerful. He was ancient *and* sired by Mikalis. A double blow of potent nyktelios genes. It also explained why Mikalis hadn't killed Saint before now, and instead had kept him locked up. Might even explain his secrecy around Saint. But when had he sired him? Was it before the Brotherhood? It had to be before because of the rules the Brotherhood all abided by. They never made more nyks. Ever. They didn't care, and they didn't drink from the vein. Simple rules, but powerful ones. What if Mikalis had broken all of them while overseeing the Brotherhood?

No, that wasn't possible. Why was Octavius listening to Saint? If anyone was lying, it was more likely to be him than Mikalis.

If only Octavius could pick up the phone and call Mikalis, and trust he would listen. Unfortunately, his apparent betrayal had burned any grace with Mikalis.

But Octavius could still call Raiden.

He paced the room, plucked Janice's stolen phone from his pocket, and dialed Raiden's number. After three rings, he answered.

"Hello?" His cheery, neat voice did something to Octavius's heart, made it shrink then pulse back to life.

"Hi."

"Octavius," he gasped. "Where are you?"

Octavius laughed a little. He wasn't going to tell him that, not yet. "I er... I didn't expect this to be so difficult," he whispered, so Saint didn't hear through the thin walls.

"Are you all right?"

Octavius dropped onto the end of the bed. He almost sobbed, which was ridiculous. Why did this hurt so much? "No." Gods, he'd had all these things he wanted to say, but now, hearing Raiden's voice, he didn't know where to begin.

"Come in."

"He'll kill me."

The line fell quiet. Raiden knew it to be true.

"Raiden, I... I just wanted to say some things I never got to say—"

"I'll meet you somewhere."

"Listen, we... had something. I know we did. Something... more. And I'm sorry I ruined it. I didn't betray you, you have to believe me."

"Octavius—"

"I know you all want me dead. Shit, most of you hate me. I never tried to be one of you, I never fit in. That wasn't me."

"I tried to help you."

"That's why I'm calling. We had something." He was going to have to say it, say the truth. He might not get another chance. "You were always there for me. The others never... they never understood. We had a bond, something... and I never wanted to hurt you."

"Octavius, you're not listening. *I know.*"

He knew... he loved him? Octavius sighed and rubbed his face. Perhaps it wasn't so bad to admit he cared, that he'd always cared. "I should have told you sooner. Everything is all screwed up. I'm trying to fix it, but it means a lot to hear your voice. I'm so damn tired, Raiden."

"I hear it in your voice. You know what else I know?"

This was it, he was going to say he loved him too, that they really did have something, that Octavius wasn't alone and never had been. He needed to hear it, ached to hear it. Kazimir had Felix, Zaine had Eric. Why couldn't Octavius have someone too? "Yeah?"

"You're so fucked."

"What?" His heart thumped in his ears, pounding like a drum. "I don't... What do you mean?"

"We have the footage, Octavius, we saw you plant the virus that brought down Atlas. You sabotaged the comms during the Sebastien mission, and you deleted the camera footage when Kazi was taken. You've been working against Mikalis this whole time—"

His heart turned to ice in his chest. "No, no, that wasn't me!"

"We trusted you. I trusted you!"

"Raiden, no. How can you believe those things? I would never betray any of you. The Brotherhood is my life, it's all I have."

"And now you don't have us." Raiden's voice shook as he added softly, "You don't have me."

Octavius covered his mouth to hide the sob. "Please," he whispered, begged.

"And you know what else I know, Octavius?"

He couldn't speak. His heart blocked his throat, and thumped in his head. It hurt so much—so much that he might shatter at any moment. "Rai, I'm sorry..."

Raiden's laugh cut down the line like a knife. "Even after all this time, you're so self-centered you can't see what's right in front of your face."

Tears wet Octavius's cheeks. He should hang up, but he

deserved this pain; he deserved everything Raiden could throw at him.

"You still there? You hear me?" Raiden asked, his tone twisting, turning dark. When he next spoke, the tremors and stutters had vanished. "Oh, Octavius. So smart, but so gullible too. I know you didn't do those things because I did them, and when I'm finished with the Brotherhood there will be nothing left but ashes."

The line died.

Octavius's tumbling thoughts screeched to a halt. His heart stopped. He stared at the phone, reeling while sitting still. Raiden had...

Raiden was the traitor?

All this time... *Raiden?!*

His friend of a dozen lifetimes, the one they'd entrusted with the inner workings of the Brotherhood? Octavius shot to his feet, redialed Raiden's number, but the phone screeched—disconnected.

His thoughts spun, taking the room with them. "Shit."

Raiden was the science guy. He knew everything about all of them, had access to confidential files. They all trusted him. Even Mikalis.

His whole world turned on its head. Raiden had betrayed him! "Fuck!"

He paced. He had to do something, call somebody. He dialed Zaine's number—the first number that came to him.

"Y'ello?"

"Zaine, it's Octavius, don't hang up! I need you to—"

"You wretched piece of shit, you had better hand yourself in right now. Where the fuck are you? If I find you before Mikalis, I'm going to rip you apart—"

"Zaine, shut up. Listen—"

"No, I'm not fucking listening to your bullshit. I never liked you, and you know what Eric told me? Yeah, how you got all up in his face for being my feeder, you snide little shit—"

"Zaine—fucking listen—"

"Fuck off."

The line cut off.

Octavius let out a growl. He dialed Zaine's number again. It clicked and went straight to his voicemail. "Zaine, do not delete this message. I called Raiden."

The connecting motel door opened, and Saint leaned against the doorjamb, all tousled and mussed in his creased suit. He'd probably just crawled out of bed. Had he heard everything Octavius had said? It didn't matter, this was more important.

Octavius dragged his gaze from him. "Raiden did all this, not me," he said in his message to Zaine. "Please, you have to believe me. We are—Raiden and I, we were close, but it was all bullshit. He set me up." Shit, he wasn't making any sense, and now Saint arched an eyebrow, as though he was judging Octavius. "I fucked up. I trusted him, I... Just look closer at Raiden. Please, I know you hate me, I know I'm an asshole, but I'm also Brotherhood, and that means something. It means something more than us. It's... everything. Memento mori."

He hung up and dialed Kazi's number. It didn't connect. He must have changed his phone. He tried Storm, but it rang out. "Fuck!" Octavius flung the phone at the wall next to Saint. it exploded into a thousand pieces. "FUCK, FUCK, FUCK!" He thumped his head and paced again. Back and forth. Raiden... It had been Raiden all along. His one and only friend.

His heart pumped, each beat brushing against razor blades. The betrayal stabbed at his chest.

"Well, I think I'm all caught up," Saint said, matter-of-factly.

Octavius dropped to his knees. He was so done, so tired, wrecked. Months on the run, months trying to figure out where it had all gone wrong, months wishing he could have told Raiden he loved him. And Raiden had just ripped out his heart. Octavius hadn't seen Raiden's truth. He'd been closer to Raiden than anyone and he hadn't seen a damn thing!

Saint crouched in front of him. "You know, before the world ends, I had planned to ride off into the sunset, but I figure the sunset can wait."

Octavius looked up and didn't care his face was wet, didn't care it was Saint who saw him like this. Nothing mattered anymore. His heart was broken.

His silver nyk eyes narrowed, vengeance in his sights. "We have a Brotherhood betrayer to kill."

"They'll never listen to me—or you. We can't get near them. Mikalis will destroy us."

Saint made an agreeable mumbling noise. "Then we'll make them listen. I'm very persuasive. Not as persuasive as you, with the witchy voodoo, but I have my ways."

"By breaking arms and crushing throats?" he asked, remembering how Saint had persuaded him to bleed a wrist for Jayden.

"There's a time for voodoo, and a time for breaking bones."

An exhausted smile tugged at Octavius's lips. No, damn it, he could not smile at Saint. He snarled it away and climbed to his feet, feeling a few thousand years older. What a sorry day it was that his only friend, his only help, came in the form of a nyktelios and his love-drunk feeder.

Jayden stood in the doorway wearing just an oversized shirt that did, at least, cover his groin.

This was Octavius's life now. This was all he had. A sleepy-eyed surfer boy and a mass murderer.

He coughed a distraught laugh. It was going to have to be enough. "They'll track that call," Octavius croaked out. "We need to leave."

"Daylight." Saint glanced toward the window. "It won't be pleasant."

"Nothing about any of this is fuckin' pleasant." Octavius nodded at Jayden. "You drive."

"Uh, sure." Jayden brightened. "Where are we going?"

Saint stood and sighed. "Somewhere you'll likely need pants."

CHAPTER 10

aine

THE MANHATTAN COFFEE shop called Dream Beans was the least likely place to house an immortal band of brothers, which made it the perfect front. Zaine nodded at the servers busy meeting the caffeine needs of New Yorkers, and headed through the back. He strode down the narrow hallway, into the storage room, then pulled the rack from the wall and pushed through a heavy security door into Atlas's new base of operations, which right now wasn't much more than Raiden and a laptop.

"Hey," he greeted. Raiden nodded, then poked his glasses back up the bridge of his nose.

Storm had arrived before Zaine and leaned against an empty bookshelf at the back of the small room, his dark mood and skin merging with the shadows. Zaine greeted him with a jerk of his chin. No Mikalis, but he hadn't been seen since London. Mikalis was on US soil though and hunting Saint, he knew that much.

"What have you got?" Storm grumbled from the gloom. He

wasn't happy. None of them were. Octavius had proven difficult to pin down, hence they'd called Zaine back to the east coast. He preferred it here, since it was closer to Eric and his work at the NYPD.

"Yeah, you're not going to like it. I got a call," Zaine said. "From Octavius. He said—"

"So did I," Raiden interrupted, flicking his eyes up from his screen. "He ranted about some conspiracy against him." It sounded as though Octavius had shared his theories with Raiden too. He truly must have been desperate. "Atlas is still rebooting but I've managed to get into the cell towers. The call came from somewhere in the Ozarks."

"Can you narrow it down?" Storm asked.

Raiden tapped his keyboard and turned his laptop so Storm could see. He moved from the back of the room and peered over Raiden's shoulder at the map. "That's thirty square miles."

Zaine took a look around Storm's bulk and saw a whole lot of forest with no large settlements.

"Yes, but..." Raiden pushed his glasses up his nose again and tapped a few keys. "Two days ago, the local police received reports of an explosion *here*." On the screen, he zoomed in on an aerial view of a building beside a lake.

"Zoom out," Zaine suggested, and watched the trees on-screen shrink. "More." The area made the perfect place to hide, but the explosion and a call from Octavius in that same location was no coincidence. Fucking Octavius. The little bitch was too smart for his own good. But that explosion was a mistake. He'd need to find somewhere to regroup. "There." Zaine tapped the screen over a tiny group of buildings. "What's that?"

Raiden tapped away and brought up pictures of a shabby single-level building. "Motel."

We've got you. "We need to get up there right now."

"I'll spin-up the chopper," Storm said, and made for the door. "You both are with me."

"My skills are better focused here," Raiden said. "I'm trying to get Atlas back online. It's proving difficult without Octavius's input. With Saint still loose, we need Atlas's eyes more than ever."

Storm nodded. "Then it's just you and I, Z. Ready up. We leave in ten."

Zaine waited a few beats after Storm had left, then turned back to Raiden. "How long until Atlas is online?"

"A few more days. I had to change some of the programming, go in a back door to work around some of Octavius's quirks. You know how he was. He had his own way of doing things. Some might say he was careless. To be honest, I fear he's been failing at his duties for a long time, and I... Well, I didn't want to say anything. I thought maybe he was just... being him, like he is sometimes."

"Yeah. Standoffish and a dick." Zaine folded his arms. During the call, Zaine had offloaded a rant at Octavius and would have said a whole lot more if the prick hadn't pissed him off within three seconds. "You and him were close?"

"Huh?" Raiden looked up. "Close? I guess. We worked together on the tech, mostly. I mean, are any of us close?"

The call had been hardly worth mentioning to Storm, but the message Octavius had left afterward hadn't sounded like Octavius at all. He'd seemed almost unhinged, even scared. And he'd said some things about Raiden. It had become clear he was getting desperate, and if he was coming undone, now was the perfect time to catch him. Before he fell too far down the nyk rabbit hole.

"What did he say to you?" Raiden asked, tapping away on his laptop and not looking up.

"Begged me to listen to his crap, that was all."

"Yes, I had the same."

Zaine considered having the team listen to it so they knew how far Octavius had fallen, but even after everything Octavius had done, something about that message felt off. It hadn't revealed any new information, only that Octavius blamed Raiden. Clearly, he'd been clutching at straws and pointing fingers because that was all he had left. Besides, they had the CCTV footage of him delivering the virus into Atlas. And he'd been in charge of comms during the

Sebastien fuckup. There were other niggly things about Octavius. He'd always been distant, and when he wasn't distant, he was a vicious, stuck-up prick who hated Eric, claimed they were all weak for loving someone other than themselves, and added nothing to the Brotherhood—except Atlas, which he'd almost destroyed.

Zaine wasn't even sure why Octavius was in the Brotherhood. Mikalis didn't even seem to like him. Although, like Raiden said, none of them liked each other. They were a brotherhood, forced together, not a fellowship. Brothers fought.

It is everything, Octavius had said in the message, as though he had cared.

Zaine glanced at Raiden busy rebooting Atlas. They had been close; perhaps Raiden should have seen something. Or perhaps there was more between them than they'd let on? Some kind of *relationship*? Raiden had kept himself distanced from the others too, always in the labs, always focused on the forensics. Could there be more to all of this? "Is there anything more we should know about you and Octavius?"

Raiden looked up. "Such as?"

Zaine's mobile pinged.

Let's go, Storm's message read.

Zaine headed for the door. It was time to weapon-up. "Call us if you crack Atlas open."

"Will do." Raiden flashed him a smile. "Have a nice flight."

CHAPTER 11

 ctavius

ALL MODERN CAR windows had UV protection, but much of the sun's powerful rays beat through the glass, wearing them down. Octavius slumped in the front passenger seat while Saint dozed in the back with his suit jacket draped over his face.

"I don't get out much. I mean, I didn't," Jayden said, comfortable behind the wheel. "I only learned to drive to go to college."

Octavius sighed through his nose. His head throbbed. Was Jayden going to try to talk to him the whole way out of state? What could he possibly say that Octavius would be interested in? How many followers he had on TikTok? Octavius didn't *do* small talk.

"Uh huh," Octavius mumbled back.

"That didn't work out, so I got some bar work in St. Louis."

"Do I look like I care?"

Jayden grimaced. "You don't like people much, do you?"

"People don't much like me."

"Maybe that's because you're mean?"

He sighed again. This was happening then. He was going to speak with Jayden as though he wasn't a feeder. At least if he talked to him, the agonizingly slow minutes might speed up. "People and me, we don't mix. It's always been that way."

Jayden mulled over that for a while, then asked, "You seem kinda angry all the time. Maybe it's a you problem? A friend of mine had a dog once—"

"You had better not be about to compare me to somebody's pet."

"No, I mean, kinda?" He screwed up his nose, then gleefully continued. "But this dog, it was a rescue, you know? When they found it, the poor thing was all kinda messed up, and angry all the time. It tried to bite everyone because that was all it knew. It had to be angry, to get by."

Octavius huffed and rubbed his forehead. He wasn't a fucking dog and he wasn't angry *all the time*. He stared out of the window at the passing tress. It was just that almost everyone turned on him, eventually, so he turned on them first. He'd survived this long because of it.

"Just sayin', it seems like you might have some... issues?" Jayden asked.

"Issues?" Octavius laughed. "What do you know about issues? You've been alive a blink compared to my existence. What issues could you possibly have in such a short life?"

Jayden fell quiet, watching the road, then said, "Must be kinda lonely, being an asshole."

"Fine," he snapped. Maybe if he told Jayden some of it, he'd shut up. "I was hunted, my whole life."

"What for?"

"For being a witch because I get inside minds. And the hair."

"Your hair is lovely. Very... Japanese anime." He waved a hand. "You have a whole sulky, emo-goth-vibe going on."

Octavius snorted. He had no idea what half of those words meant but Jayden seemed the sort to say every thought that entered his head, which in many ways made him more honest than most people. Perhaps he'd be able to tell Octavius about Saint—real information, not rumors and myths. "How did you meet Saint?"

"Oh, he stalked me," Jayden replied breezily.

"I *saved* him," came Saint's grumble from the back seat. "Not stalking."

There was a story there.

Jayden grinned. "It's a rags to riches tale, although, we don't have anything but this car and an overnight bag so... More of a Bonnie and Clyde, on the run from the law. Hm, that doesn't really work either. *Pretty Woman* maybe, but with a hot, ancient vampire as my sugar daddy."

Octavius tried to riddle out any of what Jayden had just said and failed there too.

"I was a mess," Jayden went on. "Drunk and high most nights, I guess. It seemed easier to escape that way," he said, smile fading. "I took a wrong turn out of a bar, ended up in a bad place. Some guys jumped me. I don't remember much, just that if Saint hadn't been there, I wouldn't be here now."

It sounded as though Saint had already been stalking Jayden with a view to turning him into a feeder, and the incident had given Saint the excuse he'd needed to move in. If it hadn't have been that, Saint would have found another way to lure Jayden to him. Typical nyk behavior.

"See, I saved him," Saint repeated.

Oh yeah, Saint was a real knight in shining armor. "We don't get involved," Octavius said.

"Huh?" Jayden asked.

"The Brotherhood, we don't get involved in human affairs. It's not our remit to save human lives."

Jayden frowned and glanced over.. "Like wildlife photographers?"

"What?"

"Observe, never interfere with nature, that kind of thing? If an elephant is drowning in mud, they have to let it drown, because you can't save every elephant."

Octavius blinked at him. "Yeah, I... uh... suppose."

He had an interesting way of seeing the world. Always optimistic, even in the face of darkness. Always smiling, always trying to find the good in a situation. But he had no idea what Saint had done to him. "In other words, Saint kidnapped you," Octavius said.

"He's mine," Saint growled.

Octavius ignored the typical protective nyk tone. "Don't you have people looking for you, Jayden? Family who are worried?"

"Not really. My parents disowned me since I came out. My sister is some hotshot lawyer. I hadn't heard from any of them in over a year. They probably hope I'm dead."

And that was a damn shame. Octavius had no time for feeders, but Jayden seemed to be harmless. No wonder Saint had ensnared him, like a spider catching a stupid fly. The nyk had seen how vulnerable Jayden was and singled him out. Find the weak and broken ones, then claim to help them so they worship their savior even as that savoir bleeds them dry.

Disgusting.

"I know what you're thinking." Saint pulled the jacket from his head and sat up. "And it's not like that."

"Sure," Octavius dismissed. "You took a vulnerable young man, fucked and fed from him, injected him with venom, and now he has no choice in anything he does. He's your personal blood bag until you grow bored, toss him out, and get yourself a new one."

Jayden glanced in the rearview mirror and his always-on smile faded under his concerned expression.

Saint narrowed his eyes at Octavius. "It's truly amazing how you've survived this long as the shortsighted, narrow-minded, self-centered prick I'm guessing you've always been."

"Fine, then tell me Jayden has a choice. He can pull the car up and leave, walk away right now, and he won't crave you within a few hours? After a day, he'll be crawling up the walls to get his next fix. The fact you picked an addict is so fucking transparent. You knew he'd be an easy catch."

"Is that true?" Jayden asked, gaze flicking from the mirror and Saint, then back to the road ahead. "Am I addicted to you?"

"Keep your eyes on the road—No."

"After a few days without you," Octavius went on, "he won't be able to function without your fangs in his neck and your dick up his ass."

An almost imperceptible growl rumbled from Saint. "I'm starting to see why nobody much likes you, Octavius."

"It's the truth. And you know it. Jayden should know it."

"When was the last time you had some dick up your ass?" Jayden said, bristling.

The question blindsided Octavius and shocked all thought from his head. "I... No, we're not talking about me. Or that."

"Why not? You brought it up," Jayden pushed. "Seems like you could do with a good humping. Just an observation."

"I don't need *that*. I don't do sex. It's not a thing I... want." He glanced at Saint in the mirror and wished he hadn't. The nyk smirked, probably remembering how hard Octavius had been when he'd had Saint against the wall. He felt the need to explain how sex hadn't been something he'd enjoyed for as long as he could remember, then bit the words back. He didn't need to explain anything to either of them. "We're discussing how his venom has infected you like a drug you crave, and you can't ever leave him. Do you understand that? Sometime in your future, you'll die, out of your mind with lust and madness for a creature you can't have, because he's dumped you at the side of the road. Or, he'll just kill you when he's done. Your pathetic life will be over, only having achieved being a cum-dump for a parasitic nyktelios."

"Fucking hell, Brotherhood." Saint laughed. "Who hurt you?"

Hurt him? How about *everyone*. "Fuck off. If I weren't trapped in this car, I'd get the hell away from both of you."

"Pull over," Saint said.

Jayden pulled the car to the curb along a quiet winding strip of back road.

"Go ahead then," Saint said. "Get out."

Octavius eyed the stretch of road outside. "It's daylight."

"You'll be fine under the trees. Go on. We don't need you. My life was just fine before you showed up, trying to recapture me for your fucking Lord of the Night, Mikalis. The only damn reason I haven't shattered you into a million pieces is because you saved Jayden. That's it. So leave."

Octavius swallowed. He could leave. He *should* leave. So why wasn't he? "We have an agreement. You need me to help you get closer to Mikalis without him killing you."

"Not really." Saint reclined back in the seat. "The chances of my redemption are so slim, they're not worth clinging to."

Octavius huffed. He couldn't leave. He did need them. Well, Saint, at least. And Saint needed Jayden. They were necessary. "I'm staying," he growled through clenched teeth.

Saint nodded, and Jayden pulled the car back onto the road. They rode in silence a while, until Jayden fiddled with the radio and found something Korean with a plucky upbeat note. He hummed along and tapped the wheel in time with the music.

Octavius slumped lower.

Perhaps it would be a mercy if Mikalis showed up and killed them all.

CHAPTER 12

aine

STORM LANDED the chopper at dusk on a wide patch of driveway beside the damaged lake house. As the rotor blades wound down, Zaine climbed out, ducked under fluttering police tape, and meandered through the rubble, searching for anything unusual.

It was a nice spot, right by the lake. Quiet, out of sight. The perfect place to hole up for a few days, or weeks. Or even months. Had that been Octavius's plan, just to hide? Why attempt to bring down the Brotherhood, only to hide out in the woods?

They were missing something—like a motive for Octavius's betrayal—but they'd find it.

Raiden had called while they were en route to inform them of the property's owner. The hotshot land developer in St. Louis had no idea anyone had been living in his house.

Zaine toed his boot through the debris. Any tire tracks had been obliterated by emergency service vehicles.

"Here," Storm called from down by the water.

Zaine approached and caught an old scent of blood on the breeze.

"Someone bled out here." Storm crouched by a patch of stained grass.

The debris from the explosion hadn't made it as far down as the water's edge, and there was no sign of drag marks. Whoever had lost a lot of blood here had been carried to that spot.

Zaine crouched and touched the dried blood, then the scattering of dark red flakes beside it. "He was here." He showed Storm the ashy substance on his fingers. "And he bled." A few days of daylight and Octavius's blood had disintegrated, whereas the human's blood still coated the ground.

Storm straightened and squinted back at the house. "There's no body and there were no reports of anyone being hurt or killed."

"Perhaps a fight?" Zaine considered. Whatever had happened in the house had played out on the lakeshore too.

Storm straightened and scanned the scene, then met Zaine's gaze. "Well, we know he's not alone." And he likely had himself a feeder. He'd have to. They all needed blood, and there was no way of getting it bagged this far from a city.

Feeding from the vein was a damn slippery slope, and one Zaine had found himself on more than once. It wasn't much of a stretch to go from that to full nyk.

"Let's check out the motel," Zaine said, grimly. Despite hating the prick, he didn't want to see him flip to the dark side. But the longer this went on, the more probable it seemed that Octavius would have to be put down.

Perhaps the motel would yield more promising news.

A CHOPPER LANDING in the motel parking lot wasn't something that happened often in these parts. A small crowd gathered, phones raised, taking photos. It would be all over the internet. But the furor would die down once the next shiny conspiracy theory distracted the masses. The noise of the internet was good for that, if little else.

"Hey." Zaine smiled at the woman behind the front desk. *Janice*, her badge said.

"You can't park that thing there," she grumbled.

He glanced back at the chopper and Storm's threatening bulk approaching. Zaine shrugged. "There aren't any signs saying no choppers, so..." He reached into his pocket and pulled out a photo of Octavius. "You seen this guy?"

Janice looked at the picture, then up at Zaine's face. "Are you cops?"

The bell tinkled and Storm clomped in, shrinking the tiny lobby area around them.

"We're private security," Zaine said, reeling off the usual line.

Janice scowled, unimpressed. Zaine tapped the photo. "This guy? Ringing any bells?"

"No."

"No?"

"I said no. I'm not going to miss someone looking like him, am I?" She tilted her head and eyed Storm behind Zaine. Her eyes widened a little, struggling to take in his smooth-headed, muscle-bound presence.

"Your camera's out," Storm said, his voice so low it sounded like a threat.

Zaine glanced at the corner of the ceiling, where a wire dangled from the camera. "How long has it been like that?"

"A few days, maybe?" Janice shrugged.

"Can we take a look at the footage before it went down?"

"No."

"Janice." Zaine leaned against the desk and ramped up the charm. The tall, blond Viking routine opened doors with most females. "C'mon, we just need a quick look. Nobody has to know, and then we'll be out of your hair."

"And lose my job? Just because you have a fancy helicopter, and you're all up in my face with your bodyguard, I'm not going to let two random guys look at our stuff without a warrant. You got a warrant? No, because you ain't cops."

"I'm not his bodyguard," Storm grumbled.

"All right, fine." Zaine huffed through his nose and straightened again. "Then have you seen anything out of the ordinary?"

"Like what?"

"People coming and going?"

She tucked her chin in. "It's a motel."

Storm snorted. "She's got you there."

"Some help here, big guy?"

"Ma'am." Storm stepped up to the desk, squeezing Zaine out. "The person we're looking for is armed and extremely dangerous. He also has an ability to be very persuasive. You may not even remember meeting him. So has anything happened to you, personally, or any of your staff that seems... off? Anything at all? Waking up somewhere when you don't remember how you got there, strange dreams, that kind of thing?"

"I mean, there was... something. It was kinda weird."

Zaine folded his arms. He must be losing his touch if Storm was getting witnesses to talk.

Janice tucked her hair behind her ear and bit into her lip. "A few nights ago, I was in the office here, and I... Well, I mean, it was probably nothing, but it was early in my shift, and then it was late, just like that. Hours gone. And I know I didn't sleep. I don't sleep on the job. We had one guy work here who fell asleep and some assholes stole the cash right out the register!"

She waffled some more about the need for security, and how she could use someone big and strong like Storm. Zaine left the lobby, letting her and Storm get acquainted, and questioned a few of the guests gawking at the chopper, but none of them had seen anything. One even offered Zaine five bucks for a selfie of them with the chopper in the background.

"We have a problem," Storm said, returning a few minutes later.

"A new problem, or more of the same problem?" Zaine asked, leaning against the chopper.

Storm nodded at Zaine to climb in, and as he readied the chopper, he glanced over. "Octavius fed from Janice."

"He did? Shit."

That was bad. It meant he was losing control. One step away from nyk, if he wasn't already too far gone. "Man, I was hoping he wouldn't make it worse, yah know?"

"How much worse can it get?" Storm pushed on the stick and the chopper lifted into the air with a roar of engine.

"We need Mikalis on this," Zaine said, raising his voice.

"He's already on it. Just a little... out of action for a while."

Out of action? Had something happened to Mikalis? "Meaning?"

The forest shrank beneath them and Storm angled the chopper west, away from the flightpath that would take them back to base. "While Mikalis was tracking Saint, Octavius showed up."

Zaine's heart sank. "Oh fuck."

"Oh fuck, is right. Mikalis didn't want me mentioning it to the others, but Octavius is not alone. He's likely with Saint in some way. We don't know if he's working with Saint, or if Saint is using him. But he let Saint out before the Atlas building imploded. That's one hell of a coincidence."

"You think they're working together? Shit. Two betrayers, and Octavius is drinking from the vein. I'm just going to say it, are we dealing with two powerful nyktelios, both of whom were Brotherhood?"

Storm didn't reply.

He didn't need to.

A bad situation had just gotten a whole lot worse.

CHAPTER 13

aint

THEY STOPPED for gas near dusk and Octavius did the necessary persuasion on the cashier. Intriguing little trick, that. And a powerful one in a world of suggestible humans.

Jay waited until Octavius was out of sight in the store, then twisted in the driver's seat to ask, "Is it true, what he said? Am I addicted to you?"

Fucking Octavius and his Brotherhood mantras. "If I were any nyk, then maybe, but I'm not any nyk, so no." The frown on Jay's face deepened. They'd been fine together for months and now Octavius was trying to drive a wedge between them. "Do you trust me?" Saint asked.

"Yes."

"Then *trust* me."

Octavius emerged from the store and crossed the gas station lot, passing by the pumps. He moved with long, deliberate strides, his body like a sheathed blade, poised for violence. Also, like a blade, he would cut indiscriminately. If only he'd see beyond the Brotherhood box and see the world for what it truly was. The Brotherhood stifled him. Smothered him. Restrained him. Like it did all its members.

If he were unleashed, he'd be glorious.

Saint wanted to see Octavius laugh, see him relax, see him run, see him fuck with abandon. He'd be a wild, brilliant creature. If he just relaxed and forgot all the rules keeping him chained, he might enjoy their last few weeks on this earth. He'd have to take his head out of his ass first though. Which didn't seem likely anytime soon.

"I know *hurt*, and he's hurting," Jay remarked, also watching him approach.

"Yes, he is."

That hurt went back a long way. But more recently, Raiden was the problem. Saint didn't care for the Brotherhood per se, but it seemed as though this Raiden had been undermining them for years and using Octavius's feelings for him to do it. Saint despised manipulators.

"Saint."

His name pierced his thoughts, rudely interjecting, but also tickling a shiver down his spine that wasn't unpleasant.

"Don't look over, but there's someone in the woods."

Saint looked. And at first, he didn't see anything out of the ordinary. Dusk light gave the air a strange orangey hue where it touched the trees. Mist lifted off wet branches. And there, among the mist, where it swirled, someone was trying very hard not to be seen.

"Jay, I'm going to get out of this car. I want you to pull away and keep on driving. Understand? Just keep going. I will find you later."

"What? Why?"

"Just do it." Saint opened the car door and climbed out. He took one last glance at Jay's angry, fearful face through the window and closed the door. Jay pulled the car onto the road. Its taillights blinked, and then it vanished around a corner.

"Mikalis?" Octavius whispered, stopping beside Saint.

"Yes."

"How does he keep finding us?"

Saint shook out his hands and rolled his shoulders, readying for impact. "He's my sire. He'll always find me."

Saint hadn't fed, not enough to fight Mikalis alone. He should have snacked on a motel guest when he'd had the chance. He glanced sidelong at Octavius, who did seem a little steadier than he should, considering all they'd been through. The sneaky prick had gotten blood from somewhere. *Do not drink from the vein.* Rule broken. Just a few more to go and he'd be down in the dirt with Saint.

"What?" Octavius gave him a double glance. "Why are you looking at me like that?"

"No reason whatsoever." The sneaky little wolf.

"Whatever you're smirking at—"

Octavius vanished midsentence—or more accurately, the briefest of shift in air currents indicated something was wrong before Mikalis tore Octavius from the spot beside Saint, and in less than a second, slammed him into one of the trees skirting the edges of the gas station. The tree crumpled and toppled forward, cracked in half at the trunk. Octavius knelt at its base, clutching his middle.

Where was Mikalis?

Saint spun, searching the tree line for movement in the shadows. In his peripheral vision, he noticed a few of the gas station staff emerge from the store to gawk at the fallen tree.

If Mikalis didn't care about witnesses, then Saint certainly didn't. He dropped his fangs. "Come on then, you want me? Show yourself!"

There was a blur to his right. He braced, and Mikalis slammed into him, as though a great hook had latched on to his back and tugged him through the air. He struck glass, heard it shatter, then landed inside the store against a stack of canned goods. The shelf buckled, cans rained. Saint reeled, stumbling as he doubled over, and then he saw Mikalis's shadowy blur surge forward under the bright convenience store lights. Saint snatched him by the neck. The act of getting his hand on him yanked him into physical form.

Saint swung him around and slammed him to the ground with enough force to buckle the concrete floor.

Mikalis hissed and lunged, breaking out of Saint's grip. Teeth snapped. Saint recoiled, avoiding those deadly daggers, and staggered backward. If Mikalis managed to sink those fangs in and deliver a shot of venom, it would all be over. Broken bones, Saint could heal. But he couldn't heal an envenomed heart.

He stumbled into another rack of goods, and stretching, he popped a few bones back into place.

"You're weak, Saint." Mikalis's voice filled his head, not unlike Octavius's little skill. But Mikalis's voice was a thousand times louder.

"I don't suppose you'll go easy on me?"

Mikalis shimmered into solid form in the middle of the aisle in front of him. His blue eyes blazed, his jaw-length curled hair somehow managing to look windswept *and* styled. He was as viciously handsome now as the day they'd met, long, long ago. He'd come to Saint as a god then. And nothing had changed. Mikalis *was* a god. But not one of the good ones.

Mikalis started forward, walking casually, as though he wasn't about to tear into Saint and have his ashes rain all over a no-name convenience store.

"You have a liar in your midst, Mikalis." Saint backed up.

"I see that."

"And you have the wrong perpetrator in Octavius. Maybe you should look closer to home than wasting time stalking me all over the Ozarks?"

"The mistake is mine. I should never have let you live."

The hate was real and visceral. Saint could taste its bitterness. It blinded Mikalis, made *him* weak. Saint straightened and tugged on his shirt cuffs, righting his suit. "There was a time I worshipped you. I might have still, if you'd been honest. But I can't abide manipulators."

"And I will not suffer *betrayers*."

Saint looked his sire in the eyes. "I've never betrayed you."

Mikalis's top lip pulled back in a snarl, revealing savage teeth. The weapons that would be Saint's end. Except, Saint wasn't alone, not this time.

Octavius swung a piece of metal bar and struck Mikalis on the side of the head. For any normal nyktelios, it would have knocked him sideways. But Mikalis stood firm, and the bar buckled *around* him.

Octavius staggered backwards with the bent bar in both hands. "Fuck." He dropped it with a clang and raised his hands. Mikalis turned slowly.

"I know what this looks like, but I'm not with him," Octavius gushed, backing up.

"He is," Saint said, wiping blood from his mouth. "We have an agreement."

"I didn't plan this, Mikalis. I didn't let Saint go."

He sounded weak, the little wolf, in the face of Mikalis's judgement. And that wasn't right. Octavius wasn't weak. Complicated, vicious, hard to like, but not weak.

"I thought more of you, Octavius. I *trusted* you," Mikalis snarled.

"I know! And I didn't break that trust."

Octavius's begging tone made Saint sick to his stomach. He'd sounded the same once, begging for forgiveness that would never come. Mikalis wasn't capable of forgiving.

"Raiden—I know how it sounds," Octavius rambled on. "But I'm not just blaming everyone else. You need to look at Raiden. He admitted it—"

"You're feeding from the vein, you're sharing a feeder, and you're colluding with my enemy? Why would I believe you?"

Octavius's face fell. He realized he'd never win this fight. He'd hoped, until this very moment, that he had a chance. Saint knew that grief, he'd been there, hoping that the truth would outshine all the lies. But it didn't.

Venom soured Saint's tongue.

Mikalis had his back turned, focused on Octavius.

Was Saint really going to kill Mikalis?

What choice had he left him? Kill or be killed.

He lunged, fangs bared, and reached for Mikalis's neck. Mikalis twisted and grabbed Saint's jaw, holding him aloft. Mikalis's glare burned with disgust. Even now, in these final moments, Saint's naïve heart still hoped he'd see the truth, and for Mikalis to know Saint had never wanted to hurt him. He wished for more time, wished it didn't have to end like this, wished he'd gotten Octavius his redemption.

An engine roared, light flooded the convenience store, and a car plowed through the remains of the window, slamming into Mikalis. He vanished, buried under the car.

Saint dropped to the floor, spluttering, and watched as the car plowed into more racks of food, then smacked into the convenience store's back wall, lodging there, halfway through, wheels spinning and horn blaring. Then the engine died, and the horn cut off.

The silence that followed numbed Saint to his core.

"That's your car!" Octavius dashed through the twisted shelving and yanked off the driver's door. The air bags had inflated, saving Jay's life. Octavius dragged his unconscious body from the buckled car, slung him over his shoulder, and barked at the hiding cashier to hand over his keys.

Still numb, Saint found himself climbing through the hole in the front of the store and following Octavius to the car that blipped its alarm, answering the key fob Octavius had.

Octavius opened the rear door, laid Jay inside, and climbed in behind the wheel. *"Saint, get in."*

The demand took his hand and guided him. He climbed in, still seeing Mikalis's hate-filled glare in front of his eyes as Octavius sped the car away from the gas station.

"He's not dead," Octavius said. "He's okay... Saint?"

He twisted and scanned Jay's body for any serious wounds. His heartbeat was strong. The gash on his head had caused him to lose consciousness, but he'd be all right.

Jay had saved them both.

Octavius punched the wheel. "He's never going to listen!"

Welcome to my world, Little Wolf, Saint thought. "Drive. Don't stop, don't slow, just drive."

Octavius dropped a gear, the engine roared, and the car lurched forward.

Octavius had just seen the real Mikalis, and it was exactly as Saint had said. Mikalis didn't want the truth. He just wanted them gone. And that was Saint's fault because Mikalis believed Octavius knew *everything*.

Perhaps it was time he did.

CHAPTER 14

ctavius

HE DROVE all night and into the day, hating every headache-inducing glare and stabbing flare of sunlight off passing cars. He drove until he couldn't see straight, and the car rattled to a halt on the side of the road, out of gas.

Jayden had woken during the day, complained of aches and pains, and Saint had tried to comfort him. He'd fallen silent since then. They all had.

And now they were out of the car, walking down a roadside, with no idea where they were or where they were headed.

The situation was dire.

"I can't." Jayden dropped to his ass on the soft shoulder of the road. "I gotta stop a minute." He slumped over, draped his arms over his knees, and bowed his head.

There might have been more internal damage, or he was just exhausted.

Octavius eyed Saint. "Get him up and moving."

"He needs rest."

"Mikalis will be tracking us."

"I know."

"He will kill us if he catches us."

"I know."

Why wasn't Saint even a little bit anxious? Didn't he care? Mikalis was a gods-damned force of nature and he was on their tail. Octavius was beginning to understand what the nyks felt, knowing the Brotherhood had them in their sights, and it wasn't good. "If he catches us, he will snap Jayden in half like a fucking twig. Is that what you want?"

Saint blurred all up in Octavius's face, fangs bared. *"I know."*

Octavius snarled back, threw up his arms, and started walking. He was done. They could follow or not. He was done with all of it, everyone, everything. The Brotherhood, nyks, everything. He had nothing, and so he owed nothing to anyone. He was alone, just like he'd always been. Outcast. Witch. Scorned and burned. He was a fool to think Mikalis was different.

A truck rumbled by. Octavius marched on until he heard the brakes squeak, and then he turned. The driver slammed the truck in reverse and pulled to the roadside.

"Oh, thank you so much!" Saint's accent was foreign again, playing the lost tourist act. "Our car broke down and we've been walking for miles. Do you think you can give us a lift?"

"Sure, get on in," the driver agreed.

Octavius sighed and watched Saint help Jayden climb into the truck's back seat. This couldn't end well. The driver probably wouldn't make it through the night.

Octavius started back toward them. Jayden was traumatized, and Saint had been *off* since the run-in with Mikalis. There was no way Octavius could ditch them now. He had to see this through.

"Oh, there you are." Saint grinned. "Ah, yes, my partner, sorry, did I not mention him?"

"Partner?" The man failed to hide his disgusted snarl. "Like, a couple?"

"Is that a problem?" Saint asked.

"No, I guess." The driver faced away, focusing on the road. "Get in."

Octavius climbed into the cramped half-cab beside Jayden and settled in for what would hopefully be an uneventful ride. The driver asked where they were headed, Saint gave him a bullshit story and said they'd go as far as he'd take them, and they all fell into an awkward silence.

An hour in, Jayden shifted, slumping against Octavius's side, then dozed there. His human warmth burned through Octavius's clothes, and his feeder scent tingled Octavius's senses. He'd forgotten he'd given Jayden his blood, but there was no chance of forgetting it now. Having Jayden close reminded him how, when he'd straddled him to save his life, Octavius's instincts had kicked in, demanding he take the weak and dying Jayden as his.

Octavius avoided human contact. Always.

Kazimir used to take a new one to his bed almost every weekend. Octavius had hated him for that, for being so careless, for needing sex. But trapped in the truck cab with Jayden plastered to his side, old, buried instincts began to simmer to the surface. Apparently, he wasn't as cold as he tried to be because the physical urges making themselves known didn't care Jayden belonged to Saint.

He forced the feeding thoughts from his head by thinking of Mikalis, and how Octavius was generally fucked. He'd believed he could make Mikalis see the truth, because the truth was true. He'd believed Mikalis would see that. Until now.

If Mikalis wasn't going to be reasonable, Octavius had to work on one of the others in the Brotherhood. Not Storm, he was too close to Mikalis. Zaine was possible. He had questioned Mikalis in the past. Something had happened between them, some prickly incident that had added tension to the room whenever they were together.

Zaine might be a weak point to get back inside the Brotherhood, in terms of having them listen, but considering Zaine's reaction to the phone call, it wouldn't be easy getting him to listen either.

Whatever happened, Mikalis was a lost cause.

No wonder Saint was like he was. From the back seat, Octavius could just make out the line of Saint's neck, and how his short brown hair curled at its ends, unkempt but free.

He'd loved Mikalis once. And it had all gone wrong for him too. Octavius felt that same grief-like sting in his chest. Was it really over? Had the Brotherhood given up on him?

Jayden yawned, slid down Octavius's chest, and rested his head on his lap. Octavius froze. The feeder fell asleep again in moments, but now he was *on* Octavius. His floppy blond hair lay in shaggy curls. Some rested on his neck, over his flickering pulse.

"You good?" the driver asked, glimpsing him in the rearview mirror. Octavius hadn't cared to remember his name.

"What? Yes. Fine."

Saint smirked in the side mirror. Octavius narrowed his eyes back at him. Saint grinned, as though he knew everything and was always right. Although, in Mikalis's case, he *had* been right.

They pulled into a truck stop, and the driver hopped out for a *pitstop*, as he called it.

Alone, in the dark, in the quiet of the cab, Octavius could feel Jayden's rushing blood against his thigh. His warmth beat too, like a drum, calling to Octavius. His fangs ached, eager to be freed. "You need to get Jayden off me."

Saint laughed and twisted to peer into the back. "Let him sleep. He's not doing any harm."

"He took my blood. This is... uncomfortable."

Saint's eyebrows lifted. "It was just a little blood. You can control yourself. It's not as though you're turning nyk, is it?"

How could he joke about such things? "No, I'm fine, I just... He's warm, that's all."

"Relax, we'll ride with this guy for a few more hours, then..." He trailed off. "Hm, this looks interesting."

Octavius followed his gaze to see a group of three men

approaching the truck. Their masculine swagger suggested all three were hungry for violence.

"I guess our driver doesn't much like us," Saint said in a monotone voice that had Octavius's insides flipping over and a flicker of nerves clenching his gut, but in a strange, needy way.

Violence scented the air, a heady mix of male sweat and adrenaline. "Hey, you guys. Get out of the truck!"

"Me?" Saint slid an elicit, knowing glance to Octavius, and innocently asked the men, "Is something wrong?"

Octavius shuddered a breath and tried to calm his racing heart. This scenario was triggering all of his needs and desires in peculiar ways. Hungry, tired, and confused, he wanted to climb down with Saint and tear into all three of them—wanted to do more than that. They sought violence, he could smell it on them, see it in their cocked poses, and he wanted to give them exactly that.

He tore his gaze away and stared out of the window. Jayden stirred on his lap, and that too, set his veins ablaze. Jayden was in danger. Jayden was *his*. Protect Jayden. Protect his blood source. He hadn't allowed himself to think it until now, but the feeder *was* his. He had Octavius's blood in his veins. That was why he'd damn well stayed, and why he'd rushed in and dragged him from the wrecked car, and it was why he burned up now, with these humans about to threaten them.

"Easy there, Little Wolf. I've got this." Saint's silvery eyes flashed in the dark, and he jumped down from the truck. "What seems to be the problem?"

One of the men whipped out a gun—and Saint became a blur, rushing at them like a furious wave. The men buckled, bent, fell to their knees, attacked by the unseen. One fired the gun, then the gun vanished.

A passing truck's lights swept over the scene, and Octavius saw how Saint had one of them wrapped in his arms, fangs in the man's neck, drinking him down.

The sight was a kick to the guts, a punch to the heart, and triggered all his needs and desires at once. Octavius wasn't supposed to want that. He couldn't drink from the vein, but he already had, so what was another taste? The nyk in him screamed for release. He breathed hard, pressed himself into the seat and tried to fight the pounding, desperate *need* to unleash, to let go, to surrender. The ancient beast in him thrashed for freedom. His fangs throbbed, needing the relief of sinking into human flesh.

He couldn't stop it, and didn't want to.

Sliding out from under Jayden, he dropped from the truck and rushed the nearest homophobic asshole. Octavius slammed him against the side of a truck, plunged his fangs in his throat, and the blood came, hot and fast, pumping hard, pouring into him. Need screamed for more. He clutched the man tighter in his fists and drank him down, deeper and deeper, gorging like he hadn't allowed himself to do in millennia.

"Easy there, or he'll be dead, and you'll sulk and whine for days." Saint's hand landed on Octavius's shoulder.

Octavius whirled, gasping, ablaze with heat, his body and heart on fire. Saint half smiled and wiped a drop of blood from his lips with his thumb. Octavius watched, entranced by that one smooth gesture.

The desire wasn't waning, but it was changing, morphing into something more carnal.

"We got what we needed. They'll sleep it off." Saint's eyes narrowed. "Octavius?"

What would happen if Octavius closed the distance between them, took him in his fists, and tasted his lips? There was still blood there, spilled, fresh human blood. He'd lick it from him, then feed on another, then another—

"Hey." Saint snatched his shoulder. "Reel it in, take back your control."

Control, yes. He shook his head, trying to clear this thoughts, but his veins throbbed. Damn, he was hard for Saint, ablaze with a need that one man's blood hadn't sated.

"You in there, Octavius?"

He nodded and swallowed hard. "Yes. Yeah. I'm fine."

"You've got this." Saint patted him. "It can't be easy, after drinking from blood bags for a few hundred years. Quite the sensory overload?"

It was. There had been Janice, back at the motel, but that was just a taste, a few desperate drops to get him through the days. A tiny candle flame. This was a match to a can of gasoline.

Octavius shrugged off Saint's grip. "You drive," he growled, climbing into the back of the truck. Thankfully, Saint hadn't seen his physical arousal. But Jayden was awake, and did see. The feeder's keen gaze traveled down Octavius's chest, to the sharp bump in his trousers, then flicked back up to his face, asking so many questions with his soft, emotive eyes.

Octavius shook his head. Saint couldn't know. It would make things complicated, more complicated than they already were.

"Thank you, fine gentlemen, for the truck," Saint said, pulling the truck away from the unconscious trio. "Maybe they learned something about themselves?"

"Yeah, not to pick up handsome hitchhikers." Jayden snorted and side-eyed Octavius.

Octavius shifted away, propped his head on his hand, and stared out the window at the darkness rolling by.

He was hard and hungry and wild. He was nyk.

And there was no going back.

CHAPTER 15

ctavius

WHETHER IT WAS by chance or local knowledge, Saint pulled the truck off the main road and down a forest track that brought them to a cabin with a spectacular view of a valley and a distant town.

The cabin was empty and it smelled stale. Nobody had been home for a long time.

Octavius left Saint and Jayden in the cabin and walked the overgrown yard to a half-rotted picnic table perched on the edge of a drop. He sat on the table part, boots up on the seat, and stared at the town's lights and how they tried to compete with the stars scattered above.

Jayden approached with all the stealth of an elephant through the long grass. "I er guess you want to be alone—"

"That is why I'm out here *alone*."

"Okay, I just... Saint lit the fire, and there's some food, mostly tinned food, but it's something... Although, I guess you've already eaten..."

He prattled on, trying to backpedal his way out of talking about *feeding*. He likely felt an attraction toward Octavius too. Probably thought it was normal to lust after a man he'd only met a few days ago, since he believed Saint's lies about not being addicted.

"Imagine if you've spent your whole life believing you were doing the right thing, making a difference," Octavius said, interrupting Jayden explaining how he was going to see if he could bake cookies with limited ingredients. "And then imagine your whole life spans several thousand years. Now take that time and belief, and throw it away. Everything you believe is now in ashes. You burned it all down. You have become the very monster you've been fighting against for millennia."

Jayden shuffled in the grass. "Sounds bad."

Octavius almost laughed.

"There's cocoa?" Jayden offered.

"Cocoa is not going to fix me, Jayden." He glanced behind him and was struck by how disheveled and vulnerable Jayden looked, standing there, defenseless against the world that wanted to kill him. Defenseless against the two nyks who now had him in their clutches. He didn't stand a chance. He'd die, either killed by Saint or Octavius, when feeding got out of control. Because by Nyx, Octavius wanted to taste his neck, sink his teeth in, and that... that couldn't ever happen. He... liked Jayden. Foolishly. Ridiculously. Against his better judgment and common sense. He liked the kid, and this fucked-up world was going to take him from them. It always did.

"Look," Jayden huffed, flicking his hair. "I know you think I'm some stupid himbo who's in way over his head, but I have eyes, and I'm not as ignorant as you assume. Saint says you saved my life, although I don't remember much of it—"

Octavius snorted. "We're tied together as nyk and feeder because you have my blood in you. I didn't envenom you, but frankly, it'll probably happen. Fuck, Jayden. What you think you feel is not real, none of it is real—I don't care about you—it's all chemicals in the brain. I am nyktelios, and while I look and talk

96

human, I'm not. What I am inside is designed to hunt and kill. I will do everything in my power to find and secure a food supply —*you*. It's the same with you and Saint."

Jayden moved around the table and sat on the seat slats next to Octavius legs. He stared at the view. "He says it's not like that."

"He's lying to keep you compliant. It's been like that since the dawn of time. Since prehistoric humans worshipped nyktelios as gods."

"I think you're wrong."

Now Octavius did laugh. "A human thinks *I'm* wrong. Get a few thousand years behind you and then tell me I'm wrong, and I'll listen."

"You know what I think is really happening?" He tilted his head, side-eyeing Octavius.

"I'm sure you're about to tell me."

"You're lost and hurting. Not long ago you had everything under control, and something bad happened to take that away from you. You feel like you've lost everything, including yourself. This might surprise you, but I know exactly what that feels like." He blinked soft doe eyes. "Just because I've only been alive for a few decades, it doesn't mean I don't get how you're in pain."

Octavius didn't even have the energy to argue, when Jayden wouldn't believe him. They were as different as night and day. Jayden couldn't understand what it meant to be shunned for so long that you began to believe you deserve it. That you were wrong, different, broken.

"Also." Jayden stood and brushed grass seed from his trousers. "You should come inside or I might let slip to Saint how you're hot for him."

"I'm not—that—what you saw—it was bloodlust, nothing else."

"It's okay to want to fuck him." Jayden grinned. "If you take the stick out from up your ass, you might even enjoy it."

"I told you I don't need that."

Jayden glanced back at the house, then hooked his thumbs over his trouser pockets. "When was the last time someone was kind to you, Octavius?"

Jayden's words rocked him like a physical blow. He opened his mouth to reply but had none that would suffice.

Jayden smiled a soft, understanding smile, one with warmth that touched his freckles. "Come inside." He ducked his head and ambled back to the cabin.

Octavius stared after him.

There was a slim chance he may have underestimated Jayden.

He hopped off the table and returned to the cabin. The wood burning stove blazed and the space had warmed. Saint stood at a bookcase, rifling through the selection of books, while Jayden clanged around the open-plan kitchen space, probably making cocoa.

Octavius paused by the door, stuck silent by the scene. In this brief moment, everything felt... good. Jayden poured hot water into three mugs, and Saint ran his finger down the page of a reference book. Octavius didn't hate them, he realized. He felt comfortable here. He'd spent his life pushing people away, but these two? He didn't mind being around them. What did that mean?

Nothing, it meant nothing. Just that they needed to make progress.

"We can't keep running," Octavius announced.

Saint placed the book on the shelf, and with a weary sigh, he faced Octavius. "Agreed. He will kill us both, as he seems to believe we're working together." He scratched at his neck and took a deep breath. "So, here's the thing, Mikalis thinks we're in cahoots and as there's no changing his mind, we should work with it. You've had your heart broken by the Brotherhood, and frankly, Jayden and I are all you've got. So I believe now is a great time to reveal a few fun facts that will get you killed. Are you game?"

"What facts?" Octavius asked carefully. He perched on the arm of the couch and waited.

"Mikalis is not nyktelios," Saint blurted and then winced, as though expecting a backlash.

But that didn't make any sense. He *had* to be nyktelios. They all were. What else could he be? Saint was wrong, but he'd listen. "Go on."

"So, you're sitting down, which is good..." Saint paced in front of the fireplace, with the flames blazing behind him. "Mikalis is a First. One of two warriors Nyx created to protect her."

"First what?"

"*The* First."

"The first...? Wait, the first nyktelios?"

"No. Pay attention, Octavius."

Jayden offered Octavius a mug of hot cocoa. Octavius scowled and took it, then went back to studying Saint's pacing and agitated hand gestures.

"All things began with Nyx and Erebus, Chaos and Darkness, correct?"

"According to the legends, yes."

"Erebus got out of hand, bullied Nyx, and to put him in his place, Nyx created two warriors. She made them hungry and fierce so they would *never* stop protecting her."

"Yes, the first nyktelios."

Saint stopped and looked up. "They weren't nyktelios. They were The First. They look like us, mostly. The same as we look like humans, but we're not, and they aren't nyks. They're gods. Mikalis is a First. He's a god, as old as Time, literally."

Octavius had been about to bring the mug of cocoa to his lips, but paused. "So, wait, Mikalis is a god and Nyx's... son?" That seemed a little far-fetched, even for Mikalis. He was powerful, and definitely old, but beginning of time old, worshipped as a god old?

"You don't believe me, that's fine, I don't expect you to."

"Good, because no, I don't. He's powerful, but he's a nyktelios. The fangs, the hunger—"

"Have you ever seen him feed?" Saint asked. "Or drink blood from bags, however the Brotherhood does it now?"

Octavius thought back through the many, many centuries he'd known Mikalis. He'd never fed in front of him, but that wasn't conclusive. "No, but it's only recently the Brotherhood has gathered together. We used to stay apart for much of our lives. He gets blood like the rest of us."

Jayden sat on the couch with his cocoa, enjoying story time.

"Run with it," Saint said, still pacing. "Let's see where it gets us, hm. The First, god-warriors made by Nyx to protect her from her brother, grew curious and learned how to create."

"All right."

Saint stopped and glared. "So intelligent, yet so slow. Mikalis and the other First created the nyktelios, as we know them, and they didn't stop at one. They made more and more. Why do you think Mikalis is all about the Brotherhood every single living, breathing moment he exists? This nyktelios plague is all his fault. All of it. And he knows it."

"He created the nyktelios? It's an interesting theory, but why wouldn't he just tell us, if that's the case?"

"Because you all believe he's like you, so you follow him blindly into the dark. Nyks are bad, the Brotherhood are better, etcetera etcetera. If you all learned he's a god, and he began this eternal war, are you going to march into battle alongside him, or are you going to look at him, see a god who messed up, and continues to mess up, and go your own way?"

"Wait, so you're, technically, one of the first *ever* nyktelios?"

"Yes. I told you. I'm one of his few remaining original creations, first generation. Eventually, when he took a long hard look at the clusterfuck of a world his little project was ruining, he realized he'd made a mistake and decided to wipe us all off the map. He began hunting us to extinction. This is the reason the Brotherhood was created. He's been on that same crusade since a little after Time and Order created the world you and humans live in today."

Octavius glanced at Jayden, who shrugged and said, "Sounds legit."

Saint pointed at Jayden. "Jay understands."

"Jay barely knows the alphabet," Octavius drawled.

Jayden laughed. That laugh's luscious timbre clenched desire low in Octavius's gut, forcing him to his feet and away from the feeder so he could clear his head and think about more important things than sinking his teeth into Jayden's neck.

"You're smarter than this. Why don't you believe it, Octavius? Are you so in love with the idea of your perfect leader that you can't see the truth of him?"

"Why are you so hell-bent on destroying him?"

"I'm not, I—" Saint cut himself off, then flopped onto the couch next to Jayden. "I worshipped him, as my creator, as a god. I loved him, when love was new and humans hadn't yet claimed dominion over it. I was there when he created the Brotherhood. I was the first fucking member. I watched him track and kill the others, but he didn't hunt me, so I believed..."

"You thought you were safe."

"Then like that—" Saint clicked his fingers. "—he turned on me. My love, my life, he turned around and tried to destroy it."

Octavius knew how that felt. And he had to admit, Mikalis was known for being blinkered when it came to the Brotherhood. There was the Brotherhood way, or death. All nyks must die. Never care, never make more nyks. Do not interfere in humanity. One goal. One mission. Destroy the nyktelios. Destroy his mistake?

The Brotherhood was cleaning up *his* mess. They weren't doing a good thing for humanity, they weren't saving the world. Mikalis's motives weren't as altruistic. He'd fucked up, and the Brotherhood was his cleanup crew. His *puppets*. If they succeeded, would he then turn on them, as he had Saint?

Shit, if the others knew this, if they believed it, the Brotherhood would collapse.

Octavius set the cocoa aside and drifted toward the fireplace, then to the window and back. His heart thumped, filling his head, drowning out a rattle that felt a lot like fear. None of this changed the fact that the nyktelios *were* a plague that needed to be stopped. That was still true. But the lines had blurred. The Brotherhood was only different because Mikalis made it so. He could just as easily rip it all away tomorrow.

No wonder Mikalis was trying so damn hard to kill them. The entire Brotherhood foundation was at stake.

"I think he's getting it," Jay whispered to Saint next to him.

"I'm sorry, Little Wolf," Saint said softly. "I was naïve and in love once too. I wanted you to have that a little while longer."

"We're all his mistakes," Octavius muttered, pacing like Saint had moments ago. "The entire Brotherhood is in danger... from Mikalis."

"Yes. However, he's failed in stopping the nyks, so there's that."

"What?" He stopped pacing and stared at Saint. "What do you mean, he's failed?"

"The nyktelios numbers have reached critical mass. I can feel it, and so can he. The Brotherhood cannot stop their rise. Mikalis has known it for months. The Brotherhood lost. *He* lost."

"He failed, so what does that mean, exactly?"

"It means the nyktelios will spread and consume. Order will break down. Chaos will ensue. The end of the world, basically."

While Octavius had been on the run, things had gotten *that* bad? "How long?"

"A few months. Once the general public is aware the nyktelios are among them, they'll likely do much of the destroying themselves. Humans have an enviable bloodlust, once fired up."

Jayden nodded, agreeing, as he was the only human present.

"A few months?!"

"This world exists on a delicate balance. Tip the scales, and it collapses. Chaos destroys. It's what She does."

This was too much. It couldn't be real, not all of it. Not now. Octavius couldn't think around all of this *madness*. He paced to the window and stared outside at the thick curtain of blackness. Could everything really end? "What do we do?"

"I had planned on mostly feeding and fucking and generally enjoying being free before either Mikalis killed me or the world died."

His answer was: nothing? Anger poked at Octavius's instincts. "You're one of the oldest nyks. You were made by Mikalis, Nyx's son, and you're just going to sit on your ass and let the world burn around you?"

Saint's right eyebrow arched. "I don't owe the world anything. I believe you understand what that's like."

"This world has fucked me over more times than you can imagine, but I will still fight for it because it's all we have. There's no Plan B."

Saint smiled and leaned back. He draped an arm over the couch cushions and Jayden leaned into him. "Not so much of a not-caring Brotherhood member, are you?"

"I care, yes. I care what happens to the people, and I care that it doesn't all end in chaos." Frustration and anger simmered in his veins. He had to do something. This had to be stopped. "I've always cared, it's true. I just... didn't show it."

"Because, in the past, when you gave your heart to others, it was used against you."

Octavius's next words lodged in his throat. How did Saint know that about him? Was he so obvious? "Trying to save people got me turned," he admitted, but couldn't say anymore. Even now, thousands of years later, the memory was too sharp, too vicious. It cut anew every time he looked back. So he didn't look back, and he didn't care, and he shut others out. It was easier that way.

"We are all nyktelios," Saint said. "We are all Mikalis's children. Some are mad with bloodlust, some thrive on control, some thirst for chaos, and some hide in the shadows. We are creatures of his making. The enemy you've been told to hunt and kill for millennia is just another nyktelios—like you, like me. Granted, they lack control, but we're the same."

"Fuck." Octavius slumped against the wall beside the fireplace.

"The truth hurts."

It was all a lie to control them. Mikalis was using them. It fit. That was why Mikalis was trying to kill Saint, and why he'd turned so viciously on Octavius. The members of the Brotherhood were his pawns.

And Octavius had fallen for it. All the Brotherhood had.

"I just... I need to... Some air... " He left the cabin, walked down the yard, past the table, and kept on walking, striding faster and faster, until his heart raced and the world blurred.

He ran. Ran so damn fast. If he ran hard enough, he might leave the truth behind and go back to the way things had been before. He stopped on the fringes of the nearby town, then pulled his hood up, tucked his hands into his pockets, and walked down the streets, passing a twenty-four-hour convenience store. Humans mingled; not many, as it was late. But they passed by in their cars, talked on their phones, going about their lives.

He entered the store and watched a woman drag a bored little girl along beside her. A girl who thought she had a long life ahead of her, full of dreams and potential.

Octavius almost yelled at them to run, to get far away and hide. He'd tried to save people like them before. Back then, it had been with herbs and fauna, and they'd called him a witch. More recently, it had been with computers and technology. And he'd thought he was making a difference.

It was all a lie from a god who had messed up and was trying to brush his mistakes under a cosmic rug.

He walked the town until the sun rose, and his muscles grew tight from weariness. Mikalis might have been a lie, but the Brotherhood was not. They believed in protecting the world by killing nyks and preventing chaos. That hadn't changed.

Octavius still needed to get through to them, to make them see how Raiden was undermining them and to plead his case so they knew he wasn't the traitor they all thought him to be.

He returned to the cabin to find Jayden sat reading on the couch.

"Hey." Jayden took in what must have been Octavius's tousled state. "You good?"

"Yeah. Is Saint—"

Saint emerged from the side door and Octavius nodded for him to head back outside. They met at the picnic table, and for a while Saint waited in silence, staring at the town in the valley.

It was good that he was quiet. He seemed to know when not to speak. He knew a lot and had been locked away for it.

"Nothing has changed," Octavius said.

Saint arched an eyebrow.

"I don't want to die, and you don't either, so let's begin with that."

"What do you suggest?"

"We kidnap Zaine."

"Good." Saint waited a beat, then asked, "Who is Zaine?"

"An obnoxious dick, but also one of the few in the Brotherhood who isn't afraid to question Mikalis."

"Sounds promising. When we have him, then what?"

"We make him listen."

"Is he likely to?"

"No, but it's all we've got." Octavius explained that in all likelihood the Brotherhood was searching for him alongside Mikalis. Storm could pilot a chopper, which meant Storm and at least one more would be tracking them. Storm was Mikalis's right-hand man and immovable when it came to his devotion to the Brotherhood leader. He couldn't be kidnapped and made to listen. That left Zaine or Kazimir as possible ways in. Kazimir could potentially be convinced, especially as he'd already interacted with Saint over the years, but Octavius's instincts were telling him Zaine was the more pliable target. As the youngest, he could still see outside Mikalis's orbit.

"How do we lure Zaine in without Mikalis finding us?" Saint asked.

"You lead Mikalis away, since he'll track you over me."

"Great." He grinned without humor. "Was nice knowing you, Octavius. Beneath all that—" He waved a hand at Octavius's face. "—you might actually be tolerable."

"Just lure him away, don't fight him."

"Uh huh." Saint smirked. 'To borrow Jay's wildlife analogy, you're asking a seal to lure a great white shark out to sea, but sure, I won't fight him."

Octavius's heart gave an unexpected hiccup at the thought of Saint dying by Mikalis's hand. He was nyk, he *should* die. Yet... things weren't as black and white as they'd been yesterday. And if he died, Jayden would be distraught, probably suicidal, which meant Octavius would have to step in. He rubbed an approaching ache from his forehead. "Just don't die."

Saint touched his chest. "Is that a tiny semblance of caring for me?"

"No, I just don't want the headache afterward."

They fell into a soft, comfortable silence. "Jay stays here," Saint said.

"Agreed." Even if Jayden had technically saved them both from Mikalis the last time. Now that Mikalis was aware of him, Jayden was an obvious weakness.

Also, Octavius needed to know the feeder was safe. He wouldn't be able to think straight if he feared for Jayden's life.

"Where do we set the trap?" Saint asked.

Octavius nodded toward the town. "Down there."

CHAPTER 16

aint

THEY STOOD about in a hardware store parking lot like sitting ducks. The store stayed open until midnight, for some inexplicable reason. It wasn't because of demand. The lot was empty, besides their own stolen truck.

Octavius simmered with anticipation, coiled tight as a spring. He had been sitting on the truck's hood, then he'd switched to leaning against the fender, then he'd paced, and now he was back on the hood. All the while, Saint waited in the driver's seat, facing the open door.

Beneath the sparse parking lot lighting, Octavius's hair gleamed like snow. He stared away, so Saint could admire his back and the slim line of his shoulders. To pass the time while they waited for the Brotherhood, he tried to guess Octavius's origins. The name Octavius was Greek, but he didn't look Greek—too pale, too slim. Mikalis was Greek, ancient Greek, and looked it. Octavius was... unique and was wholly surprising.

He'd heard Raiden's side of his and Octavius's last conversation, accusing Octavius of being shortsighted, self-centered, and more. And Saint had assumed the same of him. He was self-centered, but only to protect himself.

Saint would have liked to have known him. Under all that spiky exterior, there might be someone worth knowing.

He'd figured all those in the Brotherhood were lost causes, since they all followed Mikalis like blind newborn puppies. Not so with Octavius, although he was clearly still wrestling with what it all meant. And this *Zaine* sounded promising. Perhaps they weren't all mindless acolytes.

Octavius hopped down off the hood and began to circle the truck, kicking at stones. He buried his hands in his pockets, making himself smaller.

"Look after Jay," Saint said, catching Octavius passing by while on a lap around the truck.

"What?"

"If I don't make it back."

"You'll make it back." He started walking again.

Saint waited until he'd done another lap and said, "But if I don't, make sure he's safe."

"He's *your* feeder. You've already fucked him up. I can't cure that." He walked on.

Saint shook his head in disbelief. What had he just been thinking, that Octavius was better than the rest? "I haven't tainted Jay with venom."

Octavius stopped so fast, his boots skidded in the gravel. "Bullshit."

Mikalis's indoctrination was strong. "We control whether to inject venom. Most nyks don't care, but I do. I haven't warped Jay's mind. He's not addicted. His blood is clean. Whatever he feels, it's real."

"C'mon, I wasn't born yesterday. You guys fuck like rabbits and you're telling me you haven't bitten him, not once? I may be naïve in the ways of... in intimacies, but he's definitely ingested your blood, else you wouldn't have needed me to save him outside the lake house."

"By choice. He ingested it *by choice*."

"Yeah, off his head with lust for you."

Saint shrugged. "I'm not going to deny we have vigorous, fantastic sex—"

Octavius marched to the front of the truck again and leaned against the hood, arms crossed.

He had some strange hang-up about sex. Saint considered asking him how long it had been since he'd been intimate with someone, then decided against it. The Brotherhood resisted intimacy due to all the complications around venom and creating feeders, and Octavius was already uptight enough while waiting for his brothers to arrive.

The things Saint could do with that body though. He eyed him now, angled away from Saint and sprung so tight he practically buzzed. Octavius wasn't imposing, not physically. If it weren't for the white hair, he'd vanish in a crowd. With his hood up, he might have been unremarkable, until you saw his eyes. His blue eyes pierced like daggers, as though they could see your soul and didn't care for it.

Saint had mistaken that look for disdain, and he figured he wasn't alone with that assumption either. But Octavius deliberately kept everyone at arm's length. He knew what he was doing when he was a vicious prick. That just made Saint want to unravel him even more. He'd be a goddamn revelation between the sheets.

"Chopper," Octavius said, glancing over his shoulder.

Saint heard it too, the distant *thwump-thwump* of rotor blades. He jumped from the truck seat and joined Octavius. Mikalis would arrive before his Brotherhood, else their fearless leader risked his secrets spilling to the whole team. Any moment now...

"I'll make sure Jayden is safe," Octavius blurted. "You have my word."

"Ah, you *do* like him."

"I didn't say that."

"Just admit it. He's easy to like. Say the words, nobody is listening. It's just you and me, and the stars—"

"Saint!" Mikalis bellowed from the tree line.

"Scratch that." Saint pushed from the truck, rolled his shoulders, then pulled the nyktelios from within him. Wings burst from his back, fangs filled his mouth. He was going to need every weapon he had to survive this.

He strode forward, spotted Mikalis, and broke into a run toward him.

It had been a nice life. Even after so many centuries, it hadn't been enough. Given the choice, he'd have lived a thousand more. But Mikalis didn't give choices.

CHAPTER 17

ctavius

SAINT VEERED toward the forest behind the hardware store, and Mikalis took the bait and followed.

Now all Octavius had to do was separate Zaine from Storm— assuming they were the pair arriving in the chopper.

The chopper's lights blinked in the distance, coming closer.

Octavius lingered at the truck, keeping an eye on the forest, should Mikalis reappear. Saint would be fine. All he had to do was run. Restless, Octavius eyed the forest again.

No, they'd made a plan. He could not go after Saint. They'd meet later. This was going to work.

Saint would fight, wouldn't he? He'd fought Mikalis in the street, throwing him into a semi. But Octavius had been there then. And they'd fought again at the gas station. Again, with Octavius. What if Saint thought he *couldn't* win? What if he didn't want to? He'd asked him to keep Jayden safe... Did he truly not believe he was coming back?

"Damnit, Saint."

The chopper's tail dropped, the nose lifted, and the blades kicked up a maelstrom of dust in the parking lot as its skids bounced down.

Zaine's distinctive flash of blond hair confirmed what Octavius needed to see. The Brotherhood Viking jumped from the heli's cab, ducked from the downdraft, and made his way over with enough swagger in his stride to make his intentions clear. Sure enough, he blurred the last few steps, picked Octavius up by the neck, and slammed him against the truck so hard, the truck tires screeched backward on the asphalt.

"Traitor," Zaine snarled. "I should rip your heart out now."

"I'm surrendering." Octavius raised his hands, still clamped by the neck. "Take me in. I'm done."

"Damn right, you're done. Mikalis is going to execute you for this."

Mikalis, the god. The reason they each carried a hungry, vicious parasite inside them, the reason the world was going to end in a few months' time. But Octavius wasn't thinking about that. He just needed to have Zaine listen to the truth about Raiden. That was all. The rest of it was too much.

Octavius nodded and kept his hands up. "I get it, I do. I'm not fighting. See? Take me in."

Zaine muscled Octavius toward the chopper, its blades still whirring and Storm waiting in the pilot seat. Storm's glare sliced into Octavius's heart. It was sharp, not with hatred, but disappointment. Storm had always been the more reasonable one, the one who somehow balanced Mikalis's tunnel vision and the needs of each of them. It hurt, knowing he'd let Storm down. It was going to hurt a lot more in a few seconds.

"Sit your ass down," Zaine ordered.

Octavius climbed into the bench seat behind Storm. As soon as Zaine was in the front, Storm lifted the chopper into the air and climbed high into the sky.

Octavius searched the forest, but there was no sign of a battle, no sign of two ancient beings tearing into each other. Maybe Saint had already lured Mikalis far away.

"Where's Saint?" Zaine yelled over the churn of the engines.

Octavius blinked at him. "Saint?"

"Yeah, dick. You're working with him. So where is he?"

"I wasn't." Octavius turned his face away and peered out of the window. They were high now, several thousand feet. But the night was clear. He could still make out the tiny twinkling lights from towns below.

They hadn't restrained him, probably thinking there was little point this high up. They could overpower him, Storm and Zaine against him, two on one. Unless Octavius evened the odds.

He didn't want to do this, but they'd left him no choice.

"You fed from the motel clerk," Zaine was saying. When he glanced back, the disgust on his face stabbed again at Octavius's chest. This pain was why it was better to distance himself. If he cut out his own heart, nobody could do it for him.

Octavius closed his eyes and listened to the chopper's engines, its beat. He'd flown her a thousand times, knew her like the back of his hand. And he knew her breaking points, knew how to pull her out of a spin...

Octavius kicked out, buckling the back of Storm's seat, slamming him face-first into the controls. He grunted, and the chopper pitched forward and rolled over in the air, tumbling into a spin. Gravity grabbed hold, trying to fling them out. Zaine let out a yell. Octavius lunged between the front seats, cracked a fist across Storm's shocked face, and grabbed the emergency door release handle. The door flung open, and with the pull of gravity, Storm was already half out, trying to cling on.

Octavius braced against the swirling motion, caught Storm's wide-eyed expression, then kicked him hard between the eyes, booting him out of the chopper. He vanished, swallowed by the spiraling blackness and spinning stars. He'd survive the fall, but not without breaking some bones.

Octavius dropped into the pilot's seat, grabbed the control sticks, and wrestled the chopper under control.

Zaine tried to grab at him, and Octavius held up a finger. Just one finger, buying himself a couple of precious seconds.

"Can you fly a chopper?!" Octavius yelled.

"The fuck! You kicked Storm out!"

"Touch me, and we'll be heading down after him. I don't want to be minced by rotor blades, do you?!"

"You son of a bitch! What the fuck, Octavius!?" He dropped back into his seat.

"Sit down. Shut up. And listen, that's all I'm asking."

"You're a goddamned nyk!" Zaine swore under his breath. "The second we land, I'm gonna rip out your throat."

Maybe he would. "Or you could listen to what I have to say, and if you still want me dead, have a go." Octavius reached under the control and felt around for the little black box. He found it and tore it free. The tracker's location was obvious, as he'd been the one to install them on all the Brotherhood vehicles. Nobody was going to be tracking this helicopter. Not even Raiden.

Fuming, Zaine flung himself back into the seat and glowered, probably thinking up all the ways he could butcher Octavius.

But this was good. Octavius had captured Zaine. The plan was in motion.

He just hoped Saint had been successful too.

CHAPTER 18

aint

IN THE DISTANCE, the chopper spiraled toward the ground.

"C'mon, Little Wolf, get control."

One of them had to make it, because right then, Saint wasn't doing so good. He'd taken a few hits from Mikalis, and the leader's fangs had skimmed closer than he cared to think about. Running had never been an option. It was always going to end in a fight. He'd given as good as he'd gotten, and by some stroke of luck, he'd lost Mikalis in an old overgrown quarry. With any luck, Mikalis would stay lost.

Saint watched the chopper fall, then swoop up and away. Hopefully, that meant Octavius was piloting the machine.

Saint dragged his broken body in the general direction of a lumberyard where they'd agreed to meet at dawn. Vicious pangs scorched his back. He'd banished the broken wings, morphed them back into himself, but their ache remained.

He was alive, so there was that. But if Mikalis came at him

again, he had nothing left to fight him with. He wasn't even sure why he was here, traipsing through the woods fighting Mikalis and the Brotherhood, when he could be tangled with Jayden on a tropical beach somewhere. The little wolf was getting under his skin in ways that likely couldn't end well. Octavius preferred to keep a safe distance, but the more time Saint spent with him, the more he found Octavius enchanting. Behind the snarls and bitterness, he was *good*, and Octavius being good meant Saint couldn't abandon him.

He'd always had a weakness for the broken ones.

He gathered his remaining strength and blurred between the trees and through shadows, moving so fast, he covered miles in minutes. The sound of the chopper winding down steered him toward the lumberyard. He leaped the fence and scented blood among the sweet smell of cut wood. *Octavius's blood.* Instincts to protect almost brought the wildness roaring out of him.

Nobody touched Octavius.

Saint dropped the human act. Broken wings unfurled. Pain became an afterthought.

He spotted Octavius and one of the Brotherhood wrestling in the dirt. The other guy had Octavius pinned—Saint didn't need to see any more. He flew in, snatched the blond off Octavius, and slammed him to the ground with enough force to rumble the earth. The Brotherhood member cried out and clutched at Saint's arm, wriggling like a worm on the hook. Blue eyes fixed on Saint, accusing him of a thousand crimes. He tried to pry Saint off, but this one was young. A few centuries. Saint had millennia on him. He could crush him in seconds, rip out his heart, pump him full of venom. So many ways to kill a Brotherhood member.

He leaned in, and the blond stopped fighting. He stared defiantly, panting through his teeth. What did he see? A monster nyk, his final moments shining in Saint's silver eyes?

"Hurt Octavius again and die, Brotherhood."

The blond member glared back at him, but the bloodlust in his eyes faded. He knew he was beaten.

116

"Good," Saint snarled around his fangs. "Don't do anything stupid and we'll get along fine." He freed the blond's neck, patted his chest, and climbed off him, then hauled his true form back beneath his skin. The effort left him dizzy. He staggered and caught Octavius's raised eyebrow. Octavius was back on his feet and wiping blood from his lips, eyeing Saint warily, as though unsure where this went next. He didn't appear hurt, other than the cut on his lip.

"This Zaine?" Saint growled.

Octavius nodded. "Yeah."

"All right, let's get him to the kiln." Saint snatched Zaine by the ankle and dragged him toward the nearby warehouse. He didn't fight, just slid along on his ass, either accepting his fate or waiting for the right moment to strike back. The Brotherhood wasn't known for surrendering.

"You said you weren't working with him!" Zaine barked.

"I wasn't, now I am." Octavius followed along behind too. "Mikalis?" Octavius asked under his breath.

"I left him behind."

"What have you done with him?" Zaine bucked. "You hurt Mikalis and the full weight of the Brotherhood will come down on you! You are *so* fucked!"

Saint's patience was wearing thin with this one. He lunged, grabbed him by the shirt, hauled him upright, and rattled him by the shirt. "Worry about yourself, little Viking. If it were up to me, you'd already be dust. And be fucking nice to Octavius."

Zaine's smirk said it all, and all of it was wrong. "You *were* working together all this time. You got some kind of relationship going on?"

Saint rolled his eyes and pulled Zaine into the warehouse. Great stacks of felled trees were piled high and the rich smell of cut wood was almost too pungent. A giant kiln loomed off to the left, used for drying logs, and it just so happened to be a huge hunk of metal with a pressure-sealed door. Perfect for holding an angry nyktelios.

"Wait, what are you doing?" Zaine dug his heels into the wood-chip-covered floor. "You got me. I'm not going to fight."

Saint glanced at Octavius, checking he was happy to do this to one of his own. Octavius nodded and Saint let Zaine go.

Of course the idiot lunged for Octavius.

Saint was done with this shit. He plucked Zaine out of the air, tossed him into the kiln, slammed the door closed, and spun the lock. A few muffled clangs rang out from inside but otherwise, the door held.

"We don't have time for this." Octavius folded his arms. "We need to get him on our side, not turn him against us."

"Give him a few minutes to cool off in there. Or we turn up the heat." The controls looked simple enough. The big red ignition button was tempting.

"I'm not turning the kiln on. I don't like him, but I don't want to turn him to dust either. We need him."

"I'm just pointing out it's an option."

A wave of dizziness washed over him. The floor tipped, the roof slid sideways, and Saint reached out for anything to help steady him. Octavius caught him, hands on Saint, his face in front of Saint's, his eyes wide. He asked if Saint was all right, and it seemed as though Saint should reply, but the fight with Mikalis and his body's efforts to heal had drained him.

He sank to his knees, and Octavius sank with him. Gods, he was pretty. Saint hadn't cared to notice all the sharp angles of his face before, and how those soft lips were so quick to snarl. They weren't snarling now.

"I'm all right." He tried to brush him off, but missed, and dropped onto a hand instead.

"Mikalis did this."

It wasn't a question, so Saint didn't reply. He rather liked the solid feel of Octavius's hands on him, especially the one on his shoulder, propping him upright. He even liked how furious Octavius looked, knowing that fury wasn't directed at him. It was sweet, seeing how the little wolf had gotten protective.

The warehouse had stopped spinning. "I'm good, I'll be all right. I'll feed from Jay later."

Octavius hefted a sigh, then brought his wrist to his own lips and bit down. The sweet smell of his blood bloomed in the air, intoxicating and alluring. Saint knew what was happening, although he wasn't sure he understood why Octavius was helping him. His blood wasn't anywhere near the human blood he needed, but it would be enough to focus him and keep his instincts from doing something he couldn't come back from, like kill Zaine.

Saint's gaze caught Octavius's, silently asking if he was sure. It was a risk. If Saint injected venom, it would kill Octavius, but he wasn't so far gone as to lose control just yet.

Octavius nodded, and that was all the permission Saint needed. He grabbed his arm and clamped his teeth into his warm wrist. Blood spilled over Saint's tongue, smooth and thick. Octavius threw his head back, closed his eyes, and went very, very still.

He'd be all right. Saint needed this.

He tasted like an aged wine, hidden away for decades. More than that, he tasted right, as though his blood belonged to Saint and was already a part of him. He couldn't explain it, and didn't care to as the blood fed the starved parts of him, the wild, rabid parts, sating the ravenous monster within. He wanted more, so much more; he wanted to push Octavius onto his back, straddle him, and sink his teeth into his neck. *More.* He wanted to spread his legs, go down on him, make him moan, make him unravel. *More.* He wanted to feel Octavius's nails dig into his back, wanted to feel his body tremble, taste his cum, wanted all of him under him, wanted to be inside him, have him inside Saint.

"That's enough!" Octavius tore his arm free. He licked the wound clean, then raised those furious eyes back to Saint.

Lust and mischief tingled through Saint. Goddamn, he needed Octavius in his arms, right now, here on the warehouse floor, where they'd fuck and bite and Octavius's little wolf claws would sink into Saint—

Octavius hurried toward the kiln. He spun the lock and flung open the door. "Z, get out here."

Zaine ducked through the doorway and narrowed his eyes on

Saint, still sitting on the floor, then flicked his gaze to Octavius. He sniffed, scenting blood, and probably a whole lot of other things.

The Viking straightened, studied them both, and said, "I don't know what the fuck the both of you are playing at but Mikalis will end you for this."

Octavius grabbed a nearby metal chair from a conveyor belt workstation and dumped it on the floor between the three of them. "Sit your ass down."

Zaine snarled at it.

Octavius had said this one had always been defiant. Which was exactly why they'd singled him out for this, but it also made him difficult. "Sit and fucking listen for once in your life, Zaine," Octavius said.

"I don't listen to traitors."

Saint would enjoy killing him unless he smartened up in the next few minutes. Climbing to his feet, he brushed dirt from his pants. Octavius's blood had smoothed his rattling nerves and eased the hunger. "Sit. Or I get primal," Saint growled.

Zaine huffed, then dropped into the chair. He folded his arms, as stubborn as they come.

Saint backed off. This was Octavius's moment. Saint was just here to make sure the prick didn't try and attack him again. Octavius was a fighter, but when it came to the Brotherhood, he had a blind spot. He needed them to accept him, to love him, to take him back.

"Let's get this over with," Zaine said.

Octavius stared at him. "Whatever your feelings for me, we are Brotherhood, and this isn't personal—"

"Until you sabotaged us. You're not Brotherhood, you're a nyk."

Saint looked away. His fangs ached. He wanted to take the little prick and slam him into the floor a few more times. They claimed to be brothers, but they knew nothing about each other. How did Zaine not know how much Octavius cared for them? How could he not see it? Was Mikalis's hold on them so strong they honestly believed life was better if they did not care?

"I didn't plant a virus in Atlas," Octavius said, approaching Zaine. "If I were going to destroy it, I wouldn't need a virus to do it. I had access to every system. I could have undone all of it with a few keystrokes."

"We have the footage, Octavius. We've all seen it."

"Who gave you that video?"

Zaine swallowed. "It doesn't matter who gave it to us. It shows what you did."

"Who gave it to you, Zaine?"

"Raiden."

Octavius paused, letting the name hang in the air between them.

Zaine snorted. "The comms went down during the Sebastien mission. They were your responsibility. We went in blind because of you."

"Comms go down, it happens." Octavius shrugged. "You all turned on me because you wanted to. You want to believe I destroyed Atlas and undermined the Brotherhood because you hate me. You all hate me. It's easier to believe I'm a traitor than to think it might be someone else who had everyone fooled for decades."

Zaine flung a hand out at Saint. "You are literally working with *him*—the biggest traitor of all. Brotherhood-turned-nyk. Look at him. He's fucking ancient and dangerous, and he has you all tangled up with his plot to ruin us. He's using you."

Octavius leveled his glare on Zaine. "I didn't let him out, but I'm grateful for whoever did. The rest of you left me no choice. Saint is the *only* one who fucking listens."

Zaine glared back.

The little Viking needed to learn some manners. Octavius was several thousand years older than him, and Zaine looked at him as though he was dirt under his boot.

Saint circled Zaine, getting into position behind him. "You should know, Octavius is the only thing standing between me and your death, so do try and listen harder."

121

"All right, fine, let's pretend I believe you." Zaine shifted in the chair. "Why did Raiden do this, huh? What's his end game?"

"I don't know. He said, when I called him, that he was going to destroy the Brotherhood. He set all these events in motion. He freed Saint to distract Mikalis. He knocked Atlas offline. He's made it so the Brotherhood is flying blind at a time when the nyks are getting more and more powerful. I fear it's building to something he's kept hidden from us, something to do with the rising nyk numbers."

"Why don't you ask your nyk buddy there?" Zaine thumbed over his shoulder.

"He did," Saint growled. "The nyk numbers have reached critical mass. In a few weeks, they'll swarm, revealing their existence to the world, and the ensuing chaos will ruin all of humanity."

Zaine laughed. "That's madness. You can't know that."

"Yeah, he can," Octavius said, drawing Zaine's glare back to him. "Mikalis is his sire. He's also among the first nyktelios ever made. But we'll get into that later. For now, I just need you to look at me and see I'm not working against you, and neither is Saint. Raiden got inside my head. He set me up. He got in all your heads."

"You're insane. Speaking of getting inside people's heads, you fed from the motel staff and made her forget you. You're working with—your words—*the oldest nyk*. And I'm supposed to believe all this shit about you being innocent? Octavius, you wouldn't even believe you right now. Why the fuck should I?"

"You know something is off with Mikalis," Octavius said. "Information you used so he didn't make Eric disappear. You know he's not what he appears to be and neither is Saint. Neither am I. I'm not your enemy. I never was. I'm going to let you go." He pointed at the warehouse door. "You'll go back to wherever the new base is, and you're going to stop Raiden. I am not the traitor you're looking for. He is."

Zaine sighed and stared at the floor. "Why don't you tell Mikalis all this?"

Octavius glanced at Saint. Now was as good a time as any to tell them the truth. He nodded, and Octavius continued. "Mikalis believes we're together, so he thinks Saint has told me his secrets."

"Has he?"

Octavius swallowed and glanced over at Saint. "No," he lied. "I'm working with Saint because, if I hadn't partnered with him, I'd already be dust."

All right, so he wasn't telling the Brotherhood the truth. Well, at least Saint knew where he stood. Octavius was using *him*. And once he got his happy-ever-after back with the Brotherhood, he'd throw Saint under a semitruck. What had Saint expected from the Brotherhood? Certainly not a friend.

Maybe he'd been wrong about Octavius. Perhaps the little wolf had fooled him all along.

"And what does he get out of this?" Zaine tilted his head toward Saint and smirked. "Your blood?"

Saint was done here. They'd never listen to him. He'd been a fool to think he had a chance when they barely listened to Octavius, one of their own.

He turned on his heel and left the warehouse but didn't go far. He listened to their murmering voices, just in case the Viking got any ideas about attacking Octavius again.

He waited by the chopper and watched dawn break over the surrounding treetops. Somewhere in all of this, he'd assumed he and Octavius were a team. Their own Brotherhood, of sorts. He was a damned fool.

He knew better than to get attached.

CHAPTER 19

ctavius

ALL WAS GOING AS PLANNED. Zaine was listening, although whether he did anything with the information was still undetermined. At least, the plan had appeared to be working. Then Saint had walked out.

"Go back to New York, and look deeper at Raiden," Octavius told Zaine. "He's clever. It won't be easy. But you have to do this—not for me, but for the Brotherhood. Because if I'm right, then Raiden is the biggest threat to the Brotherhood since... well, since Saint."

Zaine stood, and Octavius tensed for another attack. "You get one chance," he said. "That's it."

"That's all I ask."

"All right. I'm good to go? Your nyk isn't going to go feral on me?"

"Go right ahead." Octavius watched him head for the doors.

"Saint could easily have killed you. He's not the nyk you think he is."

Zaine showed Octavius his middle finger and shoved through the door. Octavius waited a few moments, taking stock of the conversation. It felt like progress. They might pull this off.

By the time Octavius made it outside, Zaine was gone, but Saint loitered nearby. He paced in front of the chopper and didn't look over. He'd needed blood and was in pain from another beating, but Octavius figured meeting up with the Brotherhood again was the real cause of his disquiet.

"We should get back to Jay," Saint said.

"We're just going to leave the chopper here?"

"Can't risk any of the Brotherhood seeing it take off." He took a running jump at the fence, landed on the other side, and marched off into the woods.

Octavius glanced around the yard. He didn't think Zaine would follow them, not when he knew Saint could tear into him, but they should double back around a few times to lose any tails.

He followed Saint into the woods and caught up with his heavy strides. He didn't know him well, but something was wrong. Saint kept his head down and marched ahead, bristling with tension.

Octavius had only had a few months of being ostracized. Saint had had multiple centuries behind bars, during which nobody had cared enough to open his cell door and listen to him. They'd all toed Mikalis's line of never discussing who was locked in Room 3B, obeying his orders without question.

"It must be hard, seeing them again," Octavius said. "They're stubborn, I know, but they aren't all bad—"

Saint's growl cut him off. He stomped through the brush. "Don't defend them," he said. "They don't deserve it."

"I just—"

Saint whirled, blocking Octavius's path. "They don't deserve *you*," he blurted. "They tossed you out like trash. You don't need them." He breathed hard, but then, with a sigh, he turned back around and started walking again. "You're better than them."

Where was this coming from? Saint didn't know him. They'd been thrown together for a few days, survived a few close calls with Mikalis. He couldn't *know* Octavius. Why did he care? "I need them," Octavius admitted. "Without them, I'm just... a ghost." He feared it might be worse than that now. Without them, he was nyk, and even knowing nyks weren't all that different, he couldn't undo a few thousand years of indoctrination overnight.

"No." Saint spun on his heel, marched up to Octavius, and stopped, chest to chest. "You're a ghost because you've carved yourself out of the world, because your past is fucked up and it hurts. I don't need to know the details, I read it in everything you do. You desperately want their approval, but you push them away. They can't save you, only you can save you. You don't need them. You have me, you have Jay. We're your Brotherhood, if you'd have us."

The words landed hard. What did he mean, he *had* them? "What?"

Saint's expression turned stern, even vicious. "Forget them, come to the end of the world with me."

This was ridiculous. Saint didn't want him. This was a trick of some kind. "What are you talking about? Raiden is about to destroy them. They're clearly not prepared. They need me. Why are you trying to turn me against them?"

"The Brotherhood doesn't give a shit about you. If I hadn't gotten to you, Zaine would have pumped you full of venom, and you'd be dust."

"Fuck you, no. They just... They just need to look at things differently, that's all."

"They've had thousands of years to see things differently. They're never changing, Octavius. Not while Mikalis is their leader. But sure, go on your knees and beg their forgiveness, Little Wolf. Maybe they'll take you in, and perhaps they won't turn on you later for another petty reason because Mikalis deems it."

Why was he saying these things now? They had a plan, it was working. They had Zaine, and he would see how Raiden was the traitor. "You're wrong. They're good. Deep down. They'll stop Raiden, they'll take us back."

Saint snarled a laugh. "And you're deluded." He turned, threw up a hand, and walked off. "Have a nice rest of your life trying to win Mikalis's approval. Good luck with that."

This wasn't about Octavius. This was about Saint, and what the Brotherhood had done to him. What *Mikalis* had done to him. "He'll come around, he'll see you again. I'm sure of it."

Saint stopped on the trail. His shoulders slouched.

Octavius made his way up behind him. "I know he hurt you."

"This isn't about me. This is about you not seeing your true worth, Octavius, and trust me, it's not as a Brotherhood puppet." He lifted his gaze, and in the lingering darkness beneath the trees, his nyk eyes shone.

His words did strange things to Octavius's insides, made them squirm with unease and guilt. He wasn't even sure why. Perhaps because he didn't deserve such kindness, or the way Saint glared at him now, as though in awe. As though—

Saint's hands bracketed his face, and before he could pull back, his soft lips pushed against Octavius's. He hadn't expected it. Was it an attack? Octavius shoved him off and gasped. He tasted Saint on his lips, blood too, but mostly Saint's sharp bitterness.

Wait, was that a... was that a kiss?

Saint stared, breathing hard.

"Why did you do that?" Octavius touched the tingling on his lips, uncertain whether it had been an attack or a trick or something else.

"You know why."

He didn't understand.

Saint took a step closer—now so close that simmering heat radiated off him and into Octavius. They didn't touch, not yet, but he was certain it was coming, and he had no idea if he wanted that, or to lash out and push him back. His mind had fallen quiet, and his body burned, his gut clenching with a strange new sensation.

Octavius studied the ancient nyk with the shining eyes, savage fangs gleaming in the early morning light. Saint gazed back at him now, all soft and strange, with no trace of anger. Nobody looked at Octavius like that. Ever.

Saint's firm fingers caught his chin, lifted his head, and this time, when their lips met, the kiss was gentle, like a soft query, asking permission.

Octavius's heart pounded, his body came alive, every thought funneled to how that kiss felt, how warm it was, and how he needed it. He parted his lips, kissed him back, deepening their touch. Then Saint's tongue sought more of him, and the kiss hardened with hunger. Other parts of Octavius hardened too, as though his body no longer listened to reason and did as it pleased.

He wanted this. He wanted it so much that desire overwhelmed all the reasons not to want this.

He was kissing Saint. He was *hard* for Saint. He wanted to touch more of him, to explore him, wanted to feel him close. This hunger was new, but just as powerful as the thirst for blood. And by Nyx, he wanted that too. Wanted to thrust his fangs in and *take*.

But this was Saint. The Big Bad Wolf. Mikalis's *creation*.

Saint's touch stroked up Octavius's neck, and Octavius moaned into the kiss. This was too much, but not enough. He couldn't do this, but wanted more. He pushed, but Saint's warning growl had Octavius's dick going from interested to desperate in a beat. He had to stop this, but didn't want to. It couldn't happen, but he needed it to. All his needs and wants and fears turned into a storm in his head, driving him mad.

He clutched at Saint's shirt, intent on throwing him off—but he pulled him closer. His back hit a tree. Saint pressed in, his body suddenly firm and everywhere. Octavius burned for more, for skin on skin, to feel him slide against him. He dropped his head back, parted his mouth, and let his aching fangs fall, and then froze as Saint risked his own life by sweeping his tongue *between* Octavius's lips and then lapping at the four vicious teeth that could kill him.

No, this was wrong. Brotherhood did not fuck nyks. The venom, the wrongness, never care.

"*Stop!*" He pushed the command too hard, lashed it into Saint like a whip to the mind.

Saint tore away and clutched at his head. "Was that necessary?!"

"I can't... We can't..." Octavius clutched the tree behind him for a few steadying seconds and fought to get his body back under control. Then he eyed Saint, the creature, the man he wanted. He hadn't wanted physical touch in so long, he couldn't even remember when he'd last lain with another. To have Saint's hands on him, to have all the strength and power quivering under Octavius's touch... "I won't."

Saint laughed sadly and shook his head. "Fine, Little Wolf. Crawl on your belly back to Mikalis and watch him rip it open. I cannot save you from yourself."

Saint left, and the forest fell quiet again, or perhaps it was Octavius's thoughts that fell quiet, after Saint turned his head into a tinderbox of scorching lust.

Saint was... a lot to get his head around. Even more to get his tongue around.

He shuddered a sigh. He was going to go back to the cabin, and they'd either agree to move locations or hunker down there, and in a few days, Octavius would reach out to Zaine. Once he returned to the cabin, he was not going to kiss Saint, and he wasn't going to fuck him. Or be fucked. Gods, what would *that* be like? Saint's teeth in his throat, his dick filling him—

Octavius pushed from the tree and *ran*. The faster he sped, the clearer his head became. He could do this. And he'd win back his place in the Brotherhood in time to save the world. He had to do this, to prove he was good enough for them.

He made it to the cabin just as dawn broke and hurried inside. He'd tell Saint that they couldn't kiss again, and how Octavius didn't want that. But he found Saint sitting on the couch, his face buried in his hands. The coppery smell of blood lingered in the cabin air.

"What happened?"

Saint looked up, his face stricken. "Mikalis took Jay," he growled. "I'm getting him back."

CHAPTER 20

 aint

MIKALIS WOULD KILL JAY. Humans meant nothing to him. Then he'd kill Octavius and Saint. He'd brush it all under a rug so his precious Brotherhood never knew, like he did with all his secrets.

"Is Jay hurt?" Octavius asked, rushing forward. He'd come back from the woods, from the kiss, from Saint revealing too much truth, things even he hadn't known he'd felt. And now this —losing Jay.

Saint held out the note he'd found in the kitchen. He'd scented blood, the same as Octavius must have, but there were no spills or splatter marks. "Not seriously hurt, no. Not yet."

It's time to end this, the note said.

Come to me, and the feeder lives.

M.

On the back, Mikalis had written an address. Not a Brotherhood location, somewhere else, somewhere nearby and secure, away from prying Brotherhood eyes. He must have planned all of it long before Saint had lured him away.

Mikalis had wanted Saint away from the cabin so he could loop back and capture Jay, knowing Jay was Saint's weakness.

Octavius took the note and snarled as he read. "Why is he like this now?"

"He's always been like this." Saint looked up, so damn tired of running, of caring. He hadn't wanted *any* of this. He would have been easier if he was the monster, then none of this would matter.

"All right." Octavius handed the note back, and their fingers brushed. The brief touch had Saint wanting to reach out to him, to take that hand, needing contact, but Octavius was quick to pull away and then pace. This would be the moment he'd leave Saint, he'd go back to the Brotherhood. He didn't need Jay, so why risk his life for a man he saw as Saint's feeder?

"Then, we go to that address, and we get Jayden," Octavius said.

Saint must have misheard. He stared up at Octavius. A few days ago, he'd been more concerned about Octavius leaving of his own accord, but now, Octavius was prepared to stand against Mikalis to save a man he assumed to be a hopelessly addicted feeder. Why?

His ice-blue eyes landed on Saint, and for a moment, he stared back, unblinking. He *did* care about the people, and about Jay. He'd always cared. But the Brotherhood didn't care, it was one of their unbreakable vows. To care made them weak. Octavius had always had a heart, but here, now, he'd stopped hiding it.

"I mean—" He cleared his throat. "—I'll talk to Mikalis. Try to negotiate. He doesn't need to use Jayden against you."

"We tried talking." Saint stood and crossed the room to the fireplace, needing to move, to think. "Talking doesn't work."

"Then we distract him. I'll keep him busy while you free Jay?"

"He's not going to fall for that." No, there was only one way out of this. Mikalis knew it too. "I know what to do."

"Which is?"

Saint headed for the door, passing near Octavius. "Exactly what Mikalis wants."

Octavius's quick hand shot out and caught Saint's arm, pulling him to a halt. Saint met his questioning gaze, but then Octavius dropped his hand, as though he'd made a mistake in stopping him. A sharp awkwardness seemed to have fallen between them and it hadn't been there before the kiss.

It might have been a mistake, but Saint had so desperately wanted him to know his worth, and how damned precious he was. He could be loved, if he wanted it.

"Mikalis wants me," Saint said. "He doesn't care about Jay. If I give myself up, he'll let him go."

Octavius's eyebrows pinched inward. "Mikalis will kill you."

Saint smiled, hoping to alleviate some of Octavius's concern. "The world's ending anyway. I'll just miss the show."

He started for the door again, but when Octavius added, "He's just a feeder," Saint stopped. He'd thought they'd been through this.

"You'll sacrifice your own life for a feeder's?" Octavius asked.

"Jay is human, with a heart and soul, and he's one of the good ones," Saint said. "I don't need more time, not at the cost of Jay's life." If Octavius didn't understand, then there was no hope for him. It wasn't his fault. Mikalis had only showed him one side of the story.

He stepped outside into morning sunshine. Sunlight glinted off every dew drop clinging to the grass and moisture in the trees, piercing Saint's eyes like needles. The drive to the address where Mikalis was holding Jay would take a few hours. Already weak, it would be grueling. But Jay needed him.

Octavius brushed by Saint and strode into the trees. "It'll be quicker if we take the chopper."

The little wolf was coming along?

A tic of a smile lifted Saint's lips. Perhaps he hadn't scared him off with that kiss after all. And what a marvelous kiss it had been, before Octavius's overthinking had gotten between them.

He followed him, avoiding the patches of sunlight blazing through the tree canopy. When they reached the lumberyard, the main gates lay open, and a small crowd of workers had gathered around the chopper.

Saint was about to warn Octavius, when the little wolf strode on ahead. He sauntered into the open, in full view of the workers. They saw him—there was no way they couldn't see a young white-haired man striding from the woods, right at them. But every single one of the men and women inexplicably turned away, then wandered off, deciding there was no chopper and there most definitely was not a white-haired stranger in the yard.

Octavius was a damn marvel. The Brotherhood was foolish to shun him.

Saint climbed into the chopper alongside him and caught his little, sly smile. The smile he wore when he believed nobody was watching him. Octavius fired up the engines, his hands skimming the controls, and the chopper lifted into the air. "What?" he asked, glancing over.

The engines whirred, the blades thwomped. Saint stared from the tinted window as the forest shrank beneath them. "Not a damn thing." *Only that you're unique, and I hope one day, you find someone who sees how special you are.*

"You said Mikalis will always find you because he's your sire. Does that work in reverse?" Octavius asked.

"Don't you feel your sire?"

Octavius shrugged. "I killed mine right after I was turned, so no."

"You did?" Fuck, with every new revelation he became more and more alluring.

"The village I was raised in believed me to be godtouched." He gestured at his head. "There aren't many white-haired Greeks around. When I refused to be their sacrifice, they hunted me down, beat me, and tossed me in the temple with their so-called god."

"A nyktelios."

"Yeah. It had been starved and imprisoned in that temple for generations, feeding on sacrifices. The villagers thought if they kept it fed, it would bless them with bountiful harvests."

Humans had come a long way since then. Well, most of them. A worrying number were still stuck in the dark ages. "You fought," Saint said, further impressed by the young mortal man Octavius had been.

"I did. But it overpowered me, obviously, and for whatever reason, it decided to turn me. Perhaps it was tired of being alone. The process is a blur, but I know that whenever it drank from me, I touched death, but I was pulled back again with the taste of blood on my lips."

This probably wasn't the time to admit Saint's turning had been more of an erotic ritual than torture.

"During one of those near-death moments," Octavius went on, "I heard a woman's voice. She told me to fight. And if I did, she'd reward me with a gift."

Ah, that was where his brilliant mind trick came from. "The persuasion?" It took a lot for Saint to be surprised. But every day he spent with Octavius brought new surprises.

"I don't remember much," Octavius went on, while guiding the chopper through the sky. "Only that I used the gift to kill the nyk. The next time the villagers opened the temple to deliver their sacrifice, I killed them all. That village and my people were wiped from the land, after that. And the gift has forever stayed with me."

As a newly turned, unnurtured nyktelios, he'd killed the villagers. Saint couldn't blame him for that. He'd have done the same, even if he'd had control. Sacrificing people to a rabid nyktelios was monstrous to the humans *and* the nyktelios.

"So I don't know much about having a sire," Octavius admitted. "But what I do know is the others don't talk about their sires, or how they were turned, either."

Everything had gotten so warped and twisted since the creation of the nyktelios. "In Mikalis's era, sires were worshipped, beginning of course with Mikalis. His acolytes prayed they'd have his gifts bestowed upon them."

"They *prayed* to be turned into nyktelios?" Octavius asked incredulously.

"It was a different time." Saint chuckled. "Those who were chosen, as I was, became even more faithful to Mikalis. We would indulge in carnal gatherings together to strengthen our bond, sometimes a dozen of us at a time, sometimes more."

"I'm not sure I want to know," he muttered.

He'd love to see Octavius squirm in his seat as he described the days and nights he'd spent tangled in many limbs, high on sexual pleasure and free-flowing blood. "The more time spent with your sire, and the more you exchange blood, the more powerful you become. A turning is just the beginning. Most nyks separate from their sire because the old ways have been forgotten, but a nyk nurtured over time by its sire quickly gains control, unlike the rabid bloodhungry nyks the Brotherhood hunt today."

"Mikalis *nurtured* you?" He pulled a disgusted face, glancing side-on.

"Like I said, different times." Those nights had been like drug-induced dreams. No thought, just physical needs sated by and endless stream of pleasure. To be turned by Mikalis was a journey of devotion that grew into love. "I wanted to be with him, mind, body, soul."

"Do you still have those... feelings?" Octavius asked.

"I did... I want to," Saint admitted, surprised the words left his lips. "Time and betrayal ravages the most stalwart of loves." He was even more surprised *those* words left his lips, and cleared his throat when Octavius glanced over again. "Our bond is strong. He'll always be able to find me, and I can sense if he's close, or in what general direction he's in. But when I do, he feels it. Hence, when on the run, I try to avoid reaching out to him."

"Hm, like a communication tower's ping. You reach out to him and he pings back to you. I get it. Can you tell me if we get close? When we land, I want to know exactly where he is."

"Now?"

"He already knows we're coming, so whenever you're ready."

Saint closed his eyes and tentatively reached out with his senses, feeling outside the physical realm and into shadow. Mikalis was there, like a black hole, swallowing all light. He pulsed, and Saint snapped open his eyes. "He's aware we're coming, all right."

Octavius nodded. "We'll be there soon." He looked over. "I'm not letting him kill you. It's not right."

"Trying to stop Mikalis is like trying to hold back an ocean."

"He is reasonable, I know it. Lately, he's been more... forgiving."

It was admirable, but there was fighting nyks, and fighting a god. Only another god could stop a god. And none of the Brotherhood were godtouched...

Saint glanced askance at Octavius. The temple, the trapped nyk, the voice in Octavius's head while he was being turned. Those were potent circumstances. "The temple with the trapped nyk," Saint said. "Who was it dedicated to?"

Octavius took a breath and said, "Goddess of Chaos and Night. Nyx."

~

"Surrendering is not a plan," Octavius grumbled as they climbed from the chopper to the sound of the engine whirring down.

"It's the only plan we've got." Jay would die, otherwise.

They'd landed in the parking lot of a foreclosed steakhouse restaurant on the outskirts of a quiet town. Grass and weeds had grown around the boarded-up windows.

"Just let me try and speak with him..." Octavius's pace slowed as he squinted up at the brilliant blue sky. He stopped and shielded his eyes.

"What is it?" Saint couldn't see anything. Just fluffy white clouds, and bright light that produced a stabbing headache.

"Nothing." He flinched, likely feeling the effects of the sunlight too. "Let's get inside."

The deep throb of Mikalis's power beat from within the building's walls. There had been a time that beat had called Saint to him, like a moth to the flame. He wished he hadn't told Octavius the truth in the chopper. It only made the shame at Saint's failure to hold on to that love more pronounced.

"This whole thing is absurd," Octavius muttered, as he tore off a timber board and climbed inside. "We should be working together, not tearing each other apart."

Saint followed Octavius inside, through a back room stacked with chairs, and into the main restaurant area, now cleared except for Jay tied to a chair and gagged. He swung his head around, struggled against the ropes, and garbled a whole lot of words, none of which made any sense.

There didn't appear to be any sign of Mikalis, but Saint *knew* he was here, in this very room with them. Octavius hurried to Jay's side and quickly removed the gag.

"Octavius!" Jay blurted. "You came."

"Quiet," Octavius snapped, and grabbed at the ropes binding his arms to the chair.

"Leave him," Mikalis's voice boomed, assaulting them from every corner.

Octavius straightened behind Jay, placed his hands on Jay's shoulders, and searched for Mikalis in the gloom. "Let's talk."

Saint studied the darkness too, and how sunlight tried to stab through holes in the rotten boards to pierce the shadows. But the darkness was too thick. Because Mikalis *was* the shadows. He wasn't in one place, he was all around them.

"Let Jay go, and I'll surrender," Saint said, turning on the spot to get a glimpse of some solid part of him.

"No, he won't, he's not going to do that—" Octavius thrust out a hand as though he could hold Saint back. "Just—the both of you, stop. We don't need to fight."

"You should leave," Saint told him. "While you can." If Mikalis let him go. There was no use in both of them dying here, like flies in Mikalis's web.

"I'm not leaving. I have nowhere to go." Octavius's snarl made the point unarguable. "Jayden doesn't need to die, and Mikalis, you don't need to kill Saint. He's done nothing wrong."

"You're both traitors."

"I told you the truth," Saint said. "The fact you didn't like it, doesn't make me a traitor."

"It ends here."

"Because of your precious Brotherhood?" Saint asked the shadows. He gestured at Octavius. "They're better than you." Was that why Mikalis was doing this? Because he knew if they learned the truth, they'd take it out of his hands? He'd lose control. What was a god without his worshippers? "Kill me, but let Jay go."

"No!" Octavius stepped forward and narrowed his glare on a thick swirl of shadow in the far corner. "I have never betrayed you, not in the thousands of years I've served you. But for Saint, for the truth, I will."

"Then you will die with him. The Brotherhood is all. Memento mori."

Remember you must die. It was always going to end this way.

"Wait!" Octavius wet his lips and glanced desperately at Saint. "Mikalis, regardless of what we know, it doesn't matter. The nyks are rising, we've lost control of the fight, and while you're here Raiden is working to undermine everything. He let Saint out, he probably has control of Atlas. He's timed this perfectly. He wants you here, distracted by this mess. Not looking at *him*. Don't you see how perfectly we've all fallen into his trap?"

The shadows swelled, crackled apart, and Mikalis stepped from inside, blue eyes blazing. His clothes were casual, as though he'd nipped out for groceries, but there was nothing normal about the thick weight of power flexing the air around him. "I see Saint helped you find your tongue, Octavius. When I found you, you hadn't spoken a word in centuries. Did he tell you his sweet lies... that I'm not like you?"

And this was the part where Mikalis would try to turn Octavius against Saint. The bastard was a master manipulator. A low growl rumbled through Saint.

"You were one of my most stalwart Brotherhood members," Mikalis went on. "I trusted you, relied on you, treated you as my equal, and this is how you repay me?"

Mikalis approached him, but Octavius stood his ground, lifting his chin. He didn't cower, he didn't beg. Saint had never believed he would. His little wolf was a fighter.

"By looking you in the eyes and telling you the truth, by trying to save you and the Brotherhood, even knowing it will be my end? Then yes. This is how I repay you."

"The truth doesn't matter. Only the Brotherhood matters. Your actions here further undermine it. If you were the devoted Brotherhood member you claim to be, you'd step aside and let me finish this."

They stood almost toe to toe now. Octavius in his hooded top and torn trousers, Mikalis with a barrage of shadows waiting behind him.

"You've forgotten what the Brotherhood is. Or maybe it's evolved, and you haven't." Octavius's smile ticced. "We exist to stop your mistake from destroying the world, not to worship you. If you want worshippers, go get yourself some feeders and make yourself a congregation of nyk acolytes."

Mikalis bared his fangs. "I *am* the Brotherhood."

"No, you're not. And I think, deep down, you're afraid they'll realize it—"

Mikalis shot his hand out and grabbed Octavius's neck, plucking him off his feet. Saint tensed to attack in what would probably be his final fight, but Mikalis dropped Octavius and reeled backward, clutching his head. Octavius had attacked inside his mind. Mikalis lifted his glare. "Use your talent on me again and I will ensure your death is agonizing!"

Octavius rocked on his feet too, as though there were some mental battle going on between them. Saint had seen enough. Whatever happened here, he'd do everything he could to save Jay *and* Octavius.

Mikalis flew at Octavius—but Saint intercepted.

Mikalis crashed into him with all the force of a freight train. Jay's shout rang out, and then the burn of fangs sinking into his neck scorched every other sense behind white-hot fire.

Alien venom surged down his jugular, pouring into him, turning the blood in his veins to acid. He didn't fight. There was no point. He'd already lost. But Octavius would be safe, and he'd take Jay. And in Saint's long, eventful life, it was enough to die knowing Octavius would save them.

Because it was the right thing to do.

CHAPTER 21

ctavius

IT HAPPENED SO FAST, there was no time to intervene. Mikalis came for Octavius, and then Saint was there, in front of him. Mikalis crushed Saint in his arms. Fangs flashed, Jay let out a yell, but it was already too late.

Mikalis struck, killing Saint with a bite that was meant for Octavius.

All of this was wrong.

It couldn't end like this.

"*Stop!*" Octavius pushed the demand at Mikalis. It punched through his barriers, into his mind. His eyes flicked up, locked on Octavius, and he bit down *harder*.

Saint was already dead—that much venom, he'd never survive. And all of this was so fucked up, so wrong. Octavius had trusted and served Mikalis for millennia. The Brotherhood had been betrayed. He'd been betrayed, by Mikalis!

"*Stop, by Nyx, let him go!*" Octavius thrust the order like a spear.

Mikalis gasped free of Saint's neck, leaving a bloody, venom-stained wound.

"How?" Mikalis snarled.

He didn't deserve to know. *"Let him go."*

Mikalis let go, and Saint collapsed onto his hands and knees, gasping for breath. Sweat glistened on his pale face. Venom would be coursing through his veins, burning him up.

Octavius couldn't lose his focus now. It wasn't enough to stop Mikalis's bite, he had to make him stop hunting them for good, or this would never end. Saint's breathing stuttered, his whole body shook. But Octavius couldn't go to him, not yet.

It was almost over. Just one final push.

He approached Mikalis. Fury rolled off the Brotherhood leader in new, dark waves. But Octavius had told him to stop, and there he stood, unmoving. Octavius couldn't think on how, or why, the mental demand had worked now, just that it had, and he needed it to stick. *"You will not hunt us,"* Octavius sent. *"We are free to go."* He could do more, could tell him to walk into sunlight and stay there, could make him hurt, like he'd hurt them.

Mikalis sneered. "How dare you assume to control me."

"Someone needs to," a new arrival said, in a deep, rumbling voice.

Storm approached from the storage area, his muscular bulk filling the doorway. He looked good for a guy who'd fallen several thousand feet from a chopper.

The hairs on the back of Octavius's neck lifted. If Storm turned on him, he was done for.

He couldn't fight them both. But he'd try.

Storm raised his hand. "Get out of here, Octavius."

Wait, Storm was letting them go?

"Storm, stop them!" Mikalis ordered.

Storm drew in a deep breath, filling his broad chest, and sighed hard. "No."

A glimmer of something passed between them—a knowing, and a resignation. Octavius wasn't about to wait around for Storm to change his mind, or Mikalis to convince him otherwise. He dashed for Jayden and snapped his ropes. He and Jayden scooped up Saint, then carried him out of the building and bundled him into the back of the chopper. Jayden climbed in beside him.

Octavius fired up the chopper and got them into the air. He couldn't be sure if he'd done enough to stop Mikalis for good. He'd issued the demands, but whether they'd stick or not was anyone's guess.

He flew the chopper northeast, toward Chicago. There were safe houses around the Great Lakes they could rest up in. If Saint survived that long.

"How is he?" Octavius called. When Jayden didn't answer, he glanced into the back. Jayden had laid Saint over his lap and was stroking his hair. Saint's skin had turned ashen-grey and begun to shrink around his bones. The venom was killing him.

Mikalis wasn't a nyktelios. There was no way of knowing what his venom would do, or how fast it would burn through Saint. He seemed to be fighting it and wasn't yet dust, so that gave them time.

But no nyk, Brotherhood or not, ever came back from Mikalis's bite.

Saint had known the bite would be fatal. And he'd taken it for Octavius.

"He's going to live," Octavius told Jayden. The feeder looked up. Tears stained his face. "He's not dying, Jayden." The thought of losing Saint tugged at Octavius's heart, almost choking him. In just a few days, they'd been through so much, shared so much, that it felt like more. Like a lifetime.

He couldn't damn well lose him.

"Live, you sonofabitch," he sent to Saint. *"Live,"* he sent again, over and over. So Saint knew he wasn't alone.

CHAPTER 22

aine

HE STILL FUMED after returning to New York and heading into the back of the coffee shop. It had been a long time since he'd been weak, but Saint and Octavius had made him feel feeble, like a newly turned nyktelios.

They'd locked him in a fucking kiln. For a while there, he'd feared they'd meant to light it.

He plucked his phone from his pocket and dialed Eric's number. He was at work, but he always picked up.

"Hey, you good?" Eric asked, probably sensing Zaine was *not* good, despite the miles between them. Their connection had been getting more intense, more powerful. It was more than love now. Somehow they made each other stronger. Eric felt it too. His human blood was *changing*.

"Yeah, I'm good, except for getting my ass handed to me by two ex-Brotherhood nyks. You around anytime soon?" He didn't say it, but he needed Eric close, needed to breathe him in and feel as though the world was just the two of them.

"I can be. I get off in an hour. Meet you for coffee?"

"Yeah." Zaine sighed, the relief like a balm to his frayed nerves. "I just need to do some housekeeping and I'll be out."

Zaine hung up and entered the Brotherhood's temporary base, expecting to find Raiden next to his laptop. But the laptop sat open and abandoned on the main table.

He'd just take a look. He owed it to the memory of Octavius to at least follow through and do some digging on Raiden.

He stepped around the table and pulled the laptop toward him. Some kind of program ran on-screen. The progress bar read *85%*. He pressed his thumb to the built-in fingerprint reader: *Denied.*

That wasn't right.

He tried again: *Denied.*

Their thumbprints never changed, which meant he'd been locked out. What the fuck was Raiden playing at? They all needed access to Atlas, even in its limited state.

He went in search of Raiden in the rabbit warren of storage rooms and corridors that stretched behind the coffee shop frontage, but nobody was home. The temporary base was deserted.

Mikalis wasn't here either, although that wasn't a surprise. He'd be out tracking Saint.

Zaine dialed Raiden's phone. It rang until the voicemail kicked in. "Hey man, what's going on with Atlas? I need to get in and it's not reading my print. Call me back." He hung up and dialed Storm.

"Yeah?" Storm's voice reverberated through the phone.

"Do you know why my print is locked out of Atlas?"

"Not a clue. Ask Raiden."

"Oh wait, why didn't I think of that," he drawled. "Raiden's not here and he's not answering his phone."

"Where is he?"

Storm's tone had changed, turned flat, as though he was trying to hide the fact Raiden being AWOL concerned him. "How should I know? What's going on?"

"Stay there. I'm coming to you."

"Storm, what's going on—"

Storm hung up.

"Assholes, all of them." Zaine had wandered back to the ops room and the working laptop. It was still at eighty-five percent, so whatever it was doing, it was doing it slowly. Why would Raiden leave the laptop open and working if he wasn't here to monitor it?

Zaine straightened, huffed, and did not like the unsettling sense of unease trying to ruin his already pretty damn sour mood.

The ops room was quiet, apart from the laptop's humming fan.

There was no reason to believe any of this was out of the ordinary. The Brotherhood was still reeling after Octavius had fucked them over.

But as Zaine stood in the quiet, the unnerving sense of dread got worse. Something was wrong. Something big. He could feel it. He'd been feeling it for a while now, since before Octavius had locked him in a kiln. Long before that.

He dialed Eric again. "Hey, can you get here quicker. Something's up—"

"Already am." Eric said, then shoved open the door and grinned. "Hey, you look good."

"I always look good." Zaine wrapped his arms around Eric and kissed him hard. The dread eased a little, probably from relief at having Eric close. It never ceased to amaze him that this man stuck with him.

Eric molded close, eagerly responding, his mouth hot and greedy, until he gasped away with a laugh. "I missed you too. Must have been bad, huh? What happened? You didn't get Octavius?"

"No, and he is working with Saint, but some things he said... Saint is powerful, I learned that much. The two of them together are bigger than me, maybe bigger than all of us. We need Mikalis on it, but he's distracted, and then there's this." He freed Eric from his arms and showed him the laptop.

"What am I looking at?" Eric asked. "Is that Atlas?"

"What's left of it. Raiden left it open and running, and now he's disappeared."

"Disappeared like...?"

"He's not answering his phone."

Eric frowned. "Maybe he just went out?"

"Maybe, but Raiden has been working to get it all back online. It was Octavius's creation, and the prick made it so nobody else had administration access. It's been slow going. We all thought Raiden had it in hand, right?"

"All right, so why are you looking at me as though I'm missing something big here?"

"Because of what Octavius said, and I know he's a lying traitor, but..."

"But?"

Zaine sighed and propped his ass against the table's edge. "You remember how Sebastien said some things about Mikalis? About how he's not nyktelios, like the rest of us? Octavius knows something, and that's why he's been cut off. He continues to plead his innocence, but we have orders from Mikalis to bring him in, so who the fuck do we believe?"

Eric stood there in his casual NYPD detective clothes, with his badge glinting at his belt, and planted his hands on his hips. "You know I don't like Octavius, I never have, but the evidence you have against him is circumstantial. Take Mikalis out of this, and you've got one Brotherhood member accusing another with no physical proof Octavius did anything wrong."

"Yeah, he said that. Octavius claims it was personal, that Raiden used him to get access to Atlas and set him up."

"And you aren't following that lead through because...?"

"Because Mikalis ordered us to bring Octavius in dead or alive." Zaine winced. Now that he'd had time to think it through, he wasn't liking the conclusion.

Eric eyed the laptop, turning the facts over in his mind, probably looking at them from different angles. Zaine loved when he got all analytical like this, loved watching his brilliant mind unpick mysteries. "Octavius makes it difficult to like him, but he's never once stepped out of line, right?"

"True. Only Kazimir is more of a suck-up."

"Let's say we don't trust Mikalis?" They shared a glance, knowing that statement to be true. Zaine did trust Mikalis, to a point. He trusted him to protect the Brotherhood by any means necessary. Which might not include the truth. He'd been difficult with the details of the unusual blood quirk found in Eric and more recently, Felix Quaid. He'd only agreed to Eric working with them after Zaine had threatened to reveal the things he'd heard from the dying nyk, Sebastien. "Octavius finds himself in an impossible situation. Kicked out, but suddenly implicit in a plot to undermine the people who think he's turned against them. What's he going to do?"

"Find a way back in."

"That's you. He called you, told you he was set up. So, why didn't you believe him?"

"Because he threatened you, and he's a dick."

Eric smiled and applied his body between Zaine's knees, leaning in nice and close. "Cute, but I'm over it, plus I can hold my own now. He reached out to you for help, Zaine. You owe him this."

"You don't think he's lying?"

"I don't know, but shouldn't we check?"

"Even if he's teamed up with Saint?"

Eric shrugged. "I don't know anything about Saint. Apparently, nobody does. And that's Mikalis's doing. He's made it so *nobody* knows Saint. But I do know there are always two sides to every story."

Zaine encircled him, trapping him by the waist and nuzzled his neck. "Why are you so reasonable?"

"I'd be a shitty cop if I wasn't."

Zaine huffed a laugh, but it didn't last. He'd ignored Octavius's call for help. "I'm an asshole."

Eric nudged his mouth with the tease of a kiss. "Actually, you're one of the few in the Brotherhood who's not so stuck in his ways and can make a difference. Octavius knows that. He might even like you, in his own fucked-up way."

"Hm." Zaine tasted his lips, warm and inviting, and wanted nothing more than to take Eric to one of the back rooms, where they could lose themselves together, but then the laptop caught Zaine's eye.

The progress bar had increased to eighty-six percent.

He reluctantly withdrew from Eric's generous intimacy and sighed. "We need to find Raiden." And they needed to find him before that bar reached one hundred percent. Because when it did, Zaine's instincts were telling him whatever happened would ruin a whole lot more than his mood.

CHAPTER 23

ctavius

THE SAFEHOUSE STOOD on its own plot of several acres on the shore of a stormy Lake Michigan.

All the Brotherhood safehouses had medical facilities, but normal medicine wasn't going to save Saint.

"What do we do? What can I do?" Jayden stood at the floor-to-ceiling window overlooking the misty lake. "My blood? I'll feed him, I don't care how much he takes. I tried in the chopper, but I couldn't open a vein—" He hurried to the kitchen area and opened the drawers. "If I cut my wrist, he'll smell the blood, right? And he'll drink. I can do that—"

"Stop." Octavius slumped against the wall. If he sat down he'd struggle to get up again. Exhaustion had caught up with him, and the adrenaline from the fight with Mikalis had worn off an hour ago. He needed to think, but there wasn't time.

Jayden grabbed a knife. "I'll do it now."

"He'll kill you."

He looked up. "He won't. He's always careful."

Jayden didn't understand. "When he's not dying, he's careful. But right now, if he were to even wake long enough to recognize blood, he'll tear into you. It's not a choice, Jayden. It's what we are."

"I can't just fucking stand here doing nothing!" He flung the knife onto the kitchen counter and thrust his hands into his hair. "God damnit, Octavius. You don't get it. He saved me. I was lost, and *he saved me*. I can't do this fucking shit world without him." He gulped a sob, stormed outside, slammed the door, and marched to the water's edge in the swirling mist.

Octavius *did* get it. Saint had saved him too, and he was only now beginning to realize how.

He'd started out hating him, believing him to be nothing more than a blood-sucking nyk. But Saint was complicated, and far from the monster they'd all been warned about. He was amusing and bold, and he cared. He even *loved*. He loved Jayden, and he had loved Mikalis. Nyks weren't like that. Saint wasn't a nyk. He was brilliant, powerful, compelling, irritating, handsome, enigmatic, and alluring in ways Octavius couldn't remember experiencing before.

But right now, he was fighting to survive a bite that should have already killed him.

There had to be something they could do. Some way to save him.

The venom was in his blood, in his veins, beating through his heart, trying to devour him beat by beat. He wasn't yet dust so that meant Saint was fighting it. If he was fighting the venom, then there might be a way to help him fight for longer.

If they could bleed him, and have him feed, it might dilute the venom enough for Saint to gain the advantage. But out of his mind with pain and starvation, Saint would grab the nearest warm-blooded living thing and drain it in seconds. That was Jayden, and Saint had done all this to *save* Jayden.

What if Octavius took Saint's blood into him?

It would mean consuming venom. Swallowing venom was a lot less effective than having it injected into his veins, but it would still be inside him, still liable to try to destroy Octavius too. But Jayden was here, a healthy feeder. Drinking from Jay wasn't ideal, but it would help Octavius recover enough to continue bleeding Saint.

Drain Saint, dilute the venom in him, then Octavius would drink from Jayden and feed Saint, replenishing his strength. Octavius would act like a filter, filtering out the venom, and protect Jayden at the same time.

If they did this carefully, slowly, it just might work.

He owed it to Saint to try.

He left Jay outside and hurried to the bedroom.

Saint writhed on the bed, eyes squeezed closed, his face and neck wet with perspiration.

Octavius tore open Saint's shirt and loosened his trousers, anything to free him and give his body space to heal. Sweat glistened on Saint's heaving chest, but it was the ash-like pallor to his skin that concerned Octavius the most.

That and the fact his next breath might be his last. If Saint turned to dust in front of him, he might fucking lose his mind.

"Fuck." Octavius had to do this. He tore off his hooded top, leaving just a shirt underneath, and rolled up his sleeves. He'd never consumed a large amount of nyktelios blood before, and he'd only injected venom to kill them. Nyk blood wouldn't satisfy his hunger the same as fresh human blood did, which meant he wouldn't have the same loss of control as drinking from a human vein would induce. In theory.

Whatever happened, whatever he did, there was no way of making the situation any worse.

He dragged a chair to the side of the bed, took Saint's wrist in both hands, and forced his fangs to drop. Saliva pooled around his tongue. He didn't *want* to do this, and he'd need to control his own venom so he didn't add to Saint's dire state. He'd never done this before. This was... something else. He wasn't even sure what this was. It felt like blasphemy. So many things could go wrong. He could take too much and poison himself, he might accidentally inject venom, killing Saint quicker. Mikalis's venom might kill them both.

"Don't overthink it," he told himself, and bit into Saint's cool, clammy wrist.

His pair of fangs loaded with venom ached to finish killing the nyk. He pulled back on those urges, shutting them down, and fought several thousand years of habit to envenom his victims. It wasn't so bad. Just some nyk blood on his tongue, he just had to swallow—

Then the blood hit.

And it was nothing like the foul, bitter blood he'd assumed it would be. It was all the tastes of Saint slapped across his face. The kiss, the desire, the need—it rolled over him, triggering a blinding cascade of hunger. Then came the taste of Mikalis's venom—acidic, sharp, like glass on his tongue.

Instincts tried to have him recoil in disgust. He swallowed anyway, his body at war with itself. Take, drink, own, kill, envenom, destroy.

"What are you doing?!"

He wasn't sure how long he'd been drinking, just that his head spun and his body throbbed. Jayden's hand burned like a brand against his shoulder. Octavius tore free, licked Saint's wound clean, using a small amount of venom to trigger the healing process, and slumped back in the chair like a deadweight.

"Are you trying to kill him?!" Jay screeched.

"No, no..." Octavius mumbled. He shoved from the chair and stumbled toward the door. Venom sizzled through his veins, turning his body into fragile glass. "Trying... to save... him."

The floor tilted out from under him and he went down, falling into darkness.

∼

HE WOKE LATER, sprawled on a bed, fully clothed, limbs akimbo, dumped there by Jayden. His head was clearer, so there was that.

He groaned upright, and waited a few minutes for the room to stop spinning, then stumbled from the bedroom, through the house. He could hear Jayden's heartbeat, could smell him, a mixture of male and soap. He dozed on the couch, unaware and vulnerable, apart from the knife clamped in his grip.

They were going to be all right. But Octavius needed Jayden to help, or it wouldn't work.

"Jayden?" Octavius propped himself against the edge of the couch.

He jolted awake and glared. "You look like shit."

"I need you to trust me. I'm doing this to save him."

His glare softened. "Really?" he croaked, and set the knife aside.

He was a good soul, just like Saint had said. He'd come through for them. "I've been cruel to you, and I'm sorry for that. But I need your help right now. I can't save him without you."

Catching on fast, he rolled up his sleeve, exposing his wrist. "Do it. Whatever you need. We're in this together."

Octavius didn't have the strength or patience to go slow. He sank to his knees, grasped Jayden's wrist, and bit. Jayden hissed in pain. Human blood poured over Octavius's tongue and down his throat, igniting all the wild urges he'd kept in check for so long. Pleasure spilled down his spine, reviving primal needs—to bite and fuck and own humans—all over again. As he drank, the physical hunger waned, but other urges surged, making him pulse with a different kind of need.

His cock hardened, growing heavy and sensitive, but he had enough control to resist, and when he'd taken enough blood, he sealed the wound with a lick across Jayden's wrist and slumped on the floor, taking a few seconds to regain control of his senses.

Jayden sighed and dropped next to him on the couch. "How many times do we do this?"

"Until the venom is out of his system."

"Then I'd better get some groceries while I can."

While he could? "I won't hurt you." Jayden was key to making this work. Without his blood, Octavius wouldn't be strong enough to filter out the venom—to go back again and again to take as much as they needed for this to work. But he wouldn't hurt Jayden for other reasons too.

Such as, he liked him.

Jayden smiled, and his handsome sun-kissed face brightened. "I know. But if this is going to be anything like Saint's fuck-fests, I'll need the fuel."

"I... No... We won't... be doing that." Octavius cleared his throat. Sex was out of the question, despite his body's demands.

Jayden's left eyebrow shot up and he looked pointedly at Octavius's crotch. He wasn't as hard as he had been, but Jayden's gaze triggered a tantalizing thrill that had him aching for touch all over again.

Octavius climbed to his feet and headed for the kitchen. "Once I'm sure the venom is out of my system, I'll see if I can get Saint to feed from me. I suspect it'll take a few tries to rouse him. He'll need to be desperate, more desperate than he is now." He'd be rabid and out of his mind, less man, more nyk. That would be the most dangerous part of this plan. Most nyks were at their most vicious when they were dying.

"If we can wake him, why doesn't he feed from me?" Jayden asked.

"Because he'll tear out your throat."

"And he won't do that to you?" Jayden joined Octavius at the kitchen's island counter. He even seemed concerned for Octavius.

Saint was right, Jayden was a good person. A rare thing in this world, and having tasted his blood, Saint had also been truthful when he'd said Jayden wasn't a feeder. In all the months they'd been together, Saint hadn't infected him with venom. He still had his free will.

He'd chosen to be here.

Octavius had been so damn wrong about so damn much that he didn't even know where to begin with untangling it all.

"I'm more robust," Octavius said. "Just concentrate on staying fed and"—he couldn't believe he was saying this—"feeding me."

Jayden's smile turned sly and a touch of color flushed his face and neck, making his spray of freckles shine. "I guess we'll be getting real close for a while then, huh?"

He was genuinely handsome, just not in a way Octavius had cared to notice. He couldn't afford to notice now, or things could get far more complicated. "Something like that." The idea of being intimate with a human would have repulsed him less than a week ago. Now, things had changed.

In fact, everything had changed, and so fast.

Their trio was special. He hadn't had time to consider what it all meant, just that they were together and were stronger for it.

This was more than necessity.

Octavius cared for them both just as much, if not more, than he cared for the Brotherhood. He'd break every and all rules to keep them safe.

"*I'll* get the groceries," Octavius said, grabbing his hooded top. He needed to get outside, get some air; he needed space to think this all through and understand who and what he was. "Stay out of Saint's room, Jayden. He might look harmless, but Saint has never been more dangerous."

He saluted. "Got it."

With any luck, and a bit of time, they might save Saint in time to see the end of the world.

CHAPTER 24

aine

"WE'VE GOT NOTHING." Zaine sat at the meeting table with the laptop churning away off to one side. Eric sat beside him, and Storm loomed at the far end. Aiko was on his way back from London, and Kazimir and Felix were inbound. They'd arrive on US soil within a few hours.

"I've got an APB out on Raiden," Eric said, "but if he doesn't want to be found, he won't be."

Storm simmered, arms crossed, cheek twitching, as pissed off as Zaine had ever seen him. And it wasn't just Raiden missing that had him on edge. Being kicked from a chopper wouldn't have been much fun, but that wasn't it either.

Storm looked... worried. And Storm didn't do worried. Ever.

"We need Mikalis on this," Zaine said. "If Raiden is all the things Octavius said, then we're sitting here with our asses out, twiddling our thumbs."

"Mikalis is indisposed."

Zaine laughed, despite how unfunny this shitshow was. "What?"

"It's just us."

They needed Mikalis. Zaine's smile faded. He wasn't fucking around anymore. This was serious. "Saint can wait. Whatever is on that laptop might not."

"He's not coming!" Storm snapped.

Zaine clamped his jaw shut. He caught Eric's eye, and his slight shake of the head, warning him not to push.

"Are we believing Octavius now?" Eric asked. Storm ground his teeth. "I just... He built Atlas. If we can't find Raiden, then we should go straight to the source. No? He clearly wants to help."

"*You* want to ask for Octavius's help?" Storm asked, eyebrows raised.

"Right, I'm sure he'll help us, because we've all been *so* supportive of his situation," Zaine drawled.

"It's worse than that," Storm grumbled, shaking his head. "Trust me, he's not coming back, and he's not going to help us."

Zaine wasn't so sure. Now he'd come around to the idea of Octavius not being the big bad traitor Mikalis had made him out to be, the prick might prove pivotal in fixing this rapidly worsening fuckup. "Last I saw of him, he *wanted* back in, he wanted to help. If we admit he was right all along, he'll come back. I'll talk to him—"

"That was before Mikalis killed Saint," Storm said, matter-of-factly.

"He... did?" Then why the fuck was Mikalis still AWOL?

"They had... a relationship."

Wait. What? "Who did?"

"Octavius and Saint."

Wait, a relationship as in... a romantic relationship?

"Fuck me, Octavius has a heart?"

In the many centuries Zaine had known Octavius, he hadn't once reacted in any way to the idea of companionship, or even getting laid. Centuries ago, he'd been their healer, and more recently, he'd been more interested in computers than people. "How do you know this?"

"I saw them... after he kicked me from the chopper. I have wings, you know. I tracked him—"

"Again with the wings," Zaine muttered. He really needed to get a pair of those upgrades.

"I followed him, watched him, because none of this makes any goddamn sense."

Then Storm had been way ahead of them this whole time? Who knew he had brains *and* muscles?

"What I saw..." He huffed, like a big dog on a hot day. "Anyway, they were close. I don't know if Octavius freed Saint, but even if he didn't, they had formed a partnership. Mikalis took that from him, as well as everything else in marking him as a traitor. Wherever Octavius is, he's not going to help. We've burned that bridge."

If Mikalis had killed Eric, Zaine wouldn't have been sitting at that table either. *Mikalis* burned that bridge, and he had a whole lot of questions to answer. No wonder their leader was keeping his head down.

But also, thinking back to when he'd seen Saint and Octavius together, it had been brief, between them beating the shit out of Zaine and throwing him into a kiln, but there had been *something*. A connection between them. Octavius had also let Saint feed from him—Zaine had scented blood as soon as they'd let him out the kiln.

And Mikalis had killed Saint.

Octavius was out there alone, thinking nobody gave a shit about him.

Zaine wasn't the only asshole here. They all were. Why hadn't they seen the truth earlier? Why hadn't *anyone* believed Octavius?

"He might talk to me," Eric said.

Had Eric lost his mind? "Or he'll kill you as revenge for Mikalis killing Saint."

"If we can find him, he might see me as an outsider, not really Brotherhood."

"No," Zaine said, then added, "Fuck, no. He's threatened to kill you before."

"He was protecting the Brotherhood. Things have changed."

"No."

Eric gave him a sympathetic look—the damn puppy dog eyes Zaine could never resist. "You keep saying no like I'm going to obey, when we both know that's not how we work."

"*Kærasti*, please no, don't do this. I will get on my knees and beg you in front of Storm. I don't care." Octavius was lethal. He'd kill Eric before Zaine could try to stop him. And now he had reason to.

Eric hesitated. "All right, fine... But it's clear we need to find him, if we can't find Raiden. Maybe that laptop doesn't mean anything, or maybe it means we're all fucked when it reaches one hundred percent. Either way, Octavius will know."

Storm rubbed his face and tried for the fiftieth time to get his thumbprint to unlock it. *Denied.* "We sure don't know what it means."

"But we do know something is very, very wrong with the current picture," Zaine said. "We all feel it, right? It's not just me feeling as though we're on an edge, peering into the abyss?"

"You're right," Storm agreed. "I fear Octavius was right, and Raiden was the real threat, although I don't know why Raiden would turn on us. But we all missed it, and I suspect we're about to pay for that mistake."

Zaine slumped in the seat. Maybe they deserved this. "What do we know about Raiden?"

"He's blisteringly intelligent," Storm said. "Potentially a consummate liar, he's also inventive, resourceful, uses weapons, and doesn't like to get his hands dirty."

"Weapons, like?" Let it be guns. Guns Zaine knew.

"It used to be the crossbow. He's an excellent marksman. Could shoot a bolt and hit a needle across a meadow. But in the last few centuries, he was drawn to science. He sought a cure for us, for a long time, but Mikalis shut him down."

"Oh?" Zaine raised his eyebrows.

"There's no cure. It's a waste of resources," Storm explained, trotting out the backup Mikalis line. "He tortured endless nyktelios in that pursuit. He's ruthless, cunning. All traits that made him perfect for the Brotherhood."

"Until he potentially turned on us." Zaine glanced at Eric for comment. He always had something to say.

Eric rubbed at the bridge of his nose. "It's not my place, but it seems like Mikalis's judge of character needs some work."

He wasn't wrong. He'd been making a whole lot of decisions lately that didn't fly right. Eric wouldn't have had a seat at the table if it had been up to Mikalis.

"Assuming Raiden is in the wind, where would Octavius go?" Eric asked. "He's alone and hurting. What does he need?" Eric looked at them both, waiting. "You guys don't know a damn thing about him, do you."

Zaine shrank deeper into the chair. "We've never needed to. He was just *there* the whole time."

Eric rubbed his forehead. "You claim to be a Brotherhood, but you're the most fractured, shortsighted collection of emotionally stunted people I've ever met, and I put murderers behind bars for a living. You must know it weakens you? All this *never care* bullshit? Never love, never interfere? If you were an actual Brotherhood it never would have gotten this bad. You'd have known there was a traitor among you this whole time. Because real brothers *care*."

The silence was back, interrupted by the whirring laptop.

The door flew open and Kazimir sauntered in, dumped his bag to the floor, and flicked his glossy black hair like the Instagram bait he was.

"Oh good, Fabio is here," Zaine drawled. Could this day get any worse?

Kazi glowered, but his glower dissolved as he gauged the mood in the room. "What's with the laptop?"

CHAPTER 25

ctavius

HE TOOK Saint's blood like before, but this time stayed conscious and drank from Jayden's offered wrist to help his body dissolve the venom. Now they knew he could bleed the venom from Saint, it was time to try to rouse him enough to replenish his blood and let him begin to heal himself.

"Stay out of the bedroom, no matter what you hear," Octavius told Jayden.

He nodded and returned to the lounge. This couldn't end well with a blood-filled human in the room, like a beacon of savage desire.

In a good scenario, Saint would recognize Octavius wasn't human and take a small amount of blood. In a not-so-good scenario, he might lash out and try to kill Octavius. Or this might not work at all. If he didn't feed, the venom remaining in his system might continue to slowly kill him.

Octavius entered the room and bit into his wrist, just as he'd done with Jayden when he'd lain dying at the lakeside.

Saint lay on the bed, eyes closed, barely breathing. Octavius pinched Saint's cheeks, forcing his mouth open, and applied his bleeding wrist to his lips.

Overflowing blood dribbled down his cheek.

This *had* to work. He'd never known of a nyk feeding a nyk. But perhaps it was like the nurturing Saint had spoken of, like a sire caring for its offspring, keeping them safe, feeding them, controlling them, helping them learn how to be nyktelios. If this was that, then it was natural?

Saint jolted, his body in a seizure, but then his human form dissolved away in a rapid blur, revealing the ancient nyktelios on the bed, his clothes stretched and warped around elongated muscles. Claws tipped his fingers, and the wings—the leathery appendages spilled off either side of the bed. He was a true monster of legend, a creature from human nightmares.

And he was gods-be-damned magnificent up close.

Octavius held fast. Nyks didn't usually spend any lengthy amount of time exposed in their true form. There was no point to it, other than terrifying humans, and revealing it was a sign of turning feral, of desperation, either to attack or defend. Nyks exposed like this, in their feral form, were typically rabid and needed to be put down.

But he wasn't going to kill Saint, he was saving him, and to see him up close, exposed as his true self without them trying to tear strips off each other, was... beautiful. He'd never examined a pure nyktelios before.

Octavius leaned closer. Saint still had the appearance of Saint, but his face was sharper, his jaw wider, to accommodate more deadly teeth. Larger shoulders supported the wings. His chest was broader too, with larger shoulder and upper torso muscles to support flight. Longer arms meant he could embrace larger prey, with claw-tipped fingers designed to dig in and *hold*. Every inch of him had been crafted to capture and feed.

Teeth struck, sinking into Octavius's wrist, catching him unawares. Lightning buzzed up his arm.

Octavius yanked, trying to pull away, but Saint's fangs hooked in, holding him fast. He didn't *want* to pull away, but damn, what if Saint was so out of his mind, he lashed out with venom? Something Octavius should have thought about before now...

Shit, he wouldn't, would he?

"No venom, just blood. Drink," Octavius sent. Saint wouldn't have heard spoken words, but he couldn't ignore a demand in his head, even if he was too far gone to recognize it as a friend's.

His teeth widened the wound, his tongue worked, prying blood free, and Octavius shuddered. He shouldn't like it. This was for... science, yes science. To see if it could be done, and to save Saint's life, but by Nyx, the sensation of Saint's tongue probing, and the thought of where else it might probe, had his cock hardening and heavy with need.

Desire aside, this was progress. Saint was aware enough to drink, and he didn't appear to be about to launch into a killing spree. At least, Octavius hoped not.

He let him feed, watched his throat move, felt his mouth suck —until a chill spread through him, a warning to stop. He pulled, and Saint's teeth clamped down harder with a growl. Octavius pulled again, and Saint's growl deepened. His eyes opened, and their silvery sheen fixed on Octavius. Saint wasn't home. The nyktelios was a beast of hunger, nothing else mattered, and right now, it had Octavius in its sights.

Octavius tore his wrist free.

Saint lunged, and even as weak as he was, he grabbed Octavius. Octavius tried to shove him back but stumbled under his weight, and they both toppled, tangled on the floor.

Octavius flipped onto his front. Fangs scorched his neck, his vision spun, head throbbed, and other parts throbbed too. Saint's erect cock pressed against Octavius's thigh, and for a moment—a terrifying, confusing moment—he feared Saint meant to take him from behind. And he wanted it. Ached for it.

"Stop!"

Saint stopped but stayed on him, a great weight on Octavius's back.

"Let me go. Return to the bed. Rest."

Saint crawled off, climbed onto the bed, and slumped chest down, wings spread, ass up, with his clothes hanging off him in rags. Octavius stayed on the floor a while, breathing, burning, needing. He dabbed at his neck, but the bite was already healing.

If it weren't for Octavius's gift, Saint would have taken him in every way, in blood and body. And he'd... wanted him to.

Octavius waited until his own body had cooled, then swayed on his feet, took a long look at Saint's impressive nyktelios form, and stumbled from the room. "Jayden?"

"Yeah, I'm here—" Jayden's arms came around him, and Octavius folded him close, then drove his fangs into his neck, like biting into a peach. He needed blood to replenish what Saint had taken, but he needed more, he needed a release. He pinned Jayden to the hallway wall and ground his cock against the human's hip. Jayden moaned, and his hands grabbed at Octavius. Teeth in his neck, cock hard against his warmth, Octavius rocked, and fed, and swallowed, and smelled human, and consumed blood, and burned up, and thought of what it would be like to have Saint's clawed hands on his hips, his thighs slapping his ass, and his dick pounding deep inside at the same time as his fangs were buried in his neck.

He came so hard and tore his fangs free with a shout before any venom could spill in and poison Jayden. He still had *that* much control, if little else. A dampness clung to his groin. Shame rolled in. "I'm sorry." He'd *used* Jayden.

"It's all right." Jayden blinked sleepy blue eyes, and he touched Octavius's face with a warm hand. "You can dry fuck me any time." He slumped, almost falling.

Octavius scooped the man into his arms. He'd taken too damn much. Curse his own needs!

"Fuck." He carried Jayden into the lounge and draped him on the couch, then tucked a blanket over him. His heart was strong.

He'd be all right. But if Octavius didn't get this right, if he couldn't control himself, then the delicate balancing act might get them all killed.

~

THIS COULDN'T BE RUSHED. Jayden needed a few days to recover, and while he did, there was no biting, no feeding, just Jayden looking after himself. Octavius stayed quiet and waited. He *demanded* more groceries out of a gas station clerk several miles from the safehouse, making sure Jayden had everything he needed, ensuring he was fed and refueled. Nurtured.

"You should make me one of you," Jayden said from the couch. He reclined, reading a book, wearing just a t-shirt and baggy pants.

"A nyktelios?" The thought repulsed Octavius.

"Yeah."

"No."

Jayden lowered the dog-eared paperback to his chest and tilted his head, peering back at Octavius preparing steak and salad in the kitchen. He'd never needed to cook much, but there was something relaxing about busying himself while waiting for Jayden to heal. It felt good, providing for him. He preferred not to think too long on that and what it meant. Probably nothing.

"But we're a team, and I'm always going to be the weak human."

"No. And you're not weak. We rely on you, and that makes you strong." He poked the sizzling steaks around the pan.

"No, it makes me a target."

"No, listen." Octavius set the steak aside to rest and met Jayden's gaze. He'd sat up, giving the conversation his full attention. "We need you because you're human. If you're nyk, we can no longer... use you." It came out sounding wrong, but he wasn't sure how to make the truth sound any better.

"Right. I'm just a walking blood bag to you." He crossed the room to the counter and grabbed a slice of cucumber off the plate, then crunched down with a baiting smirk.

He was more than that, and he was trying to make Octavius say it. "Forgetting the fact new nyks are generally rabid, monstrous killers for several years, you'd lose what makes you special."

"My usefulness to you?"

"You're going to make me say it? Fine. You're special. You're human. You live and breathe and care. You're as complicated as you are simple. Humans, the good ones, are like..." He'd never been very good at words and was probably about to fail miserably in describing what Jayden meant to both him and Saint. "You're like a sunrise that you didn't expect, but it's so beautiful, so fleeting, you cannot help but stop and watch its colors until its flare fades under daylight."

Jayden scooped up his dinner plate, grinned, and sauntered toward the dining table. "I love you too."

The man was infuriating. "You don't need to be a nyk. It's our job to protect you, and we will."

"Hm, two big, powerful vampire monsters reliant on me eating this steak." He sat at the table and grinned as he tucked in.

Octavius chuckled. Maybe Jayden had it right all along, and the people with the real power had always been humans. Without them, the nyktelios were nothing.

"May I er... ask something, Jayden?"

"Sure, anything, fire away."

And now he'd begun, he had to continue, it was just that it was sensitive. "We are very different. You have an... enthusiasm for some things, that I.... don't. Or didn't. Until recently."

Jayden looked up, chewing slowly, and frowned as though trying to guess where the conversation was headed.

"It's just, as nyktelios—or rather, as Brotherhood, I suppose—I haven't needed to engage in..." His throat was dry, making his voice creak. "Intimacies."

"Are we talking about sex?"

Octavius winced. "Not just that. I... With Saint, I mean, there's a... need. And when I'm with him, helping him, feeding him, I see him—look at him, I mean—and I have these... feelings, and I don't know what to do with them."

"You have had a sexual partner before?"

"I don't know? I don't remember. If I have, it was fleeting. But with Saint, I'm drawn to him. I can't explain it. I look at him, and I think... things. Is it wrong?"

Jayden's smile was the kind type, soft and understanding, and exactly what Octavius needed. He didn't know how to navigate sexual needs, and while it wasn't an issue now, it might be, later. If Saint survived. He could no longer deny his desire, or shun it as a biproduct of feeding.

"It's not wrong," Jayden said.

Octavius felt like a fool. Several thousand years old, and this kid human was coaching him about sex.

Jayden's smile grew. "I knew I was right about you. You're a good guy, Octavius."

Was he a good guy? He'd never thought of himself as one. But he'd always tried to do the right thing, even when right was sometimes grey. "I'm going to try Saint again. Are you ready?"

Jayden nodded enthusiastically and kept on eating. "Also, if you ever want me to go down on you? Y'know, to take the edge off? I'm game." He slid a piece of steak off his fork into his mouth and stroked the tip of his tongue across his lips.

"I uh... I think I'm good." Octavius laughed. The pair of them, Saint and Jayden, were endless flirts.

With any luck, this might be the final time Octavius would have to feed Saint. Maybe he'd regain enough control not to kill Jayden. Once he could feed from Jayden, his recovery would be much faster. They were almost there.

As to what happened after? The Brotherhood, Raiden, rising nyks, the end of the world... They would have to face all of it, perhaps together.

He left the kitchen, and as he walked down the hallway, he considered how, even though the last few days and nights had been difficult, they'd also been the easiest and most rewarding days in many, many decades. No Mikalis, no Brotherhood, just him and Saint and Jayden. In many ways, it felt more right than the millennia he'd spent tracking down and killing nyks.

He couldn't go back to the Brotherhood. He knew that much. Could it be just the three of them until the end of days?

He entered Saint's bedroom. Saint remained on the bed, on his back, wings splayed to either side. He seemed to be sleeping. His breathing wasn't labored and his heartbeat was a steady, strong rhythm.

This was it; this time, it was going to work.

"Okay, big bad wolf." Octavius stepped over his wing and rolled up his own sleeve as he approached the bedside. "It's just you and me."

Octavius paused, studying Saint's nyktelios face. He might not get another chance to see his true appearance up close while serene, and it was worthy of admiration. Saint was pureblood nyktelios, first generation, and his proud features, killing teeth, and substantial body made a glorious sight.

Octavius's mouth dried, and a few fluttering nerves skittered in his belly. He swallowed, sat on the edge of the bed, and bit into his own wrist. There was no reason to be anxious. He'd done this before, and if Saint lashed out, he just had to demand Saint back off.

Pushing his nerves aside, he flexed his hand into a fist and turned it over, pressing the bleeding wound to Saint's warm lips. Lust shivered through him, a perfectly normal reaction. He just had to keep his desires reined in for Jayden's sake later. He could not attack him again like an out-of-control freshly turned nyk.

He wouldn't have reacted like that if he hadn't been starved of this by the Brotherhood. Saint would tell him the same. That the Brotherhood had held Octavius back—Mikalis had held him back. Deliberately.

Saint's teeth clamped in, his claw-tipped fingers grabbed Octavius's wrist, just like before, and Octavius closed his eyes, letting it happen. This was right. It even felt right, now he wasn't fighting the Brotherhood ways. Saint, Jayden, and Octavius. Nyktelios and human: feeding, protecting, thriving. Like it had been, long ago.

Saint's tongue lapped and another lustful fizzle tugged on Octavius's efforts to remain calm and controlled. He opened his eyes and stared straight into Saint's stunning silver eyes. That gaze pierced through all doubt and every single reason why this was bad, striking at the beast within. Unguarded, he had no defense against that piercing stare, and desire simmered hotter.

He had to be better, had to control this.

It wasn't about fucking; he needed Saint strong from blood so he'd be able to feed from Jayden without killing him. That was all this was. But the more he held Saint's eye, the more his needs boiled. His dick hardened, trapped uncomfortably in his pants.

Saint would know he was aroused. If Saint didn't taste arousal in his blood, he'd smell it. Nyks were creatures of need.

Just a little more, then Octavius could leave, and maybe he'd take Jayden up on his offer to suck his dick. It didn't have to become a regular thing. It wasn't that he didn't want Jayden, more that he wanted... Saint.

He tore his gaze from Saint's, but Saint's growl rumbled through the bed, and through Octavius. He wanted Octavius looking at him as he fed, but that would make the urges worse.

By Nyx, he was better than this, he had better control than this.

He lifted his eyes, and there was Saint's glare, as hungry as before, but now, when Octavius locked gazes with him, Saint's tongue swept up his wrist and continued on. He dragged his fangs up Octavius arm, not piercing skin, just scraping, moving to his inner arm, where the vein pulsed. Saint's mouth opened, and his bristling teeth slid through flesh. There was no venom. Saint had control of himself.

Now was not the time.

Saint was recovering.

Besides, Saint needed Jayden for *that*—for sex. He probably didn't even want Octavius.

177

Saint's mouth pulled, his tongue probed, and Octavius rode tantalizing waves of pleasure. It was by accident, when he looked away for a second time, that he saw how Saint's cock stretched his torn pants. Nyktelios cocks were *bigger*. Like everything about them in their true form was bigger. Octavius just hadn't really paid that much attention to nyk anatomy before. He was looking now though, his mouth watering, teeth aching to sink in while his own dick pulsed with every pull from Saint's mouth, as though Saint's hot, wet lips were sealed around Octavius's dick, sucking him off.

Saint's fangs slid from Octavius's skin, but he still gripped his arm, and then he twisted, rising onto a knee, to face Octavius. They'd been this close when they'd fought, and violence shimmered in Saint's scrutiny now too, alongside raw, desperate need.

Perhaps Octavius should shed his human appearance too, if only to protect himself.

Saint breathed hard, his fangs gleamed, his chest heaved. He was either going to sink his teeth into Octavius's neck and kill him or sink his dick into him and fuck him raw. And as Octavius looked up at the nyktelios of legend and lore, he knew there was one outcome he desperately, thoroughly, with every piece of him wanted.

Saint *moved*. But he didn't move in a way Octavius could track. He moved too fast, moved through the gloom, and from one blink to the next, he grabbed Octavius, wrestled him around so fast that the room blurred, and then he was chest down on the dresser with Saint's heavy breathing sawing at his neck. He'd stopped with Octavius bent under him.

It felt hard: the position Octavius had been thrown into, the hand between his shoulders, the dresser beneath him. But hard in a real, raw way. Hard, like it hurt, and he wanted it to so he could feel everything deep in his bones.

"Do you want me, Little Wolf?" The voice was more monster than man, and it set off a riot of chaotic need racing through Octavius's already scorched veins.

"Yes." He replied in his mind, fearing the word would leave his lips garbled.

Saint tore Octavius's trousers free. Fabric burns scorched his thighs. The pain felt good, felt real. Saint's hands clasped his ass and spread his cheeks. Cool, hard claws scraped his hips, and then Saint's probing, wet tongue skimmed his hole so damn gently that Octavius let out a whimpering moan. He needed this. It had been... too long. Forever. He needed to be fucked.

His cock was pinched against the dresser, but that felt good too, felt sharp, and as Saint's tongue swirled his dick wept pre-cum, wetting his lower abs and slicking up the dresser top. He was losing his damn mind. Venom leaked too, bitter on his tongue, and there wasn't a damn thing he could do about it. The creature he'd become raged for more, for Saint, for pain, for blood, to be fucked and taken.

And Saint answered. When his mouth vanished, he thrust his thick hardness deep inside Octavius so hard and so fast, his vision turned white and pain raced up his back, splitting him apart. He gasped, too full, too shocked. And then Saint's claws caught his hips, holding him rigid as his wide length withdrew, then slammed back in.

Octavius growled, hurting, but needing too.

Saint thrust again, and Octavius's cock slid, trapped under him, slick and sensitive.

Then Saint's teeth pierced Octavius's neck, and just like he'd dreamed, Saint fucked him hard with his teeth in his neck and his dick deep inside, and it was all Octavius could do to ride surging waves of pleasure and pain, each one threatening to rip his consciousness away.

Saint grunted at Octavius's neck with every thrust, accompanied by the wet sounds of slapping and rabid growls.

He was too much, but not enough.

More, Octavius needed more. He needed to feel all of him, his dick filling him, his teeth holding him, his hands claiming him. Pleasure and pain crested together, and Octavius came, spilling cum in spurts over the dresser and himself. He didn't care. But Saint did. His fucking turned messy, but harder, and he chased his own climax, buried deep in Octavius. He pistoned and snarled and fucked like a wild creature of chaos, until his pace stuttered and his cock spilled. He came, snarling into Octavius's neck, dick stuttering from Octavius's hole, as though each clench of Octavius's ass pained him too.

Octavius burned—at his neck, his ass—but he liked the warmth, liked the sizzling contact. He'd been so cold, so alone, so isolated.

This sex was like nothing he'd experienced, and he wanted *more*.

CHAPTER 26

 aint

By Nyx, what had he done?

Pleasure and satisfaction swelled inside him. He tasted Octavius and Jay, their sweetness dancing on his tongue, and knew he'd swallowed them, but he was also aware of how he'd just brutally fucked Octavius against a dresser, and he couldn't remember whether Octavius had consented. It wouldn't have mattered, Saint would have fucked him anyway. Octavius had been everywhere, in his head, all over his body. In his heart. He was Saint's. And to make him Saint's, he'd needed to bury his cock in him over and over, bite him and feed, so he understood he was claimed.

But as he'd become sated, well-fed and well-fucked, he'd come around from the frenzy with Octavius crushed under him, his hips bleeding under his claws, and probably bleeding from his ass too, seeing as Saint still had his dick buried in it.

Why the fuck hadn't Octavius reverted to his true form if he'd wanted this?

Because he *hadn't* wanted this.

Saint had just raped him.

The horror of it turned his veins to ice.

Octavius would never forgive him. Saint would never forgive himself. He was here, standing, breathing, because of Octavius. He'd been out of his mind with hunger, but he should have had better control.

Saint withdrew, and winced at Octavius's hiss. He glanced down at his dick and saw how it was slick with more than just saliva.

Damn his vicious needs. That was not how he'd wanted to thank Octavius for saving his life. He reached for him—Octavius's blood glistened on his claws. No, he couldn't touch him.

Octavius trembled, so fucking small. Saint's little wolf.

What should he do? Comfort him? Tell him he was sorry? Such a stupid, pathetic word. Sorry. Sorry he'd fucked him in half. Sorry he'd held him down and buried his teeth in him like an animal.

Octavius turned his head and glared over his shoulder. His face was pale, his eyes a washed-out blue, like a winter's sky. His white hair was mussed. He was wrecked. Saint had done that.

Octavius's eyebrows pinched together, scrunching in... What? Concern? He twisted, and there was his cock, barely hard at all. Further proof Saint had ruined any chance of proving to him how he was not a rabid nyk.

Saint shrugged off his true form, recoiling some from the physical change, and now he stood as a man, his clothes all torn and hanging off him, his body burning with sensation, with heat and the feel of Octavius under him. He'd wanted him since they'd met, but not like that.

"I er..." Saint croaked, then stumbled against the bed and dropped on the edge. "You can go."

He was safe to go. It was important he knew that. Saint wasn't going to imprison him.

Octavius snorted. "I can go?"

His heart twisted up in his chest. If he could rip the damn thing out and give it to him to show how sorry he was, he would. "I'm sorry—"

He snorted again, snatched up his ripped pants, and marched from the room with blood running down his thighs. Jay's concerned voice rattled outside. Octavius replied, sounding vicious. Then Jay was in the doorway, surveying the bedroom, the blood, and Saint, slumped on the bed. His face brightened. "You're alive!" He rushed in, but slowed, reading Saint's face. "What happened? Do you need to feed? You can—"

He began to raise an arm, but Saint shook his head. "No. I've fed enough. Will you..." He couldn't ask Jay to see if Octavius was all right. Octavius might lash out at him. No, that thought didn't sit right. Octavius smelled like Jay, as though they'd been *together*. As though they were one. Nyktelios and feeder. "What happened, while I was out? Are you two close?"

"No, not really." Jay sat on the edge of the bed. He looked good, healthy, bubbly. Octavius had been caring for him. "He filtered out the venom in your veins and took blood from me to keep the venom from hurting him. And it worked!"

"He consumed my blood knowing it was poisoned?"

"Yeah, then drank from me, to help fight the effects of the venom. Amazing, right?"

Then what Saint had just done was so much worse in the face of Octavius's selflessness. "Will you see if he's all right?"

"He'll be fine." Jay shrugged. "He gets prickly afterward. It'll pass."

"No, Jay. I hurt him." Saint's voice caught. "Really hurt him, and I er..." He swallowed to try to clear the knot. "I don't want you to lose him because of me."

Jay laughed at Saint's concern. "He won't go, he loves us. Trust me."

Every damn thing Jay said made his heart want to shrivel in his chest. He slumped forward and buried his face in his hands. "Please, in a little while, give him some time, and then go to him."

"Why don't *you* go to him?"

"Because I just raped him, Jay," Saint snapped. "I raped him and bled him, exactly like the monster he believes I am. I can't go to him. I can't look him in the eyes..."

Jay stood abruptly. He should run from Saint. They should both leave. Saint did not deserve them. Jay backed away and left with a delicate click of the closed door.

Saint had been so far away, drifting in nothingness for so long, poised at the edge of a precipice as though one wrong step would topple him over the edge, but then Octavius had been there, in his head and his heart, holding him back. He hadn't been alone, after being alone for so, so long. And that had meant everything because he'd known he'd had something—someone—to come back to.

"Hey." Jay ventured back inside after being gone for some time. "So, I spoke with him, and he's grumpy, as usual, but I don't think he's angry about what you did. You need to speak with him."

He did need to speak with him. Apologize, do whatever he had to so Octavius knew it had been a terrible mistake.

"Thank you."

Jay shrugged. "Are *you* okay?"

Saint stood and got a waft of his stale-smelling clothes. Besides smelling like a vagrant, he felt good. Better than good. But that was the effect of feeding and fucking like he had. "Yeah, I'll be fine. And thank you again, Jay." He reached for him and when Jay melted into his arms, his heart swelled. It meant a lot, what they'd both done for him. He'd find a way to thank them properly. "Where is Octavius?"

"In his room. He was going to take a shower, but he said to send you in."

Saint left Jay and headed down the hall, following the sounds of the shower. He knocked on the bedroom door.

"Come!"

Perhaps this was a trap, so Saint lowered his guard, leaving him open to Octavius's vengeful attack. It had to be coming. He pushed open the door and spotted how the bathroom door was ajar. Octavius's lithe figure moved behind the shower door among bellowing steam. Then he shut off the water, the door opened, and Saint looked away. He'd destroyed any right he had to admire Octavius naked, yet every piece of him ached to have him close.

After the rustle of fabric, Octavius emerged with a towel around his waist, and he used another to ruffle his wet hair. Water droplets glistened on his chest, tiny little gems that Saint ached to lick off. One drop at a time.

Octavius tossed the damp towel on the bed, keeping the one around his waist, then folded his arms and glowered. "Well?"

Where to begin? "Hear me out." Saint raised his hands. "Actually, no, there's no excuse. I was out of my mind. I just—You were there, and I knew I needed you, and I... I didn't want that." Octavius's glower sharpened. This was terrible. Saint wanted to crawl into a hole. "Fuck, I don't know what to say or do to make this right. Name it, and I'll do it."

"Get on your knees."

"What?"

"Get on your knees."

Saint dropped. If Octavius ran a blade through his heart, he'd welcome it. It was all he deserved for turning on him.

Octavius came forward and with less than a step remaining, he peered down his nose. From below, Octavius was even more enchanting. Fury radiated off him, power restrained, and Saint could feel himself getting hard again, adding insult to injury.

Octavius's cool damp fingers pinched Saint's chin, lifted his head, and then his hot, wet mouth claimed Saint's, and his tongue swept in. Fangs nicked, but it didn't matter, Octavius was kissing him, not killing him. And the kiss was as bright and devastating as any Saint had experienced.

When he straightened, Saint was left on his knees, lost in his startling blue eyes. "I'm not going to lie, I'm a little confused and a lot aroused. I see you're mad, but also, that kiss was—"

"Yes, I'm mad. You kicked me out after we fucked, and then told me you used me because *I was there*. Is that true?"

"No. What? Wait. What I did, I'm truly sorry. I hurt you—"

"Hold on, what are you apologizing for exactly?"

He was going to make him say it? "For raping you."

Octavius's mouth fell open. "You didn't—that's not what happened. If I hadn't wanted... that, I'd have fought you off." Color touched his face and chest, a beautiful flush that clashed delightfully with his silvery white hair and blue eyes. "You asked me, and I said yes."

"I did? *You* said yes?"

"You don't remember?"

"No, perhaps..." There had been a thought inside his head, a kind of freeing moment, when he'd first had Octavius in his grasp.

"I answered in your mind."

"I thought I'd dreamed it."

Octavius's lips twitched with humor. He planted a hand on his hip, stepped back, and admired Saint from head to toe with a not unwarranted smirk. "The mighty Saint, on his knees, begging for forgiveness. I like you there."

Hm. He considered standing again, now Octavius clearly wasn't enraged, but he still wasn't sure he'd earned it. "So why were you so angry?"

"I haven't experienced anything like that in forever. I wanted it, and you. I thought... I thought it meant something, but right after, with cum running down my thighs, you told me to leave."

He'd been so distraught after realizing what he'd done, he hadn't even considered that Octavius had *wanted* to be taken like that. "I'm an idiot."

"Yes, you are." Octavius chuckled. "And you need to have more faith in me. If I don't want something, I will make sure you know it *by getting inside your head.*"

Saint winced at the penetrating thoughts.

"But you were also recovering from Mikalis's bite, so just this once, you're forgiven for acting like an idiot. Now get in the shower. You need it." He sat on the end of the bed, all smug and virtually naked, then leaned back and braced his arms on either side of him, as though reminding Saint of the bounty he may or may not be allowed to touch.

Climbing to his feet, he took a shaky breath, feeling more wrecked now than when he'd been suffering from venom, but relieved too. Octavius wanted him. That was its own revelation. Did he want more than sex, did he want to be a part of Saint's life? Was that even possible? His heart flip-flopped, but he guarded it against disappointment. Love hadn't worked out so well in the past, and they didn't have much of a future. But still, Octavius wanted him.

He stripped, stepped into the shower, and turned the hot water on full. It was just a shame he'd had to wait until the end of days for Octavius to find his way into his life. Did he love a man he'd only met a few weeks ago without the aid of venom? Had it been weeks? How long had he been unconscious, fighting Mikalis's venom? Did two nyktelios even deserve such a thing as love?

The shower door opened, and Octavius stood there, naked, eyes ablaze with hunger. Before Saint could ask him to join him, he'd stepped into the small enclosed space, closed the door, and stood chest to chest under the pounding jets of water. He studied Saint's face, then reached up a wet hand and traced the lines of his jaw, then skipped his fingers down Saint's neck.

Saint snatched his hand, stopping its roaming. Octavius's eyes widened, then narrowed with sly delight. This was... good. Close and warm and intense.

"Shall we do this a little more gently this time?" Saint asked.

"Define gentle." Octavius dropped his free hand and clutched Saint's filling dick, then shoved him backwards against the cool tiles. His slick body pushed, chest on Saint's, and his thigh pinned Saint's. Octavius's mouth teased Saint's neck. He was anything but vulnerable. He had control, and he'd had it before too, despite what Saint's simple nyktelios brain had been telling him.

Saint freed his wrist, and Octavius became a writhing, hot, wet pillar of male suddenly everywhere—his mouth scorching Saint's shoulder, teeth grazing his skin, hands sliding down Saint's back, then cupping his ass. Every touch set his skin ablaze, igniting a softer yet potent desire. This wasn't a mindless, chaotic need to fuck. This was relishing in having Octavius in his hands, against his skin, between his teeth.

Hm, between his teeth... Saint slid down the tiles, bracketing Octavius's wet body, and went to his knees. Water cascaded down Octavius and ran in rivulets over lean muscle, into the V of his hips, and the proud, glistening erection was now level with Saint's mouth. This was what he wanted. He was hard for Saint. But what if he'd preferred the rough nyktelios handling, the claws, and the exaggerated size of other parts?

"Now who is overthinking?" Octavius tipped Saint's chin up.

"Do you want me as nyktelios?"

"Then, I did. But right now, I want *you* like this. I can't take another pounding."

Good, because while he'd enjoyed fucking him raw, Saint preferred this gentleness between them, and where it might lead. He liked the taste of dick too, when he drew its length between his lips and over his tongue. By the goddess, he was hard, and long, and as Saint sucked, he swallowed deep, sliding Octavius's cock between his lethal fangs. He'd wanted this since they'd met—the feisty, angry little wolf, tamed under Saint.

Octavius grabbed a fistful of hair and twisted, making Saint splutter. Not so tame, then. And knowing how hard Octavius would give in return freed the fire in Saint's veins all over again. He needed this in ways he couldn't explain. Octavius was a part of him, woven into his heart.

He'd saved Saint, but Saint had cared for Octavius long before that.

Octavius pumped, holding Saint's hair rigid, thrusting down Saint's throat, balls to his chin. He'd tilted his head, and his sharp mouth opened, his body flushed. Saint needed him on the cusp of coming, he needed him burning up and mindless. There, that precipice, that moment before ecstasy stole all his inhibitions away.

He let go of Saint's hair, raised his hands above his head, holding them in the shower's stream, and he fucked Saint's mouth with abandon. There he was, the real Octavius, the man who was free of all rules, of all lies. Free and full of life.

His thrusting hips stuttered, and he came, pulsing deeply down Saint's throat. His cum might have been the sweetest elixir Saint had ever tasted. As the aftershocks racked him, Saint rose, wiped his mouth, and thrust a messy kiss on Octavius's plump lips. His eyes blew wide, pupils full and dark and filled with desire.

"More," Octavius said.

Saint scooped his slippery body up, under his ass, and kissed him as though there was no tomorrow.

CHAPTER 27

ctavius

THERE WERE memories of long-forgotten lovers, the ghost of their touch, but none had been like Saint. He seemed to know in the moment what Octavius needed and how to satisfy those needs, either under his tongue or the stroke of his hand over Octavius's dick.

Octavius knew now why he'd kept himself behind bars, avoiding all physical contact. Because it made him feel, made him want to live, made him come alive, and made him crave pleasure like a drug. He truly had been a phantom, moving through the world, untouched and untouchable. But Saint saw him in ways he hadn't known he'd needed. In dangerous ways.

He wasn't sure, as they lay entwined, where he ended and Saint began. His cock stroked in and out, his mouth sucked, teeth grazed, hands gripped, hard and soft. Their lovemaking blurred, driven by need without thought. He wasn't sure if it was a nyk thing or just a

Saint thing, but Octavius lost himself in the hours they sought pleasure together.

As his body healed the all-over assault, it tingled in the most delightful way. According to Brotherhood creed, intimate relations with a nyktelios were forbidden, but now he'd thrown off the stifling Brotherhood shackles, he saw the world around him in a whole new light. One of feeling and hunger and lust, and perhaps even love. He'd been just another tool for Mikalis. Saint had showed him another way, a way that had to be the true way. Why else would it feel so right?

He left Saint sleeping, tugged on trousers and one of Saint's loose shirts, leaving a few buttons open, and ventured into the kitchen.

"Hey." Jayden smirked at the kitchen counter. "Want some ice cream? Sure you do. Ice cream after bone-melting sex is the best."

Jayden had heard them then. They hadn't been quiet. By Nyx, did Jayden mind Octavius had been intimate with his lover? He didn't appear angry as he collected a second bowl and grabbed the tub of ice cream from the freezer. Still, Octavius should say something. But what?

"It's fine." Jayden scooped out the ice cream.

"What is?"

"I could make you stand there a while longer, all awkward, trying to be stoic, while you figure out how to explain why you and Saint just spent the night fucking each other's brains out, or we can eat ice cream together while I explain how it's good for all of us, and how I like your smile. You should wear it more." He handed over the bowl and Octavius automatically took it. "I just care you're happy."

He didn't mind at all?

Jayden sauntered to the couch in front of the wall of glass and sat with his ice cream. "You're surprised?"

"I don't really do relationships, so I don't know how this is supposed to work."

"But you're a natural!" Jayden laughed.

Octavius snorted and carried his ice cream to the chair opposite Jayden. He sat and folded his legs beside him, scraped the spoon over the ice cream, collecting a curl, then tasted it. An explosion of honeycomb zinged on his tongue. "You bought this? It's good."

"I found some cash in a tin, and went to get groceries while you two were getting to know each other—finally! So, let me explain what we've got here." Jayden circled his spoon in the air. "It's not what most people would define as a normal relationship, but it's working, and I like it."

"Three of us?"

"Yeah. Do you like it?"

Did he like *this*? There was a lot more to that question than there seemed on the surface. This wasn't just sex. Jayden was asking about the feeding aspect too. The whole package. Nyktelios and human. Two nyktelios and one human, living as a trio. And Octavius *did* like it. He liked Jayden's gentleness, his realism, and his endless optimism, even if it was irritating at times. It helped that feeding from him had become a pleasure rather than guilt-ridden torture.

"Yes, I do like us." It surprised him to say it. Every damn day was a surprise thanks to Jayden and Saint.

"You're allowed to like it," he said. "But you need to work on not feeling guilty when you feed from me, when I'm fairly certain it was always supposed to be like this."

He was right. Again. "It's going to take a while to get used to it. I've spent a really long time despising this."

"Like I said, we'll work on it, with a whole lot of sex."

"I like the sound of that." Saint's gravelly timbre filled the big room. "Hm, ice cream."

Octavius twisted in the chair to see Saint helping himself to the ice cream Jayden had left on the counter. He had that morning after, just fallen out of bed look that suited him so well, with his ruffled dark hair and always-bright eyes.

"Octavius says he wants to fuck the two of us," Jayden said.

Octavius spluttered. "That's not—I mean, I..."

Jay chuckled, Saint snorted, and Octavius found his own little laugh bubbling free.

"Good. This is us then." Saint carried a bowl of ice cream to the couch and sat beside Jayden. "A threesome."

Then Saint was open to the idea of a polyamorous relationship too. Of course he was, he was Saint.

If any in the Brotherhood could have seen Octavius now, sitting in a living room, eating ice cream with a feeder and the big bad nyktelios that had been locked away for centuries, what would they make of it?

They'd probably kill him.

Fuck.

He was never going to be a part of them again.

While Mikalis couldn't personally hunt Octavius or Saint, he'd have the Brotherhood do it for him, and now, after Octavius had gotten inside his head, he'd double down on their efforts. Octavius now knew how the nyks felt, with the Brotherhood closing in.

All this time, they'd been wrong to kill all nyks with extreme prejudice.

"You get that look in your eye when you're thinking about the Brotherhood," Saint said, with his own kind of somber tone. "I know what it's like, I—"

A tiny spot in the glass window behind Jayden cracked, like a growing spiderweb. It seemed strange, that little crack, as though appearing from nowhere. But in a moment between seconds, Saint moved so fast he blurred—grabbing Jayden and yanking him into his arms—and in the next split second, the vicious crack from a high-powered rifle shot split the air.

Saint and Jayden jerked, and Saint collapsed on the couch with Jayden in his arms.

It happened fast yet slowly too, as though Octavius were frozen, watching the horror unfold. He flew from the chair. Blood. He smelled it before seeing it and knew Jayden had been hit. A dark patch of blood spread on Jayden's sweater, close to his heart. He gasped and wide, terrified eyes fixed on Octavius, begging for help.

Octavius grabbed his sweater, tore it open, and there was the perfect hole, just above his left nipple. Dark blood began to spill down his chest.

"Go!" Saint yelled, and at first, Octavius had no idea who Saint was ordering, because he wasn't damn well leaving them.

"He's hit."

Saint shuffled upright, clutching Jayden to him. "I've got him, go!"

Go?

The shooter.

In the woods.

A marksman. A sniper.

Raiden.

Octavius's fangs dropped. He'd kill the vicious, traitorous fiend! But Jayden... Octavius looked at Saint. He wanted to stay, to help, to make sure Jayden would be safe. That was his duty. Jayden was his too.

"He will be all right—it's above the lung." Saint shuffled Jayden around and laid him on the couch, then knelt over him. The wound continued to ooze dark blood. Jayden blinked too fast and groped for Saint's arm. "The bullet went through," Saint said.

Saint was bleeding too. The rifle round had hit Saint *first.* He'd absorbed much of the impact, and he'd heal fast. Saint had this in hand. There was nothing Octavius could do here, but he could get Raiden.

"Go, Octavius, hunt that bastard down and turn him to dust!"

Octavius bolted for the door. Saint would see Jayden was cared for. Octavius had a traitor to catch. On his way out of the door, he spotted a second crack in the side window. The two cracks indicated the bullet's rough trajectory, and Raiden couldn't have fired from too far away—too many trees. He had to be close.

How had Raiden found them? And why?

Didn't matter.

Only finding Raiden mattered. Stopping him. *Killing* him.

Early evening dew wet the brush Octavius tracked through. He kept low and traveled *fast*. Raiden would have seen him coming. In fact, he'd probably shot at Jayden to ensure Octavius would come for him. Why else would he shoot a feeder if not to lure Octavius outside? Even if this was a trap, Raiden was no fighter. The coward shot from afar or played with test tubes in the lab, preferring to keep his hands clean.

But why was he here—

Octavius heard the hiss of air milliseconds before the crack of a gunshot, and veered left, expecting the bullet to sail by. But Raiden had anticipated the move. The round smacked into his shoulder, punching him off his feet.

He fell in the grass at the forest's edge and pressed his hand over the scorching wound, grasping over his left shoulder with his right hand, searching for an exit wound. If it hadn't punctured clean through, his body would heal around it.

Fire pulsed down his chest and arm, rendering both numb. What by Nyx had Raiden shot him with? He'd been shot before, multiple times, but those gunshot wounds hadn't burned hotter with every heartbeat. Something was wrong with the round.

Octavius dug his fingers into the wound, widening it as his skin tried to knit itself closed. Heat pulsed hotter and hotter. He had to get the damn thing out.

Raiden emerged from the tree line, rifle slung at his side. He wore black and green, attempting to camouflage himself. He dropped his hood and shoved his light chestnut bangs back from over his glasses. How long had he been out there?

"It's best if you don't struggle," he said casually. "It'll just hurry the venom along."

"Venom?" Octavius panted.

Raiden pushed his glasses up the bridge of his nose, his habitual tick. He didn't even need the glasses. "Encapsulated-venom rounds," he said. "Each one has its own tiny vessel inside. On impact, venom is released. One shot isn't enough to kill someone like you, but it'll slow you down. Two shots, however? It's a little experiment I've been working on. Among other things. It's amazing what you can do with the Brotherhood's unlimited resources and nobody watching."

Fuck, he had venom in him?! Octavius tried to prop himself up on his arms, but the venom blazed through his veins. He thrust his fingers into the wound again, dug around, and snagged the projectile. He pinched it with his nails and pried it out, then tossed the deformed slug away. Raiden didn't seem concerned, but nothing much seemed to ruffle him. He was Raiden. The science guy, as Zaine had nicknamed him.

"You were painfully easy to find. The only safehouse activated in the past few months. You set the alerts up, I believe. Once one of the houses detects movement inside, it pings Atlas. Rest assured, nobody else saw it. Nobody is coming." He smiled, and the smile Octavius had once admired now looked cruel.

"Why are you doing this?" Octavius hissed as Raiden came forward. "I trusted you!"

He removed a fresh round from his pocket and slotted it into the rifle's chamber, then cocked it with force. "Venom to the heart will finish you. I don't even have to bite you." He pulled a face. "So archaic, killing with fangs, don't you think? Technology is far more elegant."

"I don't understand. I was... We were friends." Octavius's vision blurred as a fresh pulse of agony surged through him. He arched against the pain, mouth open, fangs leaking, desperate to defend himself.

"Friends? Is that what you thought? Of course you did. Poor Octavius, just looking for love in a world that hates him." Raiden crouched and pouted. "If you weren't such a toxic bitch, perhaps the Brotherhood would be here to save you. But alas, nobody is coming." He mock-winced. "Probably a good thing, as you're not exactly the stand-up Brotherhood member you used to be. Hm? Keeping a feeder?" he whispered. "Fucking a nyktelios? How far you've fallen."

"It's not like that—"

He snorted and straightened. "It's exactly like that. Not that I care. It's all coming to an end anyway and you, dear Octavius, made it all possible. I couldn't have brought about the beginning of the end without your brilliant creation."

There was only one thing Octavius had created in his very long life. Most things he destroyed, but he had one shining accomplishment on his resume. "Atlas."

"Exactly."

"What have you done?"

"Just rebooted it back up, with a few minor alterations. You should be proud. You taught me everything I needed to know."

Atlas had been the powerful information hub at the heart of the Brotherhood. Mikalis and the Brotherhood used it to monitor the human world and alter any information regarding nyktelios and the Brotherhood, helping them slip unnoticed through a tech-heavy modern world. Atlas had been offline since the explosion that had destroyed the Brotherhood's New York hub. Octavius had worked with Raiden to restore it.

He'd given Raiden access to one of the world's most advanced and sophisticated AI's.

"It's a remarkable system," Raiden said. "Able to crawl inside every network in every city, in every state, all across the world. Imagine what it could do, if it was used for more than just surgically altering a few files or erasing some unfortunate history Mikalis doesn't want humans seeing. With a few little tweaks, Atlas could... Oh, I don't know, open every locked door on the planet, erase the stock market, start a nuclear war."

"Why would you do that?"

"Chaos, Octavius." The gleam of something not quite sane shone in his eyes. "Beautiful, natural chaos. She has been away from this world for far too long."

Raiden had set into motion the end of the world Saint had warned him of? "She? You mean Nyx?" A thousand niggling little inconsistencies fell into place. The nyktelios rising, the saboteur among their ranks, the Nyxian Vesna Dragovic worming her way into Atlas HQ, claiming she knew Octavius's name, the virus mysteriously finding its way into Atlas, triggering the base's self-destruct. "You're Nyxian."

Raiden worshipped Nyx, just like the insane acolytes who had kidnapped Kazimir and used his blood to make a small army of rabid nyks. But where they'd been human worshippers, Raiden was a Brotherhood nyktelios, and perfectly placed to undermine everything the Brotherhood had done to stop chaos.

How had Mikalis let a Nyxian join the Brotherhood?

Raiden smiled, and that glimmer of insanity sharpened his blue eyes. "Nyx is coming, and neither you or the Brotherhood can stop her." He smirked, so damn smug. "I've waited a long time for this. We're all about to have our hands full in..." Raiden breathed in for a dramatic pause. "Well, we'll see, won't we."

All those people. Billions of lives. Each and every one of them was about to have their world turned upside down. It would begin slowly. Little systems would fail, then the phone networks would go down, then the broadcasters, and then, with all the computers offline, society would begin to fracture. Laws would follow. Enter the vicious, unhinged nyktelios, and the massacre would be endless. An apocalypse.

"You can stop this," Octavius said, still hoping there was some good in Raiden.

"Hm... No, actually, I can't. Once Atlas reboots, it will spread in milliseconds to every internet-connected device and begin to unravel all of humanity's interwoven technologies. It can't be stopped. Except, perhaps by you. And well..." He shouldered the rifle. "That's why I'm here. I'd say it's been a pleasure knowing you, but you really are an asshole. Goodbye, Octavius." His pressed his finger against the trigger.

"Wait!" Octavius thrust out a hand, thoughts racing, desperate to find leverage. "If Nyx is returning, she'll want Mikalis. *Her son!* I can control him."

Raiden snorted, unsurprised by the revelation of who Mikalis was. "Nice try, but you're not that powerful."

Fuck him. Octavius was done listening. *"Stop."*

Raiden's eyes widened, realization dawning.

"Turn the gun on yourself. Press it to your chest. Over your heart."

As Raiden trembled and struggled against his own body, Octavius staggered to his feet. Venom sizzled through him, but its affect had begun to wane. Whatever dosage Raiden had used, it wasn't enough to keep him down. Not now he had Saint's blood in him, and Jayden's. In fact, he felt stronger than ever.

Raiden had turned the gun toward himself. He couldn't reach the trigger though.

Octavius straightened, wincing at the thumping heat in his shoulder, and met Raiden's gaze.

"It doesn't matter what happens to me, she's coming. Nobody can stop it."

"Then there's no reason to keep you alive."

He saw it then, his fate in these final few moments, and his face paled. "Octavius, wait! Those things I said, I was... I was wrong. We are friends. I just... I'm confused. I hear voices. I can't stop them... She's in my head."

"Nyx once spoke to me too. She gave me a gift."

He blinked, and the blubbering bullshit act vanished. "She did?" he asked, as though disgusted.

Octavius slipped his finger over the rifle's trigger and tugged. The rifle barked and kicked, and Raiden staggered once, then again, and clutched at his chest. But he didn't fall.

A horrible satisfied chuckle left his lips.

"It's *my* venom inside the rounds." He laughed harder. "I'm immune. You're such a tool, Octavius." He rolled his shoulders and straightened, the shot having no more impact than a slight shove. "That's the problem with the Brotherhood. You do not see beyond what Mikalis shows you. So blind, all of you. You always have been." With a sigh, he started forward. "I almost hate to do this, because you are brilliant, and you were right about one thing. The feeders *are* making the lovestruck Brotherhood weaker."

"They... What?" Eric Sharpe and Felix Quaid were weakening Zaine and Kazimir? No, he'd believed it once. But not anymore, not now he'd felt what it meant to have someone, to be a part of something. To not be alone. There was nothing weak about love. "You're wrong."

"Wrong?!" Raiden laughed.

"*Stop!*" Octavius thrust the thought toward Raiden, but he didn't stop. His smile grew.

"Hm, tickles. Do it again."

It hadn't worked. Why hadn't it worked? Even Mikalis had buckled under his persuasion... That meant Raiden was more powerful than Mikalis? No, it wasn't possible.

"I see your thoughts all over your face." He laughed again, and between one step and the next, he began to change. Shadows poured in, and his outline blurred, swelling outward, *consuming.* "Did you think I was just the *science guy?*" His voice twisted, deepened, simmered with a growl. "Forget Saint. You should have asked Mikalis *about me.*"

Octavius wasn't waiting to learn what Raiden was about to become. He sprang off his back foot and plunged forward while casting aside his human guise. He slammed into Raiden's chest, knocking him back, then drew back his right fist and punched Raiden's indistinct form where his face should be. He hit some solid part of him, and Raiden roared. Hands crushed around Octavius's middle. Blazing silver eyes bored into his mind, then Raiden—as his true nyktelios form—slammed Octavius down into the ground.

Pain scorched up his spine, but pain was temporary. As Raiden drew back to examine his work, Octavius thrust back with his wings, launching himself forward, and slammed his forehead into Raiden's.

Raiden reeled. Octavius grabbed him, swung, and threw Raiden toward the great lake's inky black waters. He skimmed on the surface, then sank some, wings flapping in an effort to gain height.

He wasn't getting away. Not this time. He was the real traitor.

"*Your limbs are lead, your wings, broken.*"

Raiden roared and thrashed in the water, no longer so smug now he struggled to guard against Octavius's mental invasion.

Octavius waded in waist deep, grabbed him, and shoved him under the surface. He thrashed, grasping at him, then snagged on to Octavius's hair and yanked. Water slammed over Octavius's face, into his mouth, blurred his eyes, filled his ears. He struck the soft bottom of the lake, then kicked up and grabbed Raiden's leg treading water.

Water surged down Octavius's throat, into his lungs, but he pulled down, dragging Raiden with him. Drowning wouldn't kill Octavius, but it would weaken him. As it would Raiden. They thrashed in the water, beneath the surface, wings and claws. Fangs flashed, silver eyes shone. It was brutal and vicious and fast, and Raiden was monstrous, in a world where Octavius knew monsters. He saw his opening, bared his fangs, and bit down into Raiden's shoulder, missing the neck and the main artery. Venom pumped, and Raiden screeched and tore away, kicking upward.

His wings spread above, blocking light from the moon, and then he was gone, lifting from the lake with impossible strength. Octavius broke the lake's surface, gasped and gulped, but he was still alive, still breathing, and not envenomed. Raiden, however, had gotten away.

A low thumping sound drew his gaze, and low on the horizon, incoming over the trees, a chopper made its approach.

Brotherhood.

They were here to kill them all.

He had to get to Saint.

CHAPTER 28

 ay

I DON'T WANT to die, I don't want to die, I don't want to die, I don't want to die... He hadn't yet lived. He wasn't done. He loved them, loved them both. They were his miracle monsters.

It felt like falling.

Cold. So cold.

But Saint was there. He could feel him, hear him. Saint would keep him safe. Octavius too. Nothing could stop them. They'd save him.

If he could just hold on...

CHAPTER 29

aint

JAY WAS DYING.

And it was all Saint's fault.

He'd sent Octavius away, knowing the ex-Brotherhood member would never allow Jay to be turned. What other choice was there? Have Jay bleed out in Saint's arms? But when it came to it, as Jay's eyes fluttered closed and Saint held him, he couldn't do it. Jay was never meant to be like them. They were monsters, all of them. Jay was sunshine and ice cream. Jay was better and brighter.

Just a small amount of Saint's blood could turn him, and Octavius's blood too, since he'd already healed him once before.

"I'm sorry." Saint stroked his golden bangs from his face, where the strands clung to Jay's clammy skin.

Saint squeezed his eyes closed. Grief crushed his heart. This whole gods-be-damned world thrived on suffering. Why did Octavius want to save it, when living meant hurting? He couldn't condemn Jay to this. A forever sentence, in which madness never completely faded.

Another shot rang out, likely Raiden fighting Octavius.

Raiden had known to target their weakness. But Jay had been their strength, the linchpin holding them together.

"Don't leave us," he whispered against Jay's lips, stroking his face, his hair, silently urging him to hold on. If Saint lost Jay, he'd lose Octavius too, and alone again, he just might lose his mind.

Saint didn't have Octavius's ability to get inside someone's head and demand they live. He only had hope, and hope alone had never been enough. He'd hoped Mikalis would see he'd never meant to hurt him, he'd hoped he'd one day see the outside of his prison bars, he'd hoped the world would be different. But it was just the same torture over and over.

He wished he knew what he'd done that was so wrong that he deserved to have each love stripped from him.

"You have to go!" Octavius was here, racing toward them, dripping water and smelling of wet earth and blood. "The Brotherhood..." He stopped beside them. "Gods, no! You said you had this, you said—!"

"We can't save him." Saint's heart was numb. He still stroked Jay's face, listened to his shallow breaths. He was passing. It wouldn't be long now. Saint had witnessed a thousand deaths, but none gouged out his heart like this one.

Octavius's hand landed on his shoulder. Saint turned his head. Octavius's face was all bloody, his white hair streaked with mud, his clothes stained and torn. But the sadness and regret in his eyes said it all. He hadn't killed Raiden. And Saint didn't even care.

Octavius raised his right wrist to his lips.

Saint shook his head. "Don't."

His glacial eyes softened. He lowered his arm again and gazed at Jay. "We can't let him die."

"Yes, we can." Saint's voice creaked. Octavius looked at him as though he'd been betrayed and shoved himself away.

"It might not turn him. He's only consumed my blood once."

It was more than that. Blood was a large part of the turn, but so was intimacy. Octavius could not deny they'd been intimate, when he'd had to take blood from Jay to replenish himself while healing Saint.

"You said some nyks aren't rabid when they turn. Maybe he won't be? We could nurture him?"

"We'd need time and space, somewhere to truly care for him. And even if the conditions are right, it still takes months to tame a new nyktelios." Saint could hear the approaching helicopter blades.

The Brotherhood was here to kill them.

"So, you're just going to let him die?" Octavius paced and thrust his hands into his hair. "I can force you, *demand* you do it.

"But you won't."

"He asked me... He asked me to turn him, to make him nyk."

That was news to Saint, but it changed nothing. "You refused."

He paced some more, back and forth, leaving little pools of water on the floor. "Fuck! The Brotherhood is coming. *You* need to go. They will kill you and I can't fight them, Saint. One, maybe, but Raiden weakened me." His voice cracked. "I'm so fuckin' tired of running."

Saint reached out mentally for any sign of Mikalis, but nothing came back. Not even a distant point of knowing, like he'd always had. Nothing. Just a hole where his sire used to be. "Mikalis isn't with them."

"That's something... He'll never forgive what I did to him. None of them will. We're so fucked."

"Who is fucked?" Jay croaked.

Saint pulled his hands back from Jay's face and sat bolt-upright, still straddling him. Jay's heart thumped, stronger than ever. He yawned and blinked a few times. "How..." Saint mumbled. This wasn't possible.

"Jay?" Octavius shot to their side. "How are you feeling?"

"Fine, I guess, tired, and my legs are numb." He side-eyed Saint.

Saint looked down, saw he was crushing his thighs, and scrambled off. Gods, he was weak and giddy with relief.

207

"What happened?" Jay glanced between them and narrowed his eyes. "Why are you both looking at me like that? Did someone die?"

"Did you feed him?" Octavius asked Saint, heavy on the accusation.

"No, not a drop." Raising his hands, Saint backed away. What was happening here? Jay had lain dying in his arms just moments ago. It didn't make any sense. It defied nature.

Octavius lunged in and swept his hand over Jay's chest, cleaning away sticky blood.

The wound. It had gone. That wasn't possible. "I didn't give him blood," Saint said again, if only to hear the words himself. He was damn sure he hadn't fed him. But he must have. How else did a wound vanish like that?

"I know what this is," Octavius said, breaking into a grin. "Don't worry, he's going to be fine."

"Is he... nyktelios?" Saint asked, even though it was impossible to turn without blood. He'd lived a long time, but he did not know everything. Clearly, Octavius knew more than him when it came to miraculous healing.

"No, he's something else. It's good. He's going to be fine, better than fine, I think. You'll see, but right now you have to leave."

The helicopter's blades thumped louder as it circled above. Grit and leaves thrashed the windows. The Brotherhood was here.

Octavius grabbed Saint's hand and drew him away from Jay. "You have to get him out of here."

And leave Octavius? "You said you can't fight them."

"I'll hold them off. Ride off into the sunset like you wanted. You were right, you don't owe anyone anything. All right? Go and be with him. Everything is going to be fine."

He didn't want to go, not without Octavius. They were a threesome. They had something. Jay's miracle proved it. They were special. Saint had never had anything this meaningful in his whole long, damned life.

"Please," Octavius urged. "They'll kill Jay because he's a feeder, and he's meant to live. They'll imprison you. And Mikalis... he'll make an example of me, of us. You must go."

Saint kissed him—wrapped his arms around his lower back and yanked him close. Octavius's mouth opened, and his tongue swept in, and despite the noise of their approaching fate, it felt as though they were alone again, just the two of them, tangled together, warm bodies and soft lips, quivering skin and sharp teeth. By Nyx, he wanted him close, wanted to spend a lifetime with him, to learn everything he loved, and give him all he deserved. He'd been misunderstood for so long, they both had, and it wasn't right that after finding each other, they were now being torn apart.

The kiss ended slowly, and Saint's heart lurched at the thought of leaving. He bowed his head against Octavius's and lost himself in his beautiful pale-lashed eyes. "I might have loved you, Little Wolf."

His lips ticced, then he placed his hands on Saint's chest and pushed. "Go." He turned on his heel and hurried for the door, throwing it open. The sounds of the landing chopper blasted into the house with the downdraft, whipping his hair and clothes around him.

Saint hauled Jay to his feet, clutched him close, and turned to see Octavius stepping out into the chopper's searchlight.

"Will we see you again?" Saint called.

Octavius smiled over his shoulder.

"Will we?" Jay asked, softly.

Saint scooped him off his feet. "Hold on to me and close your eyes. This is going to feel... strange." He stepped from the side door, then plunged *into* shadow. Would they see Octavius again? He hadn't answered because Jay needed hope, and so did Saint. But the truth left no room for it.

In all likelihood, they'd never see their little wolf again.

CHAPTER 30

ctavius

IT WAS all going to be okay. Saint had Jayden, and Jayden was like the others. Like Eric and Felix, he was *changed* but not nyktelios. Human, but evolved. He'd heal, he'd get stronger, and he'd make Saint stronger too, just by being together. Octavius didn't understand it, none of them did, but he knew they'd be safe. Together. Saint would get to live the happy ever after Mikalis had denied him for millennia.

Octavius was ready to face his fate. To face the Brotherhood. And he supposed, face Mikalis.

He planted his feet and shielded his eyes against the chopper's downdraft as it touched down near the lake's edge.

If they listened and didn't kill him within the first few minutes, he'd help with Atlas. Not for Mikalis, but for the Brotherhood. Because they were all victims of Mikalis's lies, just like Saint had been, just like Octavius was. Although, none of them were likely to ever believe him. Except maybe Zaine, and they all knew he was an idiot.

Nerves rattled Octavius's heart. Nobody stood against Mikalis and his Brotherhood and lived.

He wished he'd had more chances to eat ice cream with Saint and Jayden. His life had lacked the joy found in little things, the small moments, the warm glances, and soft smiles.

The helicopter blades slowed. Storm climbed from the pilot seat.

As it was Storm greeting him, this would be over fast.

Octavius stood firm, cold and aching, bloody and bruised. Storm stopped a few feet in front of him and folded his broad arms. "What happened to you?"

Octavius swallowed. This had to be small talk before the beating began. "Raiden."

"You kill him?" Storm grunted.

"No."

"Huh." Storm cast his steely-eyed gaze around the forest and the safehouse, reading the scene. "He's not here?"

"No, he fled, probably heard the chopper."

"And you're here alone?"

"Absolutely."

Storm's left eyebrow arched.

What was this? They had to know he hadn't been here alone.

"Listen, about Saint—" Storm began. Octavius opened his mouth to explain how they'd never find him and shouldn't bother searching with everything else happening, but Storm held up a hand, cutting him off. "I don't know the details and frankly, don't ever want to, but for what it's worth, I'm sorry it ended that way."

"What... way?"

"Mikalis is..." Storm's mouth twisted as he chewed on words he didn't appear to be able to say. "We have more pressing matters than Saint's death. Raiden has locked everyone out of Atlas, and we have concerns he may have set into motion something... untoward."

Well. That changed things. To start with, they believed Saint was dead, which meant they wouldn't be searching for him. Relief lifted his heart, unraveling knotted nerves. But more than that, they'd begun to suspect Raiden wasn't the stand-up Brotherhood member they'd all assumed him to be. Which meant Octavius was right.

"So, let me get this straight, just so we're clear... You're not here to kill me?"

"No," Storm muttered. He didn't look pleased.

"And you want *my help* after hunting me down like a stray dog for months?"

Storm sucked in a deep breath and glowered. "That sounds about right."

Octavius took a step forward, and Storm's eyebrow arched higher. "Then... you believe me?"

"There were extenuating circumstances that conspired to lead us to believe you were a traitor, but since then, some facts have come to light that suggest otherwise."

So they weren't fully convinced of his innocence but needed someone to hack into Atlas. That sounded like the Brotherhood. "You could just apologize?"

"I can't and will not apologize for the actions of others, but for my part..." He huffed. "I am sorry."

"All right." Octavius strode by Storm and headed for the chopper.

"I've got him." He heard Storm say, probably into a comms device, alerting the others.

Octavius climbed into the front of the chopper, then caught Storm's narrow-eyed glare. "I'll just... sit in the back."

"You do that," Storm said.

Once strapped into the back, and after the chopper was in the air, Octavius watched the safehouse vanish behind them. His arm still throbbed, but the small amount of venom dragging through his veins like broken glass would clear eventually. Raiden was out there somewhere, about to rally the Nyxians and welcome the queen of night, Nyx. How had Raiden's betrayal been allowed to happen?

At least he knew Saint and Jayden were safe, and that the bunch of Brotherhood assholes might actually listen to him now. He just had to hack back into Atlas and stop it from turning the world inside out. "How did you find me?"

"We visited every safehouse within range of the chopper you stole."

That was a lot of houses. They'd be spread thin, as Raiden had planned. "Then it was luck."

"A process of elimination."

They were going to need more than luck to stop Raiden. During their brief fight, Octavius had seen what he was capable of, and he wasn't just any nyktelios. He was old, like Saint was old, like Mikalis was old.

"Where's Mikalis?"

"He's sitting this out."

"What?" Octavius laughed. Storm had to be joking. "He can't sit out the apocalypse."

Storm glanced over his shoulder. "An apocalypse?"

Octavius sighed. The Brotherhood had been kept in the dark for so long, they'd become irrelevant. Mikalis had them blindly marching to his kill-all-nyks tune, like the pied piper leading his rats, and Raiden had taken advantage of that obsession.

"You ready to listen now?" Octavius began to tell Storm everything.

THE BROTHERHOOD'S apparent new headquarters was... an independent artisan coffee shop in Manhattan—temporarily closed, according to the sign on the door. Blinds had been pulled down over the windows, preventing the outside world from peeking in, which was a good thing, as the current clientele did not look like the coffee shop sort.

Zaine and his partner, the plain-clothed detective Eric, stood together in the far corner, while Kazimir had the ex-reporter Felix tucked close against his side in one of the many couches scattered around what had once been the main coffee shop but was now a lounge/meeting/rec room. Even the edgy Aiko was here, speaking rapidly in Japanese into his phone, while he flicked a knife in his free hand.

The moment Octavius entered behind Storm, they all fell silent, so there was just the traffic hum and occasional honking horn from outside.

No Mikalis. He really was sitting this one out.

Zaine was the first to break. He headed over, weaving through the couches and café tables, then offered his hand. "We good?"

Months on the run, death threats, abuse, attempts on his life? *We good* didn't cover it.

He'd fought alongside these people for centuries, saved them, and they'd saved him. But they didn't actually know him, and he didn't know them. He'd guarded himself because it was safer, and he was beginning to understand that they all hid the hurt. That didn't excuse the bastards, or him—he *had* been an epic asshole.

Octavius gripped Zaine's hand. "Sorry I threw Eric against a wall."

"Yeah, man, you're lucky I didn't know about that until recently."

Octavius tightened his hold on the handshake. "You think you can take me, Z?"

"Right now, yeah." Zaine laughed, then let go. "You look like shit and smell like a pond. What happened, you get run through a washer?"

"I had a conversation in a lake with Raiden."

"Oh?" Zaine's eyebrows lifted, and everyone else in the room suddenly became very interested.

Storm cleared his throat. "I'll get you all up to speed, but what I need right now is for Octavius to have some alone time with Raiden's laptop, and we had all better pray to the gods he can hack inside, or we're all about to have a very exciting but short rest of our lives." He guided Octavius out of the back of the café, into a store room, and through a door into a whole other building, this one far larger than the shop front belied.

The laptop in question sat central on an oval table, with several more laptops open around it. Octavius sat down and angled Raiden's laptop toward him. Atlas was clearly counting down to Armageddon. Who knew Raiden had a flare for the dramatic.

"You need anything?" Storm asked.

"Blood. And not to be disturbed."

"We can do that."

Octavius grabbed a second laptop and opened the web browsers he'd used in the past to connect to Atlas. If he could attack Atlas from multiple angles, he might find a way in.

"And hey." Storm rubbed his face and sighed. "You think you can stop this?"

"I think I'm the only one who can try, and right now, that's the best we've got."

"You're not filling me with confidence."

"You know what you should do?" Octavius asked without looking up. He tapped away at the keys, half his mind already lost in the code. Then, with a quick smile, he flicked his eyes up to Storm. "You should trust me."

"Yeah, yeah." Storm smiled. "Trust you, when you kicked me out of a chopper."

"You were going to kill me."

"I was, and I'd have done the same as you. We all would. It's good to have you back."

"Because I'm your last resort."

"I'm sure I'm not the only one who missed your quick temper and vicious threats."

Octavius smiled as he continued working. No so long ago, he'd have lashed out at anyone who dared laugh at him. Things had changed. He'd changed. And it looked as though the Brotherhood may be changing too.

~

RAIDEN'S COUNTDOWN was drawing close to its conclusion, but Octavius had found a way inside Atlas and had begun picking the code apart around the edges, undoing all the work he'd thought he and Raiden had made progress on together.

"Hey, asshole." Zaine tossed a blood bag onto the table beside him then parked his ass in a chair next to Octavius. "You good?"

"I gave Storm instructions not to be disturbed."

"I know, and aren't you glad I'm not very good at following orders?"

He was. It had to have been Zaine that had the Brotherhood coming around. Zaine had always irritated him. His snarky mouth, his lack of respect, how careless he was, and then bringing Eric into their headquarters. An outsider, and a feeder! But it was those things that had allowed him to see outside Mikalis's creed.

Octavius hit the return key and watched Atlas peel open on the screen in front of him. "I'm in." But what he saw was not good. Atlas was already spread far and wide, its tentacles knotted into countless worldwide systems. All this time, it had been working its way into all the keyholes in all the electronic locks across the world. The countdown was ticking down to the moment it turned the locks to open.

"I'm assuming from your paler than usual face that we're still fucked."

He needed a moment to think. There had to be a way to cancel the command, to at least mitigate the damage.

He grabbed the blood bag, bit down, and almost choked on the days-old donor blood. It tasted... flat, cold, dead. He swallowed anyway, needing it, but it would take three or four bags to give him the kick just a few swallows from Jayden's vein would have given him.

"Not good, huh? Used to blood from the vein?"

Octavius downed the bag, then retracted his fangs and returned Zaine's unimpressed glower with one of his own. "I'm not getting into that with you right now."

"Sure." Zaine shrugged and leaned back in the chair. "You may not be the only one questioning certain things, that's all."

Did Zaine drink from Eric? If he did, then he knew why the blood bag had almost repulsed Octavius. "It is us changing our— your partners." He wasn't going to say feeders. A feeder was a tool. Eric wasn't Zaine's tool, Felix wasn't Kazimir's. Octavius had been so very wrong about them. "Raiden claimed their blood weakens you, but he doesn't understand because he hasn't felt it."

"And you do?"

"Yes. I do." Jayden had healed a gunshot wound to the chest. He had the same blood quirk as the rest of the Brotherhood's new human partners. They had run the numbers and looked at hospital records. Felix's and Eric's blood was unique. It *had* been changed. When they'd come into contact with a nyktelios, it had triggered a mutation, or an evolution.

"I'm sorry about Saint, man. Storm said you guys were tight—"

He waved his sympathy away. It wasn't Saint, or maybe it was, maybe it had been the three of them together that had triggered Jayden's change. "There's a different way."

"How do you mean?"

"Just that Mikalis's way is one of many."

Zaine slumped in the chair. "We've been wondering a few things for a while, Eric and me. Shit didn't add up. He deleted a bunch of Eric's blood work reports. We had to run them again. He knew Sebastien, but claimed he didn't. Some things the nyks have been saying... There's a whole lot of questions bubbling up around him, like where the fuck is he now?"

"And there's the fact he tried to kill me because I know his secrets."

"And that."

"Do the others know you have concerns?"

"No. Just Storm. I'm beginning to wonder if he's been suspicious for a lot longer than we have."

They could really have done with Mikalis on their side on this. Unless he'd never been on their side, in which case, did that make them enemies? Octavius pushed those thoughts away. They weren't helpful now.

"So, is Atlas about to kill us all?" Zaine asked.

"Not if I can slow it down." Octavius leaned forward. "I need you to track down Raiden because if I can't stop this, he's going to rise up as a nyk messiah heralding the return of Nyx, and we are not prepared."

"On it." Zaine shot from the chair. "You know, who'd have thought Raiden's the prick and you're the hero?"

"I'm still a prick," Octavius said, keeping his eyes on the code.

Zaine left with a laugh that didn't have Octavius hating him all over again.

CHAPTER 31

ctavius

ONE HOUR until the countdown reached its finale, and while Atlas had relinquished control of countless tentacles, there was no chance Octavius would unravel them all.

Storm entered the room, said nothing as the minutes ticked down, asked how bad it was, then left again. It was bad. Not apocalypse bad, but close. People would die. Octavius had untethered Atlas from military systems, and some worldwide police networks, but not all, and not the financial markets. In the next hour, as billions of dollars were erased from the market and the ripples spread across the world, chaos would simmer to the surface. Society would begin to wobble. Humans were resilient and resourceful. They'd regain order, if the nyktelios didn't rise in that window of opportunity.

Which they would.

They'd been waiting for this, building for this, rallying for this. A reckoning.

Octavius sat back as the hour turned to minutes. "Fuck." He'd done all he could, and it wasn't enough.

The countdown timer ticked down. Kazimir entered the room and loomed, then Eric joined him, and Zaine behind him.

Three, two, one...

The laptop shut off.

Octavius's heart plummeted through the floor

Nothing happened.

No sirens. No screaming. Just Manhattan's typical background murmurings. They each shared tentative, hopeful glances.

Then Eric's phone pinged. He raised it to his ear as he answered. "Yeah, Hi.... All right. I'll be right there." He hung up, stared at his phone a few beats, before saying, "The er... the department computer system has gone offline. They think it's temporary, but they want all of us in, so..."

It was the beginning.

"Be careful," Zaine said. "This is going to get worse." Eric nodded and left, his phone ringing again when he reached the other room.

An icy chill trickled down Octavius's spine at those prophetic words. *This is going to get worse.* Even he couldn't know how bad it would be. Humans had become reliant on technology, and when it was taken away, they'd have to quickly adapt.

"You have to start helping people," Felix said, approaching Kazimir's side. "You can."

"Not without exposing who and what we are," Storm replied.

"Social media is down," Kazi said, checking his phone.

"Which one?" Felix asked.

Kazi looked up. "All of them."

"The nyktelios are about to expose us." Octavius stood, and the combined weight of the Brotherhood glares landed on him, as though waiting for a solution he didn't have.

"Humans aren't ready for this," Aiko added, entering the room. "For us."

"We need a plan." Felix turned to Storm. "Nobody wants to mention the elephant who isn't in the room, but where is Mikalis?"

"I don't know," Storm admitted, his gaze skipping to Octavius. "He had an altercation with Octavius, then killed Saint, and he... left."

"He left?" Zaine asked, voice peaking.

"We can't rely on him," Octavius said. "Humans will fix their systems, and they'll do it fast. We can't get in the way of that. All we can do is coordinate against any rising nyks. That means looking for spikes in nyk activity, reports of violence, of... monsters."

"In a world where its cities are about to experience riots and anarchy, nyks aren't going to stand out."

"We've been doing it for centuries," Octavius said. "This is just... more of the same, but bigger."

"A hundred nyk attacks at once, instead of one every few weeks." Zaine shrugged. "We're about to learn how many nyk nests we've missed."

"We *have* to do this," Storm said. "We're going to war."

CHAPTER 32

 aint

HE THOUGHT about walking off into the sunset... for three minutes. There was still room in his life for that, but he wasn't going anywhere without Octavius. A sentiment Jay shared.

Traveling at speed all night, through the shadows, almost ruined him all over again, but Jay was there, willing and hot-blooded and healed, and so Saint drank from him, then set off again, reaching New York as dawn broke.

Petty theft ruined an early-morning commuter's day, but Saint figured this was a matter of helping to stop the end of the world, so John Smith—or Jonathan Ridgeway—as his credit card read, was a hero. He just didn't know it.

Saint found a back-alley motel/apartment building in a part of the city where its residents who wouldn't ask too many questions, booked a room, left the card details on file, seeing as their computer booking system was experiencing a glitch, told Jay to rest up, then set about finding Octavius—in encroaching daylight. At least the weather was abysmal, keeping the sun tucked behind heavy cloud cover while also threatening rain. He preferred the rain to blazing sunshine.

The Brotherhood worked out of New York, and he knew they liked to be close enough to the center of a city to have their finger on its pulse. He just needed to narrow it down to a neighborhood.

He sauntered into a laundromat, stole a bundle of clothes from inside that happened to include a pair of dark pants and a fine white shirt, and after switching out his old clothes in a café stall, he wandered back outside into irritating daylight. Stealing a cheap pair of sunglasses from a tourist stall was his next minor crime. He needed them more than any tourist.

Wandering aimlessly wasn't the best of plans, but he had a feeling he'd be able to sense Octavius, like he could sense Mikalis. They'd shared body and blood so often, and with heart and intensity, that they were bound, as one and the same being, like sire and offspring, but equals. He'd sense Octavius, he was sure of it.

He mentally reached out and tried to make the connection, making sure to probe carefully so he didn't accidentally tag Mikalis. But again, Mikalis wasn't there. A wave of chilling cold rolled over him, a thick sense of dread. It stuttered his pace, then passed.

Strange.

He tried again, reaching for Octavius, and felt a flicker of knowing and familiarity. He *was* close. The early morning streets were quiet. A jogger passed by. A few cars. Was it always this quiet? Long shadows cast by the tall buildings helped shield him from the worst of the subdued UV rays. He passed by an alley opening, caught a glimpse of two lovers, and walked on.

Not lovers, his instincts warned.

He stopped and ambled back a few strides.

The scent of fresh blood lingered among other, stronger scents of rotten garbage and mildew.

A nyktelios attacking in public, in daylight? A few weeks ago, he'd have ignored it. Out of control nyks weren't his problem. But then Octavius happened, and something about Octavius wanting to help people made Saint want to help them too.

"Hey." He stepped into the alley. The nyk didn't hear, or didn't care to hear, probably thinking he was the apex predator in these parts. Saint moved closer. "Hey, nyk."

The nyk lifted his head, which took some effort, since he had his fangs deep in his victim's neck. Scruffy and reeking of body odor, he didn't look like much. Nobody had nurtured this one, and his madness was apparent in his rabid snarls.

The nyk jerked his chin, sniffing the air. He dropped his victim, assuming he'd get back to his meal later. "You take a wrong turn, suit? Manhattan is that way." He jerked his head, indicating back the way Saint had walked, then started forward.

Was he *stalking* Saint? Oh dear.

Saint sighed, then smiled and reached up to remove his sunglasses. He folded them, tucked them into his pocket, and looked up. The nyk saw his eyes, saw them shimmer silver, and his shoulders dropped. He smiled. "Hey man, come to join the party, eh—?"

Saint was on him before the last words could leave his lips. He bit down, pumping enough venom to kill several nyks, then shoved him against a dumpster and licked his fangs clean. "Nyks like you give the rest of us a bad name."

Whether he heard or not didn't matter. He turned to dust in seconds, with no time to scream.

Welcome to New York. Saint brushed ash from his hands, already dirtying up his new clothes, and slipped the shades back on.

Strange. Young nyks didn't risk daylight hunts, even the rabid ones.

The slumped, panting victim caught his eye. He knelt next to the semi-conscious man, rummaged through his pockets, found his phone, dialed 911, and slotted the phone into his hand. "Tell them where you are. You'll be fine." He patted him on the shoulder and returned to the street. Manhattan was ahead, according to the nyk, the same direction he'd sensed Octavius.

Sirens wailed nearby, then faded again.

Dread slithered under his skin, as though he were being watched from the *inside*. Something was wrong, and it was more than just the empty streets and the nyk attacking in daylight.

He stopped on the sidewalk. Jay was safe, just so long as he stayed inside, but if this was the beginning of the end, then Octavius needed Saint. The Brotherhood would need him. Eyes closed, he reached out with his senses, summoning the welcome memory of Octavius's touch, his taste, his smell, and how his skin gave under the pressure of Saint's fangs, how he shivered under Saint's hands. They were so close, he could feel him now, hear his heartbeat.

And he knew exactly where Octavius was.

They'd get their sunset ending, but not before Saint found his little wolf, and knowing Octavius as he did now, he'd probably find him right in the thick of it.

CHAPTER 33

ctavius

SOCIETY WAS BEGINNING TO UNRAVEL, thread by thread. Phones, communications media, emergency services. Atlas appeared to be dead, and without a way of communicating with the system, there was no way to hack back in to undo the damage done. Given days, weeks, months perhaps, he might be able to fix this. But they didn't have that time. So the Brotherhood did what they'd been doing for thousands of years. They fought nyks.

Eric phoned Zaine to warn there were possible nyk sightings popping up all over the city, in daylight, and then the cell towers died, and most all of New York's residents found themselves alone, cut off from the rest of the world.

And the Brotherhood went to war.

Octavius traveled in one of two black panel vans, with Zaine and Storm, while Felix, Aiko, and Kazimir traveled in the second. They split up to cover more ground.

They drove by a group of men throwing concrete blocks

through a store window. Human crimes weren't their responsibility. First responders shot by with flashing lights and wailing sirens, but roads were quieter than usual for a Manhattan morning. Some taxi drivers had pulled over, locked out of tracking their fares.

Some of the cell towers came back online and Zaine's phone pinged multiple messages. "Turn right up here. Eric says there's reports of a gang of *insane rioters killing multiple people.*"

"Not our problem," Storm grumbled.

"Yeah, except Eric says one person reported seeing them *drink blood,* so right up our street. He also says, uh, and I'm quoting, *you need to do something—you can't hide from this...* I'm pretty sure he means us."

"He's right," Storm said, and swung the van down a side street, into the shade of a high-rise, and there they were—five nyks tearing people from their cars and ripping them apart. But these weren't typical nyks, these were freshly turned and rabid with hunger.

Storm screeched the van to a halt and they all decamped, ready to attack. Storm went in first, using just his claws to rip in to the nyks. Zaine plucked one off a dying human, pumped it full of venom, then discarded it to move on to the next. Octavius wiped out the first he came to without breaking his stride. Four Brotherhood on five rabid nyks meant the assault was over as quickly as it had begun, with all the nyks turned to dust in seconds.

But the damage done before they'd arrived was extensive. The local convenience store burned, its sirens screeching. Windows had been smashed. Flames reflected on the shattered glass in the street, and bodies were scattered all over.

Zaine's phone pinged again. "We got more. Let's go." Back inside the van, he reeled off a list of locations.

"How are there so many nyks?" Octavius thought aloud. "There's no way we missed this in our backyard."

Storm threw the van into gear and sped from the massacre. "When Raiden crippled Atlas months ago, he blinded us. Seems like the Nyxians have been on a recruitment drive."

"Yeah, but why come here?" Zaine asked. "And those nyks

were new. Kazi and I saw factories in Poland, set up to create nyks, and there was that one at Eagle Lake where the Nyxians tried to bleed Kazi... These nyks are like those, off their heads with hunger. You think we missed a nyk factory right under our noses?"

Storm didn't reply, probably because he was thinking the same as Octavius: They'd missed more than one. It didn't take many rabid nyks to seed chaos, and once they undermined a society, they'd quickly take over, slaughtering and turning the population. This was what the Brotherhood had been fighting to stop, and it was all collapsing under Octavius's watch.

"I should have done more." He'd spent years working alongside Raiden, even began to think of him as a friend, because he was so damned desperate for someone to see him, to care. "I should have seen what he was doing!"

"It's not your fault," Storm said. "If we'd believed you, you'd have had more time to stop Atlas."

"We all fucked up," Zaine added.

And now people were dying by the hundreds, soon to be thousands.

"It's all right, we can get on top of this," Storm said, swinging the van down a deserted side street. "But we're going to have to split up to cover more ground. Try and stay in touch by phone, but if the networks are down, just get the job done, no matter what. Consequences be damned."

"Kill every nyk, got it," Zaine drawled.

"We'll be seen," Octavius warned. The Brotherhood would be exposed for the first time in modern history.

"Yes, we will." Storm drifted the van out of the side street and into an intersection. The traffic had stopped, snarled up. Smoke drifted from the crumpled hood of one vehicle, drifting toward the sky, and sparks rained. And people ran screaming from the nyks chasing them down.

"Fucking hell," Storm said, and the Brotherhood closed in.

Octavius singled out a nyk. These ones were older, more

cunning, quicker, but just as mad as the newly turned. Whoever had made them had kept them rabid.

After the first few succumbed to bites, the others fled. Octavius chased a female running headlong down the street. She was slight and fast, but he gained on her. Daylight beat down, but for now, it didn't matter. They had to stop the chaos.

The fleeing nyk jumped a car and veered left at a quiet intersection, causing traffic to honk and skid. The damp, mildewy smell of the Hudson wet the air. They were close to the river, and getting closer.

The nyk slowed, glanced over her shoulder, and put in a burst of speed. This began to feel as though she was a lure, leading him away from the others. He dropped into a jog, and sure enough, several yards ahead, so did she.

"I wondered how long it would be before you figured it out, Brotherhood." She laughed, turning.

A trap. He scanned the neglected residential buildings several stories high. The windows were dark, no activity.

"Mikalis's little groupies are so very predictable." The nyk spread her arms. "Go on then, hero. I'm waiting."

These weren't random attacks. They were organized, to draw them out. The Brotherhood was being hunted, and the others were in danger. Octavius eased his phone from his pocket. *No signal.* He looked up at the female nyk, at her smirk, and his senses prickled, skin crawling. On either side of the street, shadows moved where nyks emerged. They came from alleyways, from buildings, from homes. This was an ambush.

He rolled his shoulders and cracked the muscles in his neck. Every member of the Brotherhood knew they'd die fighting, and they fought anyway, because they believed in the cause, even if that cause had been a lie. It still mattered. People mattered. They'd been protecting them for millennia. Not for Mikalis, but because they knew it was right. Octavius would die for the Brotherhood, and for the people it protected. He was ready.

The nyks lunged from both sides, surging in a rush. Octavius threw off any pretense of being human, flung his wings wide, and roared. He unleashed the beast inside, shutting away any human emotion, and grabbed the first nyk, sinking his fangs in before it had a chance to lash out. Venom pumped, enough to kill, and Octavius threw him away, launching a spinning kick, throwing the next nyk backward. Another lunged. Octavius swung a fist, shattering the nyk's jawbone, destroying its ability to bite.

A weight slammed onto his back. He doubled over, flung the nyk overhead, and as it slammed into the ground, he stomped on the nyk's skull, taking it out of the fight.

More came, he spun and grabbed, bit down, kicked out, punched, used his wings to hold them back, but still they came, again and again, pushing in, teeth flashing. He'd bitten so many that venom burned his mouth and made his fangs ache. Blood painted his hands and dripped from his nails, writhing wounded lay at his feet, dust clouded the air.

Yet, still they came.

A gunshot rang out, then another. Octavius caught a glimpse of Zaine among the fray, but he was soon buried under attacking nyks. Gunfire boomed, and the nyks fell, but more took their place.

Storm's roar shook the world. He barreled in, tossing nyks like dolls.

Storm and Zaine were here. They just might survive this...

Octavius ducked another swing. Hands gripped him, teeth grazed his neck. *Too damn close.* He thrust out his wings, knocking a wave of nyks back, and grabbed the fool who had tried to bite him, spun him around and tore into his neck, injecting venom. Pain scorched his right wing. He snarled free of the nyk's neck, spun and threw the disintegrating nyk at the prick with a damned axe. The envenomed nyk burst into ash, raining over the axe-wielding brute. Octavius flew at the fiend, but a second nyk came down on his back. He sensed the fangs near his neck and twisted, trying to buck his attacker off. The axe flew, and the blade slammed into his left arm, rendering it numb. And he went down, sprawled on asphalt, pinned under a nyk.

His wings were trapped beneath him, broken and bleeding. His arm hung limp—he couldn't damn well get up. He needed a pause, a second, just a moment to gather his strength. He couldn't die here.

I could have loved you, he sent out in a desperate attempt to have Saint hear his final thoughts. He maybe already did love him. It had crept up on him, and now he faced never realizing it, and never knowing what might become of Saint. The ache in his heart, the desperate need to have Saint close, it might have been the one thing he'd spent millennia searching for.

The nyk pinning him down struck fast. Octavius flung up his right arm, and its fangs sunk into his forearm. Venom spilled like broken glass into his veins.

The biggest damn nyk Octavius had ever seen swooped down from above, grabbed the nyk who still had his fangs embedded in Octavius's arm, and ripped him free.

"Memento mori, motherfucker," the beastly nyk said with a savage growl. He tore the nyk's jaw off, then struck viper-fast at its neck. The nyk burst into a cloud of dust.

Saint.

Saint was here.

Had Octavius dreamed him?

"Hello, Little Wolf." Saint reached down, and Octavius grabbed him with his good hand, staggering to his feet. He wanted to be strong, to stand tall, but nyk venom was under his skin, trying to weaken him. He clutched at Saint. He'd be dead if Saint hadn't come.

"Drink," Saint said.

Octavius smelled the blood, clamped down on Saint's offered wrist, and gulped the strengthening blood. Exhaustion lifted, setting his veins ablaze with a new desire to fight, to protect, to kill.

Renewed, he licked Saint's wrist clean and scanned the carnage in the street. Zaine and Storm were in trouble, both surrounded and about to be drowned under nyks.

Saint grinned. "Let's get medieval."

He vanished, then reappeared in a cloud of static shadow beside

Storm, and plowed into the attacking nyks. Octavius fought his way to Zaine, clearing the mob enough for Zaine to get back on his feet. Zaine nodded his thanks, and together they beat back the tide of nyks, turning the battle in their favor. As the nyk numbers dwindled, the remaining ones fled, scattering like roaches when the lights turned on.

Octavius searched for Saint among the drifts of ash and spotted him offering Storm a hand up. Storm gripped Saint's forearm and climbed to his feet, eyeing Saint with a hint of trepidation.

Saint smiled, his jaws filled with vicious teeth, and then shrugged off the monstrous guise, returning to his more subtle human form. "Good to see you again, Storm. Aren't you glad I'm not dead."

Storm grunted an acknowledgement but said no more. He had to know that without Saint's intervention, they'd all be dead.

A wave of tiredness sucked any joy and relief at seeing Saint out of Octavius. "We need to find the others."

"There shouldn't have been that many..." Zaine mumbled and ran a shaking hand through his hair, leaving bloody streaks in the blond locks. "Where the fuck did they come from?"

Covered in blood and ash, their clothes stained and torn, even they couldn't hide the weariness and shock from their faces. They needed to get out of the open and away from the evidence of the nyk massacre.

Zaine's phone chirped. "It's Kazi..." He answered. "Hey, man, you good?" Zaine looked up. "They're all right, but it was close. He's saying we should meet, not at the base. Somewhere else."

Storm huffed a great sigh and wiped blood from his right bicep, either his or the nyks'. "The fuck if I know where."

They needed to get out of the daylight and regroup, they needed Mikalis... and the bastard wasn't here. His absence was a betrayal, and now they all felt the same pain Octavius had been carrying for the past few months, and Saint's pain, carried for far longer.

"I know somewhere," Saint said. "It's mostly full of addicts and pimps. Nobody is going to notice y'all."

"Classy," Zaine said with a grin. "Kazimir will fit right in. Lead the way."

Saint nodded. "You got a vehicle nearby?"

Storm grumbled and headed back down the street, stirring up nyk ash with every step. Octavius glanced up at the windows of the buildings they passed under. Somebody would have filmed the battle. Once social media was back up and working, the footage would go viral. This wasn't like Poland, where Kazimir's dramatics had been explained away as a publicity stunt.

The truth was out there. There was no putting it back in a box.

Vampires were real.

Welcome to the end of the world.

CHAPTER 34

 aint

THERE WERE multiple empty rooms next to the one Saint had borrowed for Jayden. He figured the owners wouldn't mind the Brotherhood borrowing them. Or if they did, they could file a complaint with the ageless, immortal, efficient killers and see how far that got them.

The Brotherhood filed into the grubby entrance foyer, and the motel's manager watched them pass by, covered in blood and dirt, and didn't say a damn thing. Wise man. Seeing a bunch of beaten up gang members was probably a typical Tuesday for the neighborhood.

Octavius remained quiet, which meant he was overthinking again, but Saint gave him space and watched how the rest of the Brotherhood reacted to Saint's arrival. They didn't like it, but nobody was going to say a damn thing after he'd saved their ungrateful asses.

It was a damn shame Mikalis had kept their wings metaphorically clipped because from the small amount of battle he'd seen, they were each fine warriors in their own right. They could have been even more powerful, with the right leader.

Saint just wanted to save Octavius. When he'd found him on his back, bleeding, shattered, dying under a nyk, Saint would have set fire to the whole fucking world to save him. Damn the rest of them. Octavius was his and no wretched, freshly turned nyk would dare touch Octavius again. The same could be said for the Brotherhood. If any of them so much as looked at Octavius with hate in their eyes, they'd be getting up close and personal with Saint's fangs. He'd only helped save them because he knew Octavius wouldn't have left without them.

Saint studied the Brotherhood anew.

Storm was the second most dangerous creature in the room, besides Saint. In powerful terms, Octavius was next in line. Then Kazimir, then the quiet one with the knives, Aiko. Zaine was the youngest here, and physically the weakest, but he made up for it with enthusiasm and guns. He was also the one who had questioned the status quo first, and for that, he'd earned Saint's respect. Kazimir had shown Saint kindness throughout the years. He was one of the good ones. Storm... Saint had history with him.

He'd been present when Mikalis had locked Saint away. Storm was Mikalis's closest ally and was currently, although discreetly, watching Saint, the same as Saint was subtly sizing up Storm.

If they were going to put Saint back in a box, Storm would be the one to do it.

Saint didn't want to be here. He wanted to take Octavius next door and watch him feed from Jay because Octavius needed it. Octavius's well-being would always come first. The rest of them walked a thin line, a line Saint would cut if Octavius gave the word.

"They won't hurt you," Octavius said, sidling up to Saint, and made sure to say it loud enough so they all heard, making it half fact, half threat.

"They can try."

Half of them turned to glare. All of them were curious. The

Brotherhood nyk, the one who had turned on them, according to Mikalis.

"I'm just going to say it, where the fuck is Mikalis?" Zaine hissed.

All attention turned to Storm.

"You know as much as I do," Storm replied, his face stoic.

"That's not good enough," Kazimir said with a thin edge of anger. If Kazimir's team had experienced half of what Storm's had, then he had every right to be angry. They'd been led to the slaughter. "The one time we rely on him, the one actual time we need him, and he's nowhere to be seen. Why? Why now? Where is he, Storm?"

"I can't answer that."

"Can't or won't?" Aiko asked. A pointed question from the quiet, lethal one.

Storm's top lip curled, revealing a small hint of sharp teeth. "Bickering changes nothing—"

"Bickering?" Kazimir snorted. "This isn't bickering, it's demanding answers we have a right to know, and you know it."

"I don't have those answers. I wish I did. Mikalis has... He's not here. I don't know where he is. That's the truth. We can waste time going back and forth on where Mikalis is, but it's not going to change anything. I'm all you've got for now."

"You've got Saint," Octavius said.

Saint blinked and arched an eyebrow. This wasn't his fight, he just happened to be here. They'd all made that clear for many, many centuries.

"What?" Storm asked.

"We have Saint." Octavius stared back at them all, daring them to say something that would set a match to the gasoline of tension in the room. "Let's talk facts. Mikalis is Saint's sire, that makes him powerful—"

"The fuck—" Kazimir spluttered. "His sire?"

"Shut up and listen."

"Still a dick, Octavius?" Kazimir asked.

"And you're still an attention whore—"

Kazi launched from the couch, Zaine lunged to stop him, and Saint watched it all unfold with a tickle of amusement, like watching a trainwreck in slow motion. The fate of the world hung on this dysfunctional Brotherhood getting their shit together. It was almost as though Mikalis had held them back.

Someone rapped on the door, pausing the almost-brawl before things became too bitey. Kazimir shook Zaine off him and Octavius sheathed his fangs.

Aiko answered the door. Two humans stood in the corridor; one smelled a lot like Kazimir, likely his feeder, and the other was Jay, holding a tray of stacked cookies.

"Er, so, this guy says he's friends with... Saint," Kazimir's human said, gaze dancing, "and he brought cookies." He shrugged. "This day has been so fuckin' nuts, I figure what the hell, maybe he's for real?"

"Hi," Jay said, smiling nervously. He wore an oversized shirt and baggy sweatpants, and was as out of place as a rabbit that had hopped into a lion enclosure.

Saint fought to keep the grin off his lips and poked his tongue into his cheek as the rest of them stared, mouths open.

Kazimir's human sidestepped through the door, passing Aiko, and read the room in a few seconds. He sat next to Kazimir. "You good?"

"I am now," Kazimir said, drawing the human close and breathing him in. Interesting. They weren't all oblivious to the benefits of maintaining a symbiotic relationship with a human then.

Jay's smile cracked a little, now that he stood alone with a tray of cookies and a whole bunch of blood-hungry vampires staring at him. "Uh, so... I'll just leave these then." He handed the tray to a stunned Aiko. "So there's maple and chocolate, and cinnamon and er... Well, I couldn't really find much else, so it's just basically cinnamon and chocolate chip. Apple would have been nicer, but whoever owns the apartment we'd hijacked didn't have any apple, so... Anyway. It's nice to meet you all." He smiled again, then swallowed and shrank some.

Saint pushed from the wall and sauntered to the door. "What these Neanderthals have forgotten to say is *thank you* for thinking of them. They appreciate it. I'd invite you to stay, but until they figure out how to behave like civilized creatures, I fear you'd be at risk." He caught Jay's chin, lifted his face, and kissed him on the lips, then whispered, "Be ready later."

Jay nodded, understanding, and throwing the group a little wave, he returned to his apartment next door.

Saint closed the door, picked up a cookie from the tray Aiko still held, and said, "If any of you so much as snarl at Jayden, I will rip your fucking arms off. Cookie?"

Interestingly, they looked at Octavius, as though expecting a backlash, but instead they found a curious, sideways smile on his lips.

"I have no idea what's happening," Aiko admitted, setting the cookies down on the coffee table in the middle of the room. The others swooped in and helped themselves.

Saint caught sight of Storm's small smile too, before he saw Saint looking, and banished it, returning to his usual stoic expression. "Nightfall is going to be worse than what we experienced earlier," Storm said. "My instincts tell me the older nyks will be out in force. They're here for a reason. This isn't random. So we need to figure out what their objective is."

Zaine grabbed a cookie and made his way over to Storm. "Take it."

Storm took it and eyed the cookie.

"I doubt it bites, big guy," Zaine said. "You saw the bro who made it. I bet it's baked with fuckin' rainbows and unicorns. That right there is the best cookie you're ever gonna eat."

"Do you mind if the grown-ups talk now?" Storm asked.

"You know you love it." Zaine smirked and flopped back down in a chair.

"When is Eric getting here?" Kazi asked.

"Not for a while." Zaine's smile faded. "The NYPD is stretched, to say the least. He's helping where he can."

"We'll save him a cookie," Kazi said, leaning forward. "And we'd better order in some blood, if our supply chain is still available."

"I'll get on that," Aiko said.

"We're going to need it," Storm said, sampling his cookie. His eyebrows lifted. "All right, so let's figure out how we're going to bring down an army of nyks and survive to see the sunrise."

They finally appeared to be working together, discussing what had happened and how to better organize for the next wave. But as Saint listened and watched then work, Octavius lagged beside him. He'd taken a beating in the street, and Saint could do something about that. "Hey, Little Wolf," he whispered. "Will you come with me for a while?"

Octavius lifted tired eyes and nodded. They slipped mostly unnoticed from the room. Storm caught Saint's eye, but made no comment. Perhaps he wouldn't be such a terrible leader after all. Saint led Octavius into the apartment next door, where Jay was waiting. He stood, and his gaze fixed on Octavius. They didn't need to speak, words would just slow them down. Jay nodded and turned his face away, exposing his neck. Octavius left Saint's side and crossed the room. Without hesitating, he took Jay in his arms and licked over his jugular.

Saint circled around the pair. Octavius saw him, peeled his lips back from his fangs, and bit deeply into Jay's neck with his gaze locked on Saint's.

He'd wanted to see Octavius feed from Jay for weeks. The need, the hunger, and that moment his teeth pierced Jay's skin—a dart of lust shot down Saint's spine, spiking his own arousal.

He'd be content to just watch, if that was what Octavius wanted.

He leaned a shoulder against the wall and recalled the very familiar taste of Jay's blood on his tongue, and how that blood would be flowing down Octavius's fine throat, replenishing him, feeding him, bringing his body and mind alive. There was little like the sensation of feeding from the vein, except sex. Watching Octavius, and how Jay responded too, fired up Saint's needs, making him hungry.

Saint and Octavius were both filthy from battle. They smelled like dead nyk ash and stale blood. The raw, viciousness of battle, and the softness of Octavius's glances afterward...

Saint looked away. He had to. Because if Octavius knew how he felt, he'd invite him over there, and he needed to feed more than Saint needed to fuck. Probably.

He closed his eyes, willing his blood to cool. Jay's moans grew louder, his human body responding, not from venom, but from pure, primal need all of his own. He'd be hard, and clutching at Octavius. But Octavius didn't do sex when he fed. Which was a damn shame. Saint would have liked to have watched that too— watch Octavius grip Jay's hips and pump into him. What a sight, his little wolf, and his sunshine, performing for him and each other.

He adjusted his pants around a throbbing erection. Perhaps watching hadn't been such a great idea.

"You want in?" Octavius asked in his mind. He'd seen Saint move and locked gazes with him.

Saint wanted *in*, in multiple ways, but what was Octavius offering? "You need to heal," Saint said, sounding gruffer than he should. This wasn't for him. Octavius needed blood and rest. He probably did not need Saint going down on him, or Saint brutally fucking him, since he'd need to recover his strength.

"Come here," Octavius demanded.

Saint freed a growl, both hating how he could command Saint to obey, yet loving it too.

He pushed from the wall and sauntered over, stopping behind Jay, with Octavius's crystalline eyes watching him the whole way. But then Octavius seemed to falter. His gaze skipped, unsure.

"Kiss him," Saint said, leaning in to press against Jay's back. Jay murmured his agreement and shifted his hips, grinding his ass against Saint's cock.

Octavius withdrew his fangs, licked up the wound with a small

243

amount of venom to seal it, and brushed his cheek over Jay's. This was new for Octavius, hence the hesitation in his eyes, but there was curiosity in his gaze too. He wanted this but didn't understand it.

Jay turned his face and teased a kiss against the corner of Octavius's mouth. Octavius opened and answered Jay's query, brushing his lips over Jay's. Hm, there were few pleasures in life that compared to kissing a warm and willing human.

"There was a moment earlier, when I thought I'd lost you both," Octavius said into Saint's thoughts.

Fuck going slow. He'd been trapped behind bars forever and never thought he'd feel so close to another soul again as he did with Octavius. Saint clutched the back of Octavius's head and slammed a kiss on his lips, with Jay pressed between them.

"Never," he thought back, unsure if Octavius could hear thoughts but knowing he'd feel it in their kiss. Having Octavius brought him to life again, made him want to fight for this world, even made him want to fight for the Brotherhood—something he'd vowed never to do again.

Saint eased back, breaking the kiss in a way that promised more, and dragged the tips of his fangs over the raw, still healing bite mark on Jay's neck. A shudder ran through Jay, and then through Saint. Octavius must have felt it too.

"I just..." Jay gasped. "I need to do this, been wanting to do this..." He went to his knees in front of Octavius, and Octavius— his expression serious and severe—let Jay free his dick from his pants and slide the thick member between his lips.

The moment Octavius looked up, straight at Saint, Saint knew he'd lost his heart to the pair of them. They were so different, yet so perfect. Octavius's glacial hardness, and Jay's endless warmth. There had never been so brilliant a match, and by some miracle, they were both wonderfully Saint's.

Octavius let his head fall back. His smooth throat undulated, temptation personified, and his dangerous fangs gleamed between parted lips. Gods, he was a vision of nyktelios beauty and lethality, all wrapped up in a lithe body and sharp mind.

Saint circled behind Octavius. There were things he could do to him that would make him lose his mind to lust, but after fucking him raw once, he'd try a more subtle approach this time. Inching Octavius's trousers down, off his hips, he captured him around the waist and nuzzled his neck, below his ear. "Let me pleasure you."

His breath hitched. "I don't know how much more I can take."

"Let's find out." Saint clutched Octavius's ass in both hands and squeezed. Right now, he had his cock down Jay's throat, and while Saint knew how Jay could do wonderful things with his tongue, Saint was focused elsewhere. He licked his fingers, then slid them down, between Octavius's ass cheeks. Octavius wasn't so naive as to not suspect what Saint had in mind, but he was new to such intimacies.

Saint clutched his hip with one hand, holding him against his chest, and teased his fingers over Octavius's hole, testing to see if he wanted more. His whimpered moan suggested more would be welcome. Saint was going to make him come with his fingers riding him hard and Octavius's cock down Jay's throat. What better way to relax after a bloodthirsty battle?

This was how it should be, with love and sex and feeding—indulging, caring. They were stronger together, and finally Octavius had begun to embrace the truth, instead of fearing it.

There had always been a better way. And now Octavius knew Saint would always be here for him, forever.

CHAPTER 35

ctavius

THE COOKIES HAD DONE IT. Jayden's ridiculous interruption, and the Brotherhood's alarmed but accepting response to having freshly baked cookies delivered to their door, had let Octavius know that they were all safe together. The same as he knew now, with Jayden's hot, sucking mouth on his dick and Saint's firm, probing fingers stroking a part of him that sent electric sparks up his spine, that this was right.

He surrendered himself to the two most precious people in his life, one a savage killer and the other a ray of brilliant sunshine.

He'd known, deep down, that there would be love out there for him; even when he'd stopped looking, when he'd pushed others away, he'd still held a tiny kernel of hope. He loved Jayden's ridiculous enthusiasm, loved his hope-filled perspective and his endless optimism, and right now, he loved his mouth, sucking and stroking and swirling around his dick. He loved Saint's ruthlessness, his straightforward thinking, and his protectiveness, even though

Octavius didn't need protecting. Right now though, he loved Saint's breath on his neck and his fingers sliding in and out, riding him toward ecstasy. They were made for each other, as though fate had brought them together. He would have laughed at any Brotherhood member if they'd suggested such a thing, would have accused them of being weak.

He'd been such a fool.

Gods, he was going to come.

He gently pushed Jayden back and tried to catch his breath. "Wait..."

"Hm, no," Jayden teased. "You're going to come and we all know it." He straightened but stayed on his knees, wiping his thumb across his lips, his smirk as wicked as Saint's growl.

Saint's fingers stroked, inching Octavius toward what would be a blinding climax. Jayden grasped his jutting dick and pumped, and it was all Octavius could do to ride the waves and chase the cresting high. Jayden opened his peachy lips and sucked the sensitive tip of Octavius's dick, as his hand pumped and Saint stroked, and all at once, the pleasure was too much to contain. He came, bucking, trembling, with Saint clutching him close and Jayden on his knees, mouth open, cum pearly on his lips, and there he stayed, lost and adrift, but found and home too.

There was no knowing what sundown would bring. But right now, he drifted in blissful satisfaction, irrevocably entwined with the two men he loved.

Jayden rose to his full height, licked his lips, and slammed a shocking salty kiss on Octavius's mouth. "I'm famished," he said with a sly grin.

"I thought you just ate," Saint drawled, then sucked on Octavius's ear as he withdrew his fingers. Octavius gasped; they were going to ruin him.

"An appetizer for later." Jayden giggled, then moved from the small lounge area to rattle around the tiny kitchen.

"I'm going to take a shower and get out of these wrecked

clothes," Saint said. Heading down the small hall, he crooked a finger. "Octavius, come with me."

Go with him? With the aftershocks of the orgasm still tingling through him, he'd have gone anywhere with either of them, but a shower was perfect.

They barely fit in the small cubicle, but even that concern melted away as Saint lathered up the soap and smothered Octavius's back and shoulders, then massaged deeply. He couldn't fail to notice Saint's eager erection, but he didn't seem that interested in satisfying himself.

He caught Octavius looking. "You may suck my dick later, Little Wolf."

They may not have many laters left, and Octavius was beginning to salivate over the thought of having Saint inside him, or watching Saint take Jayden. *That* idea made his insides writhe in new and breathless ways.

"Hm, what are you thinking that has your heart racing and your cock taking notice?"

Octavius rinsed his face under the hot jets of water, then grasped the soap from Saint's hand and shoved him back against the tiles. "Just how much I'd like to watch you with Jayden."

Saint fell quiet and stared, which meant he was trying to figure out how best to reply without scaring Octavius off. He wasn't as stoic and mysterious as he believed, at least not to Octavius.

"And feed?" Saint asked.

Octavius swept his soapy hands up Saint's muscular chest, then flicked a nipple and marveled at Saint's hiss. "And feed. If Jayden is up to it."

"What if I take Jay while he swallows you?"

"At once? Together?"

"Yes, together."

"Jayden will do that?"

Saint grinned. "My sweet little innocent wolf."

Octavius narrowed his glare, sucked on Saint's right nipple, then bit down.

"Gah, fuck!" Octavius let go, and Saint snorted a laugh. "Yes, he'll suck you off while I fuck him. Getting him to stop will be the difficult part."

"The we should do it soon. It's nearly sundown." Octavius stepped from the shower, dripping wet, flung a towel around his waist, and left the bathroom.

"That's the only towel!" Saint called.

"Oh, is it?" Octavius teased, leaving the bathroom.

He found Jayden in the lounge area, tucking into a bag of chips while watching TV. The broadcast towers must have been reestablished. But that wasn't the reason Jayden had fallen silent, or why Octavius's heart stopped in his chest.

Raiden was on the news, looking unassuming and respectable under studio lighting, with his glasses perched on his nose and a laptop in front of him. The ticker across the bottom of the screen read: *The nyktelios threat: Stay indoors. Curfew in affect. Dr. Galanis Raiden.*

"Is that the Brotherhood's Raiden?"

"Yes," Octavius snarled, then dashed to next door and burst inside.

"Man, of all the horrors we've witnessed today, seeing you in just a towel is right up there." Zaine gestured, indicating the top of the list, and grinned.

"Turn on the TV," Octavius ordered. "Channel Nine."

No more jokes came from Zaine when he saw Raiden's face on the screen. *"The real source of the problem is a secular group known as the Brotherhood. Seen here..."*

The screen cut to shaky phone footage of their earlier battle in the street, and of course, to anyone not paying attention, the nyks appeared to be distressed human beings, while Octavius, Saint, Storm, and Zaine all resembled monstrous fanged nightmares made real. At least the footage was so frantic that their faces weren't recognizable.

"That mother-fucking asshole," Zaine hissed. "Seriously. That guy, they believe *that guy...*"

"I mean, you all did, so..." Felix added unhelpfully, then trailed off, sensing the mood in the room wasn't in his favor. "Too soon. Right." He winced and stared at the screen. "It's the glasses, maybe? They make him look respectable, harmless. Like someone we should trust." He stopped and glanced around at the rest of them staring. "I'm just adding a perspective."

"What's Raiden doing?" Kazimir asked. "Why draw attention to us?"

Storm gave a heavy sigh, as though he was long ago done with all of this shit. "For the same reason he's had us all chasing our tails for months. The humans will pour their resources into finding and stopping *us*, meaning we're distracted while he does whatever he's doing."

"Do we still not know what his plan is?" Zaine asked.

"He's bringing Nyx back," Octavius said, cold in his towel, dripping water all over the floor. "Somewhere in the city, somewhere close. I thought we'd never see him again after the fight at the safehouse, but he's here, in New York, which means whatever his endgame is, that's here too. And the nyks being here... It all fits. He's a Nyxian, and he's going to bring Nyx back."

"Can he do that?" Felix asked, bouncing his gaze from member to member. "Can he bring Nyx to life?"

All their gazes landed on Storm, who was the only one who could answer that kind of question.

"We are manifestations of Nyx's power," Storm said. "We exist, then so must she."

"A god," Felix said. "Just so we're clear. You're all talking about summoning an actual god?"

"Not a god," Storm replied. "A primordial being."

"Oh, a primordial being. That's okay then." Felix gripped the back of the couch behind Kazimir. "Is nobody else worried? None of you look all that concerned. Is it just me?"

"I'm pretty sure we're all screaming on the inside," Zaine said, then took his phone from his pocket. "Come on, Eric... Pick up."

Raiden was turning the population of New York against them at a time when they were trying to protect the people. Damn him.

"We need to find and stop Raiden," Aiko said, flicking a butterfly knife between his fingers.

"Except we don't know where he is. Do we?" Kazimir asked.

Everyone stared at Octavius because he'd been the closest to Raiden. But he didn't know anything. None of them did. "When we fought the nyks, they were close to the river, to the docks. Find me a laptop and I'll see what's in the area and why the nyks were concentrated there."

"Or it was just a trap," Kazi said.

"Or both. Raiden is efficient, but he'll also want the attention, he'll want us to notice what he's doing. He wants us to figure it out. Where's the fun in destroying the world if the people you hate the most don't know how you did it?"

"You think he hates us that much?" Kazimir asked.

"We all hate each other." Octavius rolled his eyes and turned on his heel. "Find me a laptop."

"Only if you find some clothes!" Zaine yelled.

～

"OUR THREESOME IS GOING to have to wait. Raiden is here," Octavius said, returning to Jayden's room.

"In New York?" Saint stood in the kitchen, naked from head to toe. He grabbed an apple from a fruit bowl and crunched noisily. Octavius missed a stride while staring—Saint had a body made to be desired. Firm, muscular thighs, gorgeous hips, and a semi-erect dick that appeared to be growing under Octavius's gaze.

"We were having a threesome?" Jayden asked, looking up from his bag of chips.

The mention of a threesome and Saint's unashamed display of masculinity stalled Octavius. "I... ugh... Only if you want to."

"Pfft, like you have to ask. Have you met me? I've been begging Saint for a threesome since we met you."

"You have?"

"You've been busy," Saint said. "I didn't want to leap ahead and scare you off by suggesting I fuck you both right after we'd met. You were just as likely to kill me as fuck me, back then."

"We're discussing this—" He pointed at Saint, then Jayden, because Saint with *everything* on display was too damn distracting. "—later." He focused on Jayden, the sensible one in the room. "Do we have any clothes or are we going into battle naked?"

"It would save time," Saint mused.

Was he joking? Octavius couldn't tell. He huffed and rubbed his face. Raiden was here. They needed to focus.

"We have clothes," Jayden said. "I'll grab some for you."

"Thank you." Octavius dropped to the end of the couch. Raiden's interview about the nyktelios threat was playing on the TV again. He looked like the pillar of the scientific community and absolutely trustworthy. Felix was right. He'd fooled them all.

"It's not your fault," Saint said, approaching from behind.

"How do you always know what I'm thinking?"

"You wear your thoughts all over your face." Saint knelt and leaned against his leg. "None of them saw his duplicity. It wasn't just you."

"Do you think Mikalis knew?"

At the mention of Mikalis, Saint lost his smile. "I think Mikalis has always had his own agenda, and trying to second-guess him is impossible."

"We're floundering, Saint. The Brotherhood is barely together."

"And he's not here. I know. But you've got me, and Storm, and the other guys, Blondie and whatever they're called."

Octavius snorted. "You know their names."

"Yeah, the mouthy blond one, the one who loves himself, the one with the knives, the big guy, the human. They're not much, compared to you." Saint smiled. "You don't need Mikalis."

"The same goes for you."

He rubbed his face and nodded. "I know, it just took me a few thousand years to realize it."

"I don't understand why Mikalis would throw it all away like this, why he's not here..."

"You've forgotten the number one Brotherhood rule: never care. He's not here because he does not care about me, or any of you, or the people. He never has."

It had always been a part of the Brotherhood creed, but none of them had *not* cared. Except Mikalis. Octavius couldn't believe it. Even now, with the evidence staring him in the face. Mikalis had assumed the worst of him, called him a traitor, tried to kill him, yet Octavius still wanted to believe Mikalis was on their side. It didn't make sense that he'd throw away thousands of years of the Brotherhood, for what? Just because he thought he'd killed Saint? Just because Octavius and Zaine dared question him? Surely Mikalis wasn't that shallow.

"Here's some clothes, at least some that might fit you," Jayden said, returning with a bundle in his arms. "Saint, I know it's a hate-crime, but you're going to have to wear jeans."

"I'll fight naked." Saint snarled in disgust as he stood.

"Really? Oh. Uh, I suppose you could do that—"

Saint laughed and took the jeans, then kissed Jayden on the forehead. "You're adorable. Don't ever change."

Octavius dressed, and as he finished towel-drying his hair, a knock at the door signaled Storm's arrival with a laptop under his arm.

He handed it over. "Is Saint here?"

Saint emerged and almost missed a step as he spotted Storm in the living area.

Octavius carried the laptop to the coffee table and set it up while keeping Storm and Saint in his peripheral vision, just above the screen. There weren't many people Saint was wary around, but Storm was one of them. They clearly had a past.

Octavius loaded several maps of the docks on the laptop.

Storm cleared his throat. "You need any blood?"

"No, we have that covered," Saint said, his voice flat, all emotion tucked away.

Storm worked his jaw, either around his fangs or around the words he didn't want to say. He glanced across the room at Jayden flicking through the channels on the TV. "I need to know you're on our side," Storm said. "I can't be watching for a dagger in the back while trying to keep everyone safe."

Saint shrugged. "You know I don't use daggers."

Storm's droll look turned into a glower. "I don't agree with how you do things, but I appreciate you're here. If it wasn't for your arrival earlier, we would have... struggled."

"You're welcome. Now tell me what you haven't told the others. What happened with Mikalis after he tried to kill me at the old steakhouse?"

Storm stiffened. Octavius tapped a few keys, but the maps no longer held his interest. He needed to see Saint grill Storm. Saint might have been the only one who knew Storm well enough to get answers out of him, even if Storm did tower over him in height *and* width.

"He believed he *had* killed you. We all did," Storm said.

"And he left?"

"Right."

Saint snorted. "We know he's not that emotionally fragile. Whatever happened, you're not telling me or them for a reason. I just don't know what that reason is."

Storm's cheek flickered. "Can you sense him, as your sire?"

"No, I haven't been able to since the steakhouse."

Was Saint's severing of the link between sire and offspring due to Octavius getting inside Mikalis's head? No, it couldn't be that. Octavius had demanded Mikalis no longer hunt them, not that Mikalis cut off Saint.

Storm appeared troubled and took a few moments before saying, "I have faith in Mikalis. I'd ask you to trust me, but I know I don't deserve your trust."

A hint of fang showed through Saint's snarl. "Never again."

They had history, for sure, and it sounded as though Storm had burned Saint in the past. Octavius wasn't surprised. Given a choice,

Storm would always choose Mikalis, and Saint hadn't. That made them enemies.

"Then are you with us, Saint?" Storm asked.

Saint thrust a hand into his jeans pocket and leaned against the kitchen counter. "Am I with the Brotherhood?" He glanced up and met Octavius's gaze. "For as long as Octavius is, yes." When he met Storm's glare again, he said, "Am I with Mikalis? You already know the answer."

"Good enough." Storm turned his heavy glare onto Octavius. "We have an hour before sundown."

"On it," Octavius acknowledged. He couldn't hack into Atlas now it was offline, but the Atlas data had been stored in an isolated server. He could get into that and look for Vesna's files, the Nyxian who had helped destroy the Brotherhood's compound. Felix Quaid had told him Vesna had been worthy of more scrutiny. Octavius hadn't listened then, but he was now. The Nyxian cult leader had property all over the US and Europe. If she'd had more land in New York, it might coincide with the concentration of nyks. Information like that, Raiden could have hidden. They had little else to go on and when the sun set, the older, more powerful nyks would be crawling from the shadows.

"He knows why Mikalis isn't here," Saint said after Storm had left. He approached Octavius, and folded his arms.

"You can read Storm?"

"He said to trust *him*, not to trust Mikalis. He knows Mikalis isn't coming. They were always inseparable. Storm would cut off his own arm if Mikalis ordered it." Saint didn't bother to hide his emotions now, and his disgust at Storm's devotion was obvious.

They *had* been close. "What did he do to you?"

Saint's smirk faded and all the light humor snuffed out of is eyes. Octavius almost wished he hadn't asked. "We fought. Ferociously. He won."

Shit. Octavius lifted his gaze from the laptop screen. "What did you fight over?"

256

"Mikalis ordered him to imprison me, so he did. Without question."

Octavius didn't need to know the details. He knew what it felt like when the people you loved turned on you. "I'm sorry."

"It was a long time ago."

"Everything always is. Doesn't change the hurt though."

"No." Saint moved to the filthy window behind Octavius. "But I'm out now. I met you, and Jay. The Brotherhood appears to be changing. It's not all bad."

If only they'd met before, when events weren't so dire. They may have had more time to explore whatever this was between the three of them. All that time, Saint had been close but out of reach behind bars. The unspoken secret. All those years, Storm had known who Saint was and hadn't said a word.

Jayden smirked and asked, "Did you and the big guy ever... you know?" He raised his eyebrows.

Saint's laugh rumbled. "What makes you ask?"

Jayden gave his hand a wave. "I'm sensing some physical tension there."

"Technically? No. Although, in the early era, the lines blurred some. It wasn't like now. Gender and desires were fluid. Fucking, feeding, sex, it was all the same. Octavius would have hated it."

Octavius laughed to himself. Storm with anyone was an image he did not want in his head, and Saint's *technically* could mean a whole array of different sexual scenarios. "Is there anything you didn't try and fuck?"

"Not if it had a heartbeat and was willing."

He wished he'd never asked but chuckled anyway, at himself, at Saint and at Jayden, and the crazy trio they'd become. Despite the chaos raging outside, he'd never felt more at ease. "What happens after?" Octavius asked, but as his heart cinched, he ran his gaze down the list of Vesna's properties, needing to pull back from the fear of losing the precious thing they had together.

"What do you mean?" Saint asked.

257

"Say we stop Raiden, we kill the nyks, the Brotherhood goes on. What do we do?"

Saint focused on Octavius in that way he did, pinning him down. "What do *you* want?"

He wasn't even sure. Have a relationship with Saint and Jayden? How would that work? Saint wouldn't stay with the Brotherhood. They'd never come around to the situation they had with Jayden, breaking the rules, drinking from the vein. It went against everything they fought for. Octavius and Saint were nyks, and when this chaos was all over, they couldn't be a part of the Brotherhood.

Octavius wasn't sure he could go back to drinking from blood bags. It didn't feel right. Having Jayden as a feeder felt *natural* because Jayden consented. But the Brotherhood wouldn't see it that way. Storm would never allow such blatant disregard for the rules.

Several of Vesna Dragovic's addresses listed in numerical order stood out among the hundreds listed on screen. Octavius opened Google maps and zoomed in on the structures, adjacent to a pier stretching out into the Hudson. They definitely hadn't been aware of these premises before.

Why would Vesna need multiple New York warehouses? Perhaps more interestingly, the largest of the warehouses, surrounded by Vesna's properties, wasn't owned by her. Her holdings created a ring around a much larger property.

Whatever the Nyxian had stored there, it couldn't be good considering their operation to create more nyks at Eagle Lake.

"I think we've got something here."

Saint leaned over Octavius's shoulder. "What am I looking at?"

"It's a map of downtown Manhattan. These are all old warehouses, marked for redevelopment, but building work in that zone never seems to get off the ground. You see all these little buildings? These are connected to a Nyxian operation we didn't know about."

Saint tapped the screen over the larger warehouse, the one not highlighted, in the middle of the rest. "What's this one?"

"She doesn't own that one."

"Seems strange all these properties surround it."

"Yeah, it does seem strange."

"Who owns it?"

Octavius opened a new window. "I can check who it's registered to. Give me a second..." He opened the city records, logged in, and searched for the address. Land ownership was public record, if you knew where to look. It was how Felix Quaid had tracked down all of Vesna's properties in the past.

A company name showed as the building's owner. Octavius read it, then read it again. "This doesn't make any sense."

"What? Who owns it?"

"Atlas Enterprises. We've owned it since before these records became digitized. It's not unusual, I guess. The Brotherhood owns a lot of property all over the world, safehouses, storage centers, weapons caches."

"But it's damn strange they own the largest warehouse in an area crawling with nyks, that happens to be surrounded by Nyxian property. Right?"

And Octavius hadn't known about it. None of them had. It hadn't appeared on their official properties list. He'd only found it now because he'd searched the public records, not their own internal documents. "Someone deleted the paper trail. Raiden, maybe. He could easily have hidden the evidence."

"Whatever is there, we've got time before sundown to take a look," Saint said, grabbing a jacket from Jayden's leftover pile of clothes. "Bring Zaine. I trust the Viking."

"Shouldn't we all go?"

"And walk into another trap? No, we get a look at what we're dealing with first."

Octavius tossed Jayden his phone. "Just in case you need to reach us."

"Okay." He shrugged. "I'll just stay here and, I don't know, bake more cookies, I guess."

A flush of protective warmth radiated through Octavius's chest. He bent and kissed Jayden on the mouth. Jayden leaned into the kiss, hungry for more.

"You had better come back," Jayden warned when the kiss ended, and Octavius lingered, lost in his soft eyes. "You owe me a threesome."

Octavius ruffled Jayden's hair, loving its bounce and the way Jayden screwed up his face. "*Do not* leave this apartment. You'll be safe here until we get back."

Jayden flopped back in the couch and arched a sultry eyebrow. "I'll be waiting, boys."

"He's got us both wrapped around his little finger," Saint said, once they were both outside in the hallway.

"He has." Octavius chuckled as he entered the Brotherhood's apartment.

"The world must be ending if Octavius can laugh," Kazimir drawled.

Only Kazi, Felix, and Aiko were in the room. "Where's Zaine?" Octavius asked.

"He went to find Eric," Kazi replied. "He wasn't answering his phone, so Z was losing his mind." They all shared concerned glances, even Aiko, who rarely showed any kind of emotion. For a Brotherhood who didn't care, they sure seemed to.

"When did he leave?" Saint asked.

"Not long ago."

"We'll catch up to him," Saint said, heading back outside.

"We have an address near the nyk ambush earlier." Octavius beckoned for Kazi to hand over his phone, then opened the maps app and dropped a pin on the warehouse location. "We're going to take a look. Wait here. It's likely to be heavily guarded and we need intel before we attempt to raid it. Where's Storm? He should know about this."

Aiko frowned and hopped down off the table. "We thought he was with you."

"He was, but he left..." He'd show up. Storm was the most reliable of all of them. "All right, we good? We'll be back at sundown."

"You'd better be," Kazimir grumbled. Aiko and Felix agreed, and Octavius left them checking the address on Kazi's phone and met

Saint in the empty hallway. "Let's find Zaine and Eric and get down there."

"We're going to have to travel fast," Saint said, and offered his hand. "You ever traveled through shadow?"

Octavius clasped his hand with Saint's, marveling at its firm strength. "No."

"All right, don't let go of my hand. Do you know where Zaine is headed?"

"Eric's precinct."

"Take a breath. Once in the shadows, things will look different. Try and focus, and pull me the way you want to go. We won't be able to talk, there's no sound. Although your persuasion might work. Just... don't get lost in there."

Why did he look worried? Before Octavius could stop to think about what they were about to do, shadows crawled across the hallway walls and gathered in front of Saint, pooling like ink, and then Saint stepped through, leading Octavius with him.

The lack of sound hit first, as though he'd been plunged underwater.

The same corridor stretched in front of them, but all the colors warped and drained away, like a painting left in the rain. Saint's eyes, shimmering in the dark, questioned if he was all right. All his edges were blurred, his face smudged away, as though if he stood still for too long, he'd disappear. A strange kind of pressure pushed against Octavius's chest, as though the shadows knew he was here and they wanted him *out*. He nodded but hoped this wouldn't take long. Instincts warned this wasn't his world, and he shouldn't stay.

He moved forward, leading Saint by the hand, but as he envisaged where they needed to go, the corridor swirled and blurred, washing away. The lack of anything solid and real unbalanced him, but Saint squeezed his hand, keeping him anchored. The world around them reformed into a street corner he knew well, just a few blocks from Eric's police department. They'd traveled blocks in seconds.

His heart seized. He stumbled, gasped. The shadows shrank around him, trying to suffocate, or eject him.

Saint yanked him out of the shadows, where the ground was hard, the air smelled like wet asphalt, and his heart galloped, trying to escape his chest.

"Fuck." He reached out to brace himself against a wall, and Saint's arm looped around him, clutching him close. His senses buzzed, his skin electric. "Let's not do that again."

Saint threw him his wicked smile. "I didn't say it was going to be enjoyable."

"Some warning would have been nice."

"You'd still have done it, and there wasn't time. We're here."

A few cop cars appeared to have been abandoned outside the precinct steps, along with several civilian cars.

"Hey, you walk through shadows now?" Zaine said, striding over. "While I get the panel van?" He thumbed over his shoulder at the black van parked half on the sidewalk a little ways down the street. "I so need a raise."

"I don't recommend it," Octavius said. His insides still felt like liquid. "Where's Sharpe?"

Zaine nodded toward the precinct. "He's coming out, said we should stay back. The cops are looking for people to blame, and as Raiden made us semi-famous, we're on the hit list. We should get in the van."

As they climbed into the van, Zaine in the front, Octavius explained about the Brotherhood warehouse.

"If Raiden wanted to hide the fact Atlas owned the warehouse," Zaine said, "he could have given it to Vesna, or registered ownership under a different company name altogether. Why leave our name all over it?"

"He deleted the files off Atlas, so he didn't need to hide it."

Zaine's mouth turned downward. "*Someone* deleted the files." His gaze lifted, and his weariness vanished. "Give me a second..." He left the van and hurried over to the man striding down the steps.

"That Eric Sharpe, the cop?" Saint asked.

Octavius nodded. Sharpe's detective's badge hung on a strap around his neck. he wore casual clothes, all creased from the long night. Short, messy brown hair brought out the warmth in his eyes.

Zaine and Eric exchanged a few words, both of them appearing concerned, and then Eric took Zaine in his arms and whatever was said between them was lost in their intimacy.

"Huh," Saint remarked. "He's human, and Mikalis allowed this?"

"He *was* human, and Mikalis only allowed it because Zaine knew which buttons to press."

"Was human?" Saint tore his gaze from the couple and turned toward Octavius. "Then he's not human?"

"You know how Jayden was able to heal that gunshot wound to the chest? Eric Sharpe has the same ability, as does Felix Quaid. I've been meaning to tell you, but with *everything*, there hasn't been time."

"Wait, that wasn't some kind of miracle?"

"No, maybe, we don't know. Something is changing the blood of certain individual human beings when they come into contact with nyktelios, and it's not venom changing them. They're not feeders. They're like Jayden is to us. They're... special."

Saint blinked and stared again at Eric and Zaine. They'd separated and were making their way back to the van, deep in conversation. "Mikalis is aware of this?"

"Yes, he didn't like it, but once Felix exhibited the same abilities as Eric, he couldn't ignore it. And now there's Jayden, so..."

"They're godtouched."

"What?" Octavius asked. He'd always hated that term. Godtouched. For him, it meant his fate had been sealed by the villagers who'd sought to sacrifice him. No good had ever come from the word. "Godtouched?"

"There's no other explanation, humans don't suddenly become immortal. They're being changed by the gods for a reason."

"Could it be to weaken us?" As Octavius had feared, and Raiden had latched on to.

Saint shrugged. "Do they look weak?"

Eric laughed at something Zaine said. They walked beside each other, at ease, but more than that. Anyone only had to glimpse at them and see the way they admired each other to know they were in love.

They weren't weak. If anything, Eric seemed rejuvenated now alongside Zaine.

"They aren't weak." Since Eric had waltzed into the ops room and upset the status quo, Octavius had feared the man's presence would damage the Brotherhood. Then along came Felix Quaid, who had somehow tamed Kazimir, and again, Octavius had feared the humans would change the Brotherhood by infecting it with their weaknesses. But he'd been looking at it all wrong. Humans, with all their messy emotions and brilliant lust for life... They weren't weak. They were everything the Brotherhood lacked.

"Hey," Eric said, sliding into the front passenger seat as Zaine got behind the wheel. "You guys good? Saint, right?" Eric offered his hand between the front seats for Saint to shake. "I tried to get into your prison cell once. Kazimir almost pitched a fit."

Saint shook Eric's hand, his smile growing.

"It's good to see all the rumors weren't true," Eric said, getting settled in the front.

"Some are." Saint grinned.

Eric laughed, and Octavius watched all this with a strange tinge of jealousy. How was Saint able to click with people, despite what and who he was? Octavius had never been good at being social. He didn't know *how* to people.

Saint's hand landed on Octavius's knee and gave a reassuring squeeze.

"Things have settled down in the city now communications have been restored," Eric explained as Zaine got the van underway. "But shit got real crazy for a while there. I doubt Mikalis is going to be able to brush all this under a rug. Seems like your existence and the fact vampires are real is common knowledge now."

"There's no rug big enough to cover all this shit," Zaine muttered.

"If we don't stop the wave of nyks," Octavius said, "there won't be much left to cover up."

"Any news on where Mikalis is?" Eric asked.

"No," Zaine growled. "Wherever he is, he's walking on thin ice. Storm is having a hard time covering for him."

"Maybe Mikalis will pull a rabbit out of a hat?" Eric asked.

"Yeah, maybe..."

None of them seemed too convinced of a last-minute rescue. Mikalis's bridges were burned. The Brotherhood had needed its leader, and the fact he wasn't here told them all they needed to know. Saint's sideways glance to Octavius confirmed it.

They were on their own.

CHAPTER 36

 aint

A HINT of sweet decay hung in the air around the docks and the Nyxian's warehouses. The warm, wet breeze shifted scents around, but the smell of nyktelios among the heavier smells of river water was strong.

They left the van a block away and walked toward the Hudson as the sun set in the west, bleeding its remaining daylight across New York's arterial river.

"Let's split up," Zaine said. "But stay close. We don't want to get drawn into a fight too soon. Meet back at the van in ten." Zaine veered left with Eric while Octavius walked alongside Saint toward the first of the warehouses.

From the exterior, the buildings appeared to have been abandoned for years. Grass had taken root through the construction fences and an old warning sign had faded from weathering. They spotted a hole in the rusted fence, used by local wildlife and drug dealers, and Saint ducked through. Once on the other side, the story of neglect and abandonment seemed to go on. A few rusted cars sat on bricks, their wheels long ago stolen. But Saint wasn't buying. Fresh tire tracks led from the main gate, where grass hadn't grown. The warehouses were used, and recently.

"You said these Nyx worshippers were creating nyks on an industrial scale?" Saint asked.

"Yeah, we shut down two of their industrial locations. The operation in Poland almost killed Kazimir."

"Why?" Saint lowered his voice. "Do they truly believe more nyks are going to raise their god?"

"Something like that," Octavius said. "Raiden, clearly with an ulterior motive, researched them. They believe that chaos will feed Nyx, bringing her back, and the nyks are her creations, so more nyks equals more chaos equals a grateful chaos god."

A *clang* rang out from one of the buildings. Saint crouched in the grass, and Octavius knelt next to him.

After a few moments of quiet, and no movement from the warehouse, Octavius said, "But Mikalis made the nyktelios, she only made the Firsts. She made Mikalis."

"Right. Their logic is flawed."

"Logic generally is with religious zealots."

Beyond the warehouse, a pontoon dock stretched onto the water. A barge had been moored to it.

"Looks as though they've been getting deliveries," Octavius said, following Saint's gaze.

"Perhaps these newly turned nyks were shipped in from elsewhere?"

"Could be. Let's get a closer look."

They needed to get inside that central warehouse but getting close meant slipping past the exterior buildings without being seen. Saint could move through the shadows, but it was risky. He wouldn't be able to see if there were any guards waiting near where he'd exit, and it would mean leaving Octavius.

"I'm going to take a look through the shadows," he said.

Octavius grimaced.

"You stay here."

Octavius's frown made it clear he didn't like that idea either. Saint smiled and kissed his snarl. "I want nothing more than to pull you close and drown you in pleasure, Little Wolf. Do not worry, I'll be right back." And with that, he stepped back into cool, soundless shadow.

Octavius's frowning expression swirled away with the rest of him, like a vanishing ghost. He hated to do this, hated leaving him, but it would only be a moment.

Saint turned toward the warehouses, maneuvered around the blurred edges of the outer buildings, and approached the higher walls of the Brotherhood-owned warehouse. Inky darkness beat in waves from inside its walls, as though the shadows were a living, breathing thing, calling to the nyks.

He drew closer, moving among shifting colors and blurred lines. Then, in an area away from any doors and windows and what he hoped was a location that wasn't being watched, he stepped from the shadows, back into solid, damp reality. Sound washed back in first, bringing with it combined low-level murmurings from a crowd.

He sidled toward a side door, careful to keep low, and got a look through the corner of the door's broken window.

Nyks filled the warehouse, wall to wall. Thousands of them. All standing motionless, all mumbling, and all facing a scaffold erected in the center, where a figure reclined in a tattered old armchair, like a king on a broken throne.

Mikalis.

All the betrayal and dread Saint had tried to push aside slammed into him, stealing his breath.

It didn't make any sense. Why would Mikalis be here, why would he lead the nyks? He wasn't attacking them. His whole reason for creating the Brotherhood had been to destroy the very creatures surrounding him—*worshipping* him.

It couldn't be as Saint was seeing. There had to be something else happening here.

But one thing was certain, this would destroy the Brotherhood.

Behind Mikalis, waves of shadows poured in, painting an ink-black picture of enormous dark wings. Wings that consumed the night and beat in hypnotic rhythm, as though keeping time with Mikalis's heartbeat.

If Saint walked in there, if he demanded answers, would it save the Brotherhood, or condemn them?

Mikalis lifted his head. All-black eyes swirled with eternal darkness. A darkness that had always been in him, just below the surface. But now it was here, living, breathing, consuming, *feeding*.

Saint suddenly knew who Mikalis was. Who he'd always been.

He wasn't nyktelios, he wasn't a First. He'd existed before the gods. Cast out, banished, locked away for the brutal crimes he'd committed against Nyx. But he wasn't lost. He was right here, gaining strength, being worshipped, feeding on darkness. Because he *was* darkness.

Erebus lived.

Mikalis turned his head. His all-black, hungry-eyed glare speared into Saint, rocking him on his feet. Saint dropped and pressed his back to the wall, breathless, fangs bared, heart racing. He had to get back. He had to warn them all.

They'd never believe him.

The shadows crackled apart a few steps in front of Saint, and Mikalis stepped from within. A brief moment of confusion crossed his face, but he quicky banished it. He looked down his nose at Saint, like a god peering at an ant. If there had ever been a time to beg his sire to spare him, this was it.

Mikalis struck.

CHAPTER 37

 ctavius

IT HAD BEEN TOO LONG.

Saint had said he'd just be a few moments. It had been longer than that. A lot longer. The sun had set. Octavius should never have let him go alone, should have followed him into the shadows, should have been with him.

"What the fuck, Octavius?" Zaine ducked under the fence. "We've been waiting for you. There are nyks all over. We need to—"

"Saint's missing."

He expected Zaine to leave, to brush him off, to tell him Saint could look after himself, to demand they go back to the others.

He paced a few strides, aware of Zaine's glare tracking his every step. This was it. This was the moment he'd have to choose Saint or the Brotherhood, and he'd choose Saint, every time. No hesitation. "I'm not leaving him, Z."

"And I'm not leaving you, so here we are." Zaine tapped out a message on his phone and dropped it back into his pocket. "Eric will contact the others and tell them what we've found. You and me are going after Saint."

Octavius stopped pacing, unsure if he'd heard correctly. "You don't understand, I have to help him."

Zaine smiled. "I know, and I *do* understand."

"Wait, you're helping me?"

Zaine sighed, planted a hand on his hip, and cleared his throat. "I fucked up, okay? You're Brotherhood. Probably more Brotherhood than I am. I owe you, and we all owe Saint after that ambush earlier, so here I am. We can stand here all night and talk it out, or we can go do what we do best, and that's protect our own."

Zaine was going to help him and Saint?

Octavius had thought he'd lost them, lost everything he'd cared for, everything he'd fought for, lost his family. But he needed them right now, and they were here for him, in Zaine.

"Oh Jesus, don't get all teary-eyed. Fuck, Octavius. I might just start liking you. Where'd you last see your man?"

"He went through the shadows toward the main warehouse. Wait—*My man?*"

Zaine huffed a sigh and drew both his guns from their holsters. "Hold on to your wings because we're about to fuck up this party."

Guns were a terrible idea. "We can't go in guns blazing."

Zaine shrugged, Desert Eagles akimbo. "The chances of finding Saint and getting him out without any bloodshed are exactly zero. Until I get wings and whatever other upgrades y'all ancient assholes have, I'm taking the guns."

All right, he'd wanted Zaine's help, and now he had it. But he also wanted to make it out alive. "Follow me." He led him through the long grass, keeping low, and snuck between the smaller outer warehouses, toward the large, looming building nearer the waterfront. "What did you mean, my man?" Octavius whispered, glancing behind him to catch Zaine's knowing smirk.

"Don't try and tell me you're not a thing. The apartments have real thin walls."

Octavius hurried to the nearest wall and shadows deep enough to hide them. "'Thin walls'?" And then it occurred to him how the others had heard him, Jayden, and Saint engaged in intimacies, when he'd had his cock down Jayden's throat, and Saint had his fingers in places that brought a flush of heat to Octavius's face. "You heard that?" he whispered.

"You didn't know?" Zaine snickered. "It was pretty awkward, especially as we were all sucking on blood bags while you were getting your rocks off next door."

If they hadn't been in the middle of nyk territory, Octavius would have dug a hole and buried himself in it, then he caught Zaine's grin in the low light and the shame fizzled away.

"No shade, man," Zaine said. "If I'd been alone with Eric, we'd have been going at it too. Besides, you've been less of a dick since getting some. I knew you just needed a good fucking. Congratulations."

"I hate you." He was also pretty sure Zaine's attempt at humor was to distract him from the fact Saint was in trouble.

Zaine's grin bloomed. "Good, we wouldn't want to make it weird by actually liking each other."

A car rumbled up to the outer gates, waiting with its engine running, and as the gates clattered open, the car ventured into the warehouse yards. Octavius and Zaine were well-hidden behind stacks of crates, but from their location, the driver as visible.

"Raiden," Zaine growled, hunkering down in the grass. If they could see him, he'd be able to see them too, if he knew where to look.

The car vanished behind one of the outer buildings, then rumbled into sight again. Its high beams swept over a bank of old oil drums, and then the vehicle came to a halt. Raiden cut the engine and climbed out, then leaned back against the car's hood, waiting for something.

"We can take him," Zaine said. "You and me, right now."

"Let's wait, see what happens."

Raiden removed his glasses and examined them in the ambient light, then folded his fingers around them and crushed the glasses to bits of broken metal and glass. He sprinkled the remains on the ground, discarding his lies.

A figure emerged from the gloom, appearing from the thickest shadows near the river.

"Goddamnit, that's Mikalis," Octavius hissed. If he was here, then Saint really was in danger.

"Fuck, is he *meeting* with Raiden?"

They weren't fighting. The wind whipped their conversation out across the river, far from earshot, but they seemed to be amicably meeting.

"The fuck? Why isn't Mikalis bitch-slapping his skinny ass?"

Because they were working together. That was why and how Raiden had been able to undermine the Brotherhood all this time without being discovered. Because Mikalis already knew who and what he was.

Octavius didn't want to believe the worst, but the evidence was stacking up.

"He's not working with the Nyxians..." Zaine said, his thoughts catching up with Octavius's. "No way, that's not Mikalis."

"It does explain why he's not helping us, and how he didn't spot Raiden was one of them. He knew—"

"No way, man. He's a slippery sonofabitch, but he wouldn't betray us like that. This has to be part of a plan, some kind of ruse he's acting out."

"So why not tell us?"

"I don't know... But he's not one of *them*."

He admired Zaine's optimism, but he hadn't had to try to fight Mikalis for survival. "Regardless, we need to find Saint before Mikalis does." Assuming he hadn't already found Saint and killed him. No, Octavius would have felt it. He and Saint were close, as close as two souls could get. He'd know if he was gone.

Octavius nodded toward the main warehouse. "Let's go, while they're preoccupied."

They tracked along the outside wall of the neighboring building, then dashed across a narrow side path, and hurried under an old set of exterior fire escape stairs to the nearest grimy window.

"Shit," Zaine muttered, peering inside.

Octavius saw them too. A whole lot of nyks, hundreds of them, all gathered around a scaffold tower. A tower sporting a single, oddly placed, tattered armchair aloft.

"There's your man. It's not good."

Octavius followed Zaine's line of sight and spotted Saint, strung up on the scaffold, tied by his wrists and ankles and gagged. His head was bowed, suggesting he was unconscious. Streaks of blood stained his neck, shining against pale skin. He'd been bitten.

A growl simmered deep inside Octavius. He'd kill them all. Every last fucking nyk.

"Easy," Zaine warned. "We need to think this through. There are a whole lot of nyks between us and him. He's not dust, so that's good. And when he wakes up, those ropes aren't going to hold him for long."

He knew all that, he knew the reasonable thing to do was wait and call the others for backup. "I need to get in there."

"I know, I hear yah. But also, *army of fuckin' nyks*. Let's not do anything rash."

"Raiden did this," Octavius hissed. Fury and adrenaline scorched his every nerve. There weren't that many nyks. They didn't even appear to be active; they stood about, waiting. Probably for whatever Raiden had planned. If they were newly turned, then Zaine and Octavius could kill them. Or...

"Do you think we can sneak through?" Octavius asked.

"'Sneak through'? Sneak through what? The ocean of nyks? What? No. Octavius, no."

He could do it, just slip inside and sneak his way through. Once he reached Saint, he'd rouse him with some blood, and then every single nyk in this fucking warehouse was dust.

"Octavius? Hey, don't do it. The others will be on their way soon—"

"Raiden and Mikalis are outside *now*. This is our chance."

"Our chance to what? *Die?*"

Octavius gave the window frame a shove. The rotted wood surrounding it shifted. It would give way, he just had to jimmy it out.

"Stop. We're not doing this. We're going to wait—"

Octavius gave the window another jerk, and this time, it came away in his hands. He hauled it out and laid it against the wall.

"You know I said we were friends? I lied. If you go in there, I'm going to have to follow you, and I gave Eric my word I wouldn't do anything stupid. Walking into a warehouse full of nyks is pretty fuckin' stupid."

Octavius heaved himself up and through the gap in the wall where the window used to be, then inch by inch, lowered himself down the other side.

The nyks hadn't moved. They swayed some, murmuring what sounded like a prayer of some kind. These were young nyks, not long turned, but they weren't rabid. Not yet, at least. They almost seemed to be sleeping with their eyes open, as though caught in a trance.

Octavius snuck between them and glanced back to see Zaine glaring daggers his waybut following him through the forest of entranced nyks. They just had to make it to the scaffold, right in the middle of the warehouse, before Raiden showed up to unleash the nyks. Assuming that's what they were all waiting for.

Kazimir had set fire to the horde of nyks in Eagle Lake. There wasn't much combustible material here, but perhaps they could lure them to another warehouse that did have flammable items in storage. There would be a way to kill them, but first, they had to free Saint.

"This is impressive." Raiden's voice filled the vast space. "Is this all of them?"

"The third barge was delayed," Mikalis replied. "We should have enough."

Octavius froze and stood in line among the nyks, hoping to blend in. Behind him, if he was smart, Zaine would freeze too.

"I thought that one was dead." Raiden narrowed his eyes on Saint, hanging from the poles.

"So did I." Mikalis jumped onto the platform and regarded Saint's slumped form. "He never did learn when to yield."

"Is he safe there? He's not going to wake up?"

"No, he's quite safe." Mikalis stopped at the front edge of the scaffold platform and scanned the crowd of nyks. Octavius willed him to keep his gaze away. He could mentally force him to ignore him, but if he tried, and failed, he'd know Octavius was near. "Well then, Raiden. Good work. It's time we began."

Raiden clapped his hands once and laughed. "Finally! I've been waiting a long time for this." He spun and studied the crowd of nyks, his face full of pride.

Mikalis glanced at Raiden's back and a strange lopsided smile tilted his lips, a smile Raiden didn't see. One of cruelty, and something else. Something like victory. Mikalis *had* been working a ruse, but Octavius wasn't sure if the lie was in their favor. Or just Mikalis's.

The Brotherhood leader spread his arms, tilted his head back, and every shadow in the warehouse rushed to him, pouring like water into his being, like a black hole swallowing all light. Behind him, great arched wings rose, and the shadows beat in waves.

The nyks' chanting grew louder, and their swaying quickened. Octavius hadn't expected it, and by the time he'd realized he was the only one not chanting and rocking, Mikalis's dark-flooded gaze picked him out of the crowd. His wings snapped together and vanished in a cloud of static.

"You," Mikalis said.

"Oh fuck," came Zaine's reply, and then a gunshot boomed.

The bullet whizzed past Octavius, zipped over the heads of the gathered nyks, and slammed into Raiden's forehead, throwing him back against a scaffold pole, rattling the entire frame around Mikalis and Saint.

Octavius bolted between the waking nyks, leaped onto the first platform, and grabbed the ropes holding Saint's right wrist.

The blow came out of nowhere, striking him in the middle and then tossing him across the warehouse. He had less than a second to brace before he barreled into the nyks, toppling them under and over him.

He skidded along the floor, chest burning from the blow, then rolled to a halt, rattled and burning.

Mikalis had struck him.

"Take this as your one and only warning," the Brotherhood leader warned. "Come for me again, Octavius, and I will kill you."

Octavius spluttered around a few broken ribs and climbed to his feet. The nyks were turning toward him, waking from their collective trance. Zaine stood several nyks to his right, eyes wide with shock, and near the platform, Raiden staggered back to his feet. The bullet wound in his forehead stitched itself closed as Raiden stretched his neck, popping muscles and rolling his shoulders.

"Mikalis, what is this?" Zaine asked. "You're here to stop these nyks, right?"

"Stop them?" Mikalis's eyes shone their inky gleam. "And why would I want to do that?"

"Idiots." Raiden snorted. "Catch up, boys. You're on the wrong side of this war."

Zaine aimed a gun at Raiden again. "The next one goes in your heart."

Raiden spread his arms. "Your bullets can't hurt me."

"Oh really?" Zaine jerked an eyebrow. "Let's test that theory, science guy." He fired, and just like the previous shot, the bullet raced ahead and slammed into Raiden's chest. And just like before, Raiden slammed back, hitting the scaffold.

Saint's limp head lifted. Octavius caught the movement in the corner of his yes. *Yes, wake up.*

Raiden choked on a laugh, stumbled forward, and grinned, baring his fangs. "You were always the dumb one."

Zaine shrugged. "I mostly lean into the blond himbo act. You'd be surprised what it gets you. Like access to your experiments because you think I'm too young to be a threat."

What was Zaine playing at. Wasting bullets, buying time? Distracting them all so that Saint might regain consciousness?

Raiden's smile faltered. He coughed, then reached for his head. "What... the..."

"Encapsulated-venom rounds," Zaine said smugly. "Nice upgrade, except I made a few modifications of my own. That tightness in your chest, that buzzing in your veins. That's my venom racing through your nervous system. Hurts like a bitch, doesn't it."

Raiden lifted his head, bared his fangs, and flung out his arms, this time throwing his ancient wings open with them. His human guise vanished, and the true nyktelios took over.

"Get to Saint," Zaine said to Octavius, cocking his guns. "I've got this."

"Enough!" Mikalis snapped his fingers with a resounding *click*, and the crowd of nyks burst to life. Octavius threw off his own human visage and clashed with the surging wall of nyks. It didn't matter how many came at him, he'd kill them all. *"Back,"* he sent the demand into the first, like an arrow to the brain. *"Yield,"* to another. *"Stop."* And each one he punched his fangs into and delivered a lethal shot of venom.

But there were many, and even as he killed them, more swarmed in, getting closer and closer, crowding him, crushing him. *"Stop-yield-surrender."*

Then Mikalis appeared in a blink. He clamped his cold hand around Octavius's throat and hauled him off his feet. "I warned you." And he struck, sinking ice-cold fangs into Octavius's neck.

"No!" Saint screamed, and all the world went dark.

CHAPTER 38

 aint

THE THUDDING in Saint's head was nothing compared to the ache in his heart. Octavius lay out cold on the scaffold boards, dumped there by Mikalis, as pale as a corpse and barely breathing.

"Enough interruptions!" Mikalis snarled, and flung open his arms and his wings, beginning to feed on the darkness all over again. Zaine clashed with Raiden among the nyks, and while all of those things were important, Saint couldn't take his eyes from Octavius. He didn't care about Mikalis, or Zaine, or the end of the world. He just needed to know Octavius would be all right.

Wake up, he silently begged. But Octavius lay there, discarded like trash, used by Mikalis, like all the Brotherhood had been used to shield Mikalis's lies.

The nyks settled, returning to their eerie rhythmic chanting.

If Saint could just get free... but Mikalis had drained him, almost killed him, and if Saint let go of the last threads of control, he might kill them all in his madness, including Octavius. He needed him back, needed him to be awake, his hope in a world of endless despair.

Come on, Little Wolf.

I know you're in there.

Live. Fight. Like you always have.

One of us has to make it out alive.

Octavius was at his strongest with his back against a wall. He would wake up. He just needed time. Saint poured all his hope into those thoughts.

"Mikalis, this is not the way." Saint growled the words, dragging them up from semi-consciousness.

Mikalis didn't respond; he stood, arms spread, wings pulsing, absorbing whatever power the nyks were giving him, taking the darkness into himself. Erebus *was* darkness. He was taking back what had been taken from him. And whatever that meant for this world, it could not be good if the nyktelios were its fuel.

"Mikalis, I loved and trusted you, as they all still do. Whatever this is, whatever you think you need, it's not worth the demise of the Brotherhood."

There, a glance, a side-eyed flicker of recognition. It wasn't much, but it was enough to know Mikalis was listening. And if he was listening, there was a chance Saint might get through to him.

Zaine let out a cry, and Saint peered through his swimming vision to see Raiden had slashed open Zaine's chest and had him pinned to the wall. The Viking's guns were gone. He thrashed, fangs bared, but even weakened by venom, Raiden was the stronger nyktelios.

They were losing this fight.

It couldn't end like this. Not with betrayal. Not again. "I always loved you," Saint spluttered. He was losing himself, losing control. "You saved each of them, and they love you—"

"I'm doing this for them!" Mikalis snapped.

For them? How was any of this for the Brotherhood?

"Yes!" Raiden roared, leaping onto the platform. "She's coming. Do you feel it? Our queen is almost here. Chaos and night, so pure, so violent, so hungry. She's close. Yes, Mikalis! More! Welcome her home!"

Mikalis's back arched, his wings stretched wider, and the darkness had him locked in its embrace.

Then they were both summoning Nyx.

This world and its humans didn't stand a chance.

A vicious bolt of lightning slammed through the warehouse roof and struck the floor, sending sparks dancing into every nyk. The beat of power from Mikalis's wings intensified, flooding the air, and a pool of darkness gathered, growing from the hole in the roof. A vast, clawed hand reached out, then another. A creature emerged, inch by inch from the pulsing gateway, liquid dark in a vast shimmering humanoid form.

When the gunshot rang out, it didn't seem consequential. It was already too late. She was here, and so was the end of all things. But then Mikalis stumbled, and his great wings stuttered, their rhythm falling out of synchronicity with the chanting and the pulsing gateway.

Saint dragged his fading gaze back to the platform, where Octavius now stood.

He hadn't shot Mikalis. Zaine had done that from among the crowd, where Raiden had left him. But Octavius had his hand out, his stare locked on Mikalis, and Saint knew Octavius was in Mikalis's head, fighting for his life, and the lives of everyone in this ungrateful world.

As he watched, Mikalis stumbled some more, he wavered, tried to catch himself, then fell to his knees.

"What?" Raiden whirled. "You vicious little prick, get out of his head!"

Raiden strode toward Octavius.

By the gods, and all the vicious darkness in all the worlds, nobody hurt Octavius and lived. Saint roared, and from deep inside, he pulled every facet of his nyktelios being to the surface. The ropes holding him burst, and he swooped down on Raiden.

"Kill him," Octavius's voice demanded, thrust into Saint's head,

and he obeyed. Raiden was nothing in Saint's grip, just the creature who had thought to kill the man Saint loved, and nobody dared hurt Saint's little wolf.

Saint clamped Raiden in his arms, heard the sweet sound of the fiend's pathetic screams, and bit into his neck, snipping that scream off. Then he crunched down harder, pumping more and more venom, harder still, until he got hold of the traitor, one hand on his shoulder, the other in his hair, and yanked, ripping Raiden apart. Now there were no more screams. His head dangled, his body sagged, and then both pieces dissolved into ash and rained across the enraptured nyks.

"Kill them all," Octavius demanded.

Saint scanned the hundreds of nyks and smiled.

CHAPTER 39

ctavius

MIKALIS WAS IN HIS HEAD, but Octavius was also hooked deep in Mikalis's, and there they fought, locked together, pushing and pulling, vying for control.

He saw in his mind's eye how Saint tore Raiden apart, and then how Saint tore into the nyks, ripping them asunder, one by one, in a flurry of blood and claws, fangs and venom. He was devastating, wild, rabid, and horrifyingly beautiful. Pride made his heart swell. Saint was Octavius's, in heart and mind and soul. They were one.

"Yield!" Mikalis pushed into Octavius.

"Stop this madness!" Octavius pushed back. *"This is not you!"* He didn't know what this was, just that the Mikalis who had found him silent and broken, a ghost in the world, and had saved him so long ago, would never betray them. He still believed it. *Hoped* it.

Mikalis, already on his knees, slumped onto a hand.

"Surrender."

"Octavius, no! Do not do this. Believe in—" Mikalis's mental assault spluttered.

Octavius understood this had to end. The huge, pulsing primal being of complete darkness was almost through the gateway. But with Mikalis on his knees, and the nyks falling under Saint's wrath, the gateway had begun to contract. The tide was turning. They were winning.

Mikalis's wings dissolved into static sparks and vanished, leaving him on his hands and knees, panting and weakened.

"It's over," Octavius said aloud. He freed Mikalis's mind and stumbled backwards. Exhaustion tried to drop him to his knees too, but it wasn't over. He cast his gaze out across the ash-covered warehouse. "Saint... stop." And Saint did, as the nyk dust fell like rain around him. Zaine was there, Storm too, and Kazimir, Aiko, Felix, and Eric—all here, coated in nyk dust, weary as they picked each other up, but alive.

It was over.

Raiden was gone, torn in two.

The nyks were dust.

Mikalis's rasps filled the silence. "What have you done?"

The laugh that bubbled from above was the sound of thunder, the sound of earthquakes; it was all the storms in nature poured into one being and unleashed upon the world. Octavius looked up, and there she was. Nyx, a god before gods existed, the night sky brought to life, and hunger flashed in her starlit eyes.

She poured down from the collapsing gateway and slammed through and over the scaffold, blasting over Octavius like a vicious wave of black, glacial ice, stealing his thoughts, his breath from his lungs, and the beats from his heart.

In a long, vicious wail, she was turned into a whirling vortex of darkness, and then she vanished in a scatter of static sparks. The sparks rained to the dusty floor, and she was gone, pulled back to wherever she'd come from.

But the spot where Mikalis had knelt was empty.

No, not empty. Octavius staggered forward, knelt, and picked up the black rose. Ice had frozen its petals stiff, but as his warm fingers touched the rose, the ice melted, and the rose wilted, then died, curling over and turning to ash that fell though his fingers.

It was done, wasn't it?

It was over?

It had to be done, because he had nothing left in him.

"Love you," he sent to Saint. And when he collapsed, there was only silence.

CHAPTER 40

ctavius

GROWLS and shouts accompanied waves of consciousness. He seemed to be moving but couldn't rouse himself to understand it, or care. When blood touched his lips, he opened his mouth, clamped onto the soft, warm flesh, and drank. No venom. That was important. He knew this blood, knew the body it belonged to. Warm, compliant, forgiving. He needed to protect it at all costs. Jayden.

When a third joined them, tucking himself against Octavius's back, Octavius's senses buzzed alive, drinking in every sensitive brush of his hand, every sweep of his tongue over bare skin. He became a creature of need, and those needs were being serviced, his hunger met by the two men on either side of him. He gave himself to them, and would die for them, as he knew they would die for him. There was no better feeling than knowing they were safe.

Octavius blinked back into the present moment. An aching weariness kept him from springing from the bed, that and the satis-fied heaviness, the feeling of safety.

Jayden was tucked against his chest, head bowed, snoring lightly. Saint took up much of the bed to his right, arm and leg thrown akimbo, fast asleep with fangs out, unashamedly naked.

There wasn't anywhere else he'd rather wake up, than sandwiched between the two most important people in his life. He blinked at the ceiling, listening to their breathing, their heartbeats, and how they beat in sync with his. He'd fed, probably from them both, and the pleasant throb in his neck and his cock suggested Saint had fed too.

Against all the odds, they had survived. They'd survived Mikalis and the god he'd been trying to summon.

A niggling thread of unease tried to sprinkle ice on his contented thoughts. He shoved it aside. They'd done everything they could, Raiden was dead, and they'd won. He'd take that win and relish it a little while longer.

So, this was them. Jayden, Octavius, and Saint. This was his life now. He wasn't Brotherhood, he couldn't be that with Saint for a lover and Jayden to share between them, at least that's how Storm would see it.

If the Brotherhood still existed...

Mikalis had been on that platform, and then gone... vanished. *Taken* back through that gateway. Just a rose left in his place.

Good.

Mikalis deserved it.

Was Storm their leader now?

Or...

He glanced over at Saint, with his ruffled hair, his mouth open, fangs carelessly extended, as though he'd crashed after a wild party. Saint couldn't lead them, could he? No, they'd never accept him. Storm would never agree. Storm was the natural leader. But what if they did allow them to stay? Would Saint want to?

He didn't want to face the difficult questions the last few months had left them with. What he really wanted was to stay entangled with these two for a few days and hide from the future and whatever it brought. The fallout from all this would be... world changing.

Vampires were real.

The Brotherhood existed.

Humans were going to be a problem.

Or maybe not. Octavius had walked among them for a long time, and they were nothing if not resilient.

"Hm, you're awake," Saint grumbled in his rough bedroom voice, and nuzzled Octavius's neck. He rolled onto his side and draped his arm over Octavius's middle, trapping him. As he didn't complain, Saint's shamelessly skimmed his hand over Octavius's chest, down his shallow abs, and grasped his erect dick. He sucked on Octavius's shoulder and lazily stroked, then Jayden woke, his eyes sleepy, his hair a golden bird's nest, and his mouth finding Octavius's. He suspected, from his own aching body, that they may have already done this a few times, but he had no memory of it. This time, he planned to enjoy it.

Octavius lowered both hands to either side of him and found his two prizes. Two firm cocks. He stroked them both as Saint pumped his. Saint's teeth pierced his neck, and Jayden's tongue plunged into his mouth, and with pleasure racing through his veins, he fell into the ecstasy, lost to their thrall.

He wasn't sure what he'd done to deserve such devotion, but he'd take it, and offer it right back, smother them both with affection. Lust and hunger pulled tight, threatening to break him apart, and he wasn't ready to end it. Easing Saint off his neck, Octavius rolled onto his knees and shuffled downward, then took Jayden's beautiful cock between his lips, between his fangs, as Jayden had done with him once before.

Saint stroked down his back. The bed dipped, and then both Saint's hands were on Octavius's ass, kneading, spreading, promising more. Octavius's cock throbbed as it hung low beneath him. He needed Saint buried deep inside him. *"Do it."*

Saint's growl was all unhinged nyk, and Octavius loved to hear it. Saint reached under him, grasped Octavius's dick, and pumped fast, until Octavius raced toward climax all over again. He didn't want to come, but gods, he thirsted for it, for the devastating release.

Saint let go, spread Octavius's ass with confident ease, and pushed in, pushed deep, and it was all Octavius could do to keep up his efforts to suck Jayden's dick, tasting its salty pre-cum while Jayden trembled and bucked under him and Saint rode him. Each sliding pressure pushed Octavius's mindless desire higher again.

"Your mouth... I love it," Jayden gasped. "Yes, so close, so close, more, suck me harder."

Hearing Jayden voice his pleasure pushed Octavius's even higher, teetering him on the edge. He tried to hold himself there, to keep from coming, but the sound of Saint slapping against him, and Jayden's moan, and then the spurting of cum on his tongue, tipped him over the edge. The pressure broke, his release spilled, and Octavius came, his cock pulsing its load over Jayden's legs, as Jay came down his throat, and Saint growled and pumped and thrust wildly, coming with a ragged, stuttering cry.

They were done, high on sex, bodies tingling.

Saint kissed the back of Octavius's neck, then dragged the tips of his fangs down his spine.

"Damn." Octavius shuddered from the aftershocks and every new electric touch Saint gave him. Saint pulled his cock from within Octavius while Octavius was still reeling from the come-down, then he scooped Octavius around the waist and dragged him back between him and Jayden. Jayden shuffled close, wriggling into Octavius's embrace, and Saint breathed against his neck.

"Hm," Jayden purred. "I got my threesome."

He'd gotten more than that. Was now the best time to tell him due to his contact with Saint and Octavius, he was changing, he'd heal almost any wound, he'd gain strength, and he'd stop aging?

Octavius stroked his hair and hoped whatever godtouched meant that it didn't change Jayden. He really was the sunshine, the hope and light both Saint and Octavius craved.

He'd have to be told, but not yet. Perhaps after cookies.

They dozed awhile, but with every passing minute, Octavius's mind turned over the potential futures. Whatever waited for them, he couldn't fathom how they'd fit.

He had to talk with Storm.

He left Saint and Jayden sleeping, showered, threw on any clothes he could find that didn't smell like burned nyk, and headed next door to find the others had left. They'd cleared out, leaving cash on the side table for the owner and a simple thank-you note.

They'd left without a word to Octavius.

Octavius tucked his hands into his pockets and returned to their own borrowed apartment. He found his phone among Jayden's clothes and opened a message from Z.

Come to the old compound.

When you're ready.

Need to talk.

Z.

That didn't sound hopeful. The old compound was the Atlas Enterprises base in the city suburbs. It had been a sprawling collection of shiny buildings masquerading as a technologies company before Raiden's sabotage had blown it all to bits. Why would they go back there?

As far as Octavius knew, there was nothing left, just burned-out buildings.

He headed back into the bedroom to wake Jayden and Saint, but they were both so deeply asleep, Octavius didn't have the heart to ruin it with Brotherhood bullshit.

He left a note and headed out.

CHAPTER 41

 aint

HE'D BEEN LOST, for a while, and had known only hunger, and fear, and the need to kill, to fight, to protect. They'd tried to take Octavius, and he'd fought. Then Storm had been there, like a lighthouse *in* a storm, his namesake. And he'd said three words: *Octavius needs you.* That was all it had taken to ground him again, to regain control. He'd brought Octavius back to the apartment and nurtured him, loved him, in every and any way he could. Jay hadn't hesitated, and together, they'd brought each other back.

So when Saint woke, he sensed Octavius had left.

He wasn't in the apartment and wasn't next door either. Saint found his note—*Gone to the Brotherhood*—and scrunched it in his fist.

They would try to turn Octavius against Saint. They'd want him back. They *needed* him.

"What's wrong?" Jay asked, probably woken by Saint's growl.

"Nothing. Stay here—Actually, no. Get dressed and come with me. You're a part of this too."

They left the apartment, heading out into a wet and raining nighttime street. Clean-up crews worked to clear the streets of debris. Saint passed them by and roamed a little, before getting a fix on Octavius's general direction, then stepping into shadows with Jay tucked close.

They emerged in a leafy suburb, untouched by the recent chaos in Manhattan. Saint honed in on Octavius's location, walking from the suburbs, down a quiet tree-lined road, until arriving at a vast building site. Security floodlights cast halos all around the grounds. A huge bent and broken sign read: *Atlas Enterprises.* Except the L was missing. The compound had seen better days.

This was the Brotherhood's old headquarters. Now he was back, he remembered fleeing from the area moments before an explosion had destroyed it. From the scaffold towers and parked trucks, it appeared the compound was being rebuilt.

Saint had spent decades trapped in a glass box here, hidden from the world, punished for daring to speak the truth.

"You okay?" Jay asked. He hung back, sensitive to the unsettling quiet of the place.

"Yeah. Stick close to me, all right? Don't trust the people here."

Jay nodded, then followed Saint through a section of tangled and broken fence.

They'd taken Octavius. He'd known they would. The Brotherhood was on its knees, barely a Brotherhood at all. They needed Octavius. Damn them, they couldn't have him. He belonged with Jay, with Saint. They'd betrayed him, tried to kill him.

Octavius owed them nothing.

The wide, sweeping roads had been repaired, and a few several story buildings were close to being completed but weren't yet finished. Plastic wrapping flapped in the breeze and the bright floodlights buzzed. Rain fell in streaks through the halos of light, making all the edges and surfaces shine. He hated the smell of it, hated the modern sharpness, hated everything about this place.

Storm's recognizable bulk blocked the glass doors of the main building.

He stood with his arms crossed in a puddle of light thrown from the building behind him, watching Saint approach.

It just had to be Storm, didn't it.

Saint worked his jaw, keeping his fangs retracted, for now, and approached the towering bear of a man. "Get out of the way."

"You're not going in there."

Saint nodded at Jay behind him, told him to stay back and waited for him to back up, before turning toward Storm again. He stopped in front of the new Brotherhood leader and had to look up to meet his glare. The bastard had always been taller. "Keep me from him, and you and I will finish that fight you started long ago."

"It was finished then," Storm said, his voice thick but hollow, devoid of emotion. "I don't trust you, and until I do, you stay out here."

"You don't trust me?" Saint snorted a laugh. "You know, I thought we were close once. But the second Mikalis turned on me —" Saint clicked his fingers. "—so did you."

Storm blinked slowly.

"This is so typical of you. Use me to get what you want, then slam the door in my face. Do they know you'll do the same to them, just like Mikalis has?"

Storm's silent snarl revealed gleaming fangs. "I gave you the benefit of the doubt, I let you into our ranks, despite the fact you're blatantly a nyk—"

Unbelievable. "And what the fuck are you, Storm? Do they think you're the immovable stalwart leader who has always done right by them? They don't know you. They don't know where you come from or what you're truly capable of, *Storm*. I have one feeder, and you call me a nyk. *You* leveled continents. You are more monster than I ever was but I'm the one who's punished, and my only crime was loving you and Mikalis, like a fool." He stepped closer, squaring up to Storm, getting in his face. "I should thank you, you showed me the Brotherhood's true colors, but if you take Octavius from me, I will burn this place to the

297

ground for a second time and I will hunt every last one of you fuckers." His fangs extended, lending his threat teeth. "He is desperate for your approval, for your love. He doesn't yet know how toxic that love is."

Gods, if they took Octavius from him, he'd lose his damn mind. He needed his little wolf. Without Octavius, there was little left in this world worth fighting for. If they seduced Octavius away with their bullshit lies, he'd show them how nyk he could be.

"Step back," Saint growled.

"I'm protecting Octavius from you—"

That was it, that was the final trigger. Saint reached for Storm, lightning-fast, and grabbed the big guy by the neck, but Storm was no push over. He'd been expecting it.

Storm brought his arms up, knocked away Saint's hold, and threw a punch that, had it hit Saint, he'd have been face down on the asphalt. But Saint backstepped, avoiding the swing, then lunged and tackled Storm in the gut. He plowed forward, smashing through the glass doors, and slammed the big guy into a new illuminated Atlas sign. Sparks rained, the sign shattered, and Storm swung another fist, this time knocking Saint flat to the floor.

His skull buzzed, ears ringing. Someone else was here. One of the others. Saint shoved his jaw back into place and levered himself off the floor. The black-haired beauty, Kazimir, hung back, probably ready to barrel in and pin Saint down once Storm had worked out his issues.

He wasn't going back in their box. Ever.

Storm glowered. "I don't want to hurt you."

Saint licked blood from inside his cheek. "A few millennia too late, Storm."

The others were here. Zaine and Eric, Felix too, and Aiko. This was what was left of them. Nothing, really. The Brotherhood was done for, and these were its death throes. Saint was beating on a dying animal.

"What the hell is this?!" Octavius shoved between Zaine and Kazimir, blue eyes flashing furious menace. "Saint, get outside!"

298

"What?"

"I'll be right there." His tone softened, but not much. "Go. I need to talk with Storm."

Saint staggered, rocked by Octavius's dismissal more than Storm's assault. As the others looked on, he backed over broken glass, then turned away from their hard stares and left the building to find Jay waiting on the other side of the road, arms folded, chewing on a fingernail.

"You okay?"

"No."

"Can we leave?"

"No... Not without Octavius."

"Is he.. coming with us?" Jay asked, trying to hide the hiccup in his voice.

Octavius wasn't going to stay, was he? No, he wasn't that much of a fool to run back to them after everything they'd done to him, and to Saint. He knew the truth. The Brotherhood was done. It was time to move on.

Saint paced, then dropped onto the wet grass and draped his arms over his knees. He loved Octavius. He'd rip out his heart and give it to him if it meant he'd stay with him and Jay. He deserved a happy ending.

Jay dropped onto the grass beside him. "Octavius is smart. He'll do the right thing."

On his own, he was. "They can be manipulative. They need him, and he's spent his whole life trying to be one of them. Why would he say no? For us? We only met a few weeks ago."

"You're scared, Saint, but you didn't see him when he brought you back. He won't throw what we have away. I trust him."

Saint breathed in through his nose and side-eyed Jay. He really was scared. He'd loved and lost before. His heart couldn't take it again.

"I'm scared too," Jay added. "I'm so fuckin' scared, Saint. But not for me. For you, for them, for this world. It's changing, and I don't know where it's going to end. I feel so helpless, all the time. What the fuck can I do? Bake cookies?"

"I won't let anything bad happen to you."

"Shouldn't that be my choice?"

He hadn't stopped to think about Jay's feelings in all of this. He'd always been so willing, so accommodating, but Saint had torn him from his world and thrown him into one full of monsters, and he had wanted it then, but now? "What *do* you want?"

Jay plucked at a stem of grass. "I think I want my life back, but I want you too. I want to study at college, maybe go to culinary school, open a restaurant—I want to be worth something more than, you know... a convenient snack for you."

"I can..." Saint's voice creaked a little. He growled to clear it. "I can see to it you have that." It wasn't fair, how he'd taken Jay from his life, even if that life had been about to self-destruct. He was good now and deserved a second chance at starting over.

"But I don't want to lose you." Jay's soft blue eyes widened. "I still want this, us."

Saint nodded so he didn't have to hear his own voice break up again. "So uh... You should know that back in the safehouse, you were shot, and you died—nearly died. But being around nyks, being around me and Octavius, has changed you. Inside. It wasn't intentional, and wasn't venom, nothing like that. It's something none of us understand yet."

Jay blinked, and cast his gaze toward the broken glass doors, where Octavius still talked with Storm. "I kinda knew, I guess. I thought I was imagining it. I feel different too, when I'm around you both. Like I'm strong, and wired, or... untouchable."

"We'll figure it out, even if it's just the two of us."

Octavius strode from the building. He didn't seem pleased, but most times he kept his smiles for special occasions, and this didn't seem like one of those. He stopped on the road and peered down at Saint on the grass.

He was going to stay goodbye. He didn't even need to say the words. Saint's heart knew it inside and began to break. He closed

300

his eyes. "How can you do this?" It hurt, it hurt like he was losing pieces of himself, right there on the side of the road.

Octavius sighed. "You need to see something. Come inside." He glanced back at the others loitering in the lobby area. "They won't stop you. Just try not to attack Storm."

Saint narrowed his eyes and glared past Octavius at the Atlas building. "There's nothing in there for me."

Octavius slumped onto the grass beside Saint, on the opposite side to Jay. He stared at the building too, and the rain pummeled them as though trying to wash all three of them away.

Water dripped from his locks of white hair and clung to his fine lashes. He was lovely, even wet and bedraggled. *Especially* wet and bedraggled. Smart and prickly and like an unleashed force of nature in bed.

"When Mikalis wasn't with us," Octavius explained, "he was here, overseeing the rebuilding of the compound, and the building of... something else."

Saint didn't give a shit about any of that. "Leave with me. Right now. Walk away, Octavius. They don't..." He dragged a hand down his wet face and guarded his heart for the words that would come next. "They don't love you like I do. They will use you, they always have. And when done, they'll lock you away, or dust you, or bury you in a hole somewhere. It's what they do."

"You love me?" His smile emerged, wet with rain.

"Look at you, acting all surprised, as though you didn't already know."

"The Big Bad Wolf is in love with me?" His grin grew, thawing all that ice he wore as armor.

"You're brilliant, compassionate, quick to anger, sometimes a dick, but you'll never quit. I admire you, Little Wolf. And love you."

Octavius laughed softly, but that laugh soon faded. "I can't leave."

"I know." He'd always known, but he'd *hoped*.

"Saint, Mikalis was building a cage, like the cage he kept you in, but bigger and reenforced. It looks as though it's designed to hold a... monster."

"Or a god," Saint mused aloud. Mikalis was Erebus. And those theatrics back in the warehouse... There was no way all this was over.

Octavius nodded. "What if... we were wrong? What if I was wrong? I can't stop thinking about his last words, 'What have you done?' I know I did the right thing, I stopped him, we stopped Raiden, and you destroyed most of the nyks, but... what if I missed something? What if it's not over?"

Octavius would never rest. His instincts were telling him something was wrong, and he had to see that through. Jay was right, when he'd said Octavius would do the right thing. He'd always right the wrongs. Saint almost wished he was more like him, but for now, he'd have to settle for loving him instead.

He almost told him that Mikalis was Erebus, but it wouldn't change anything. It would only strengthen his desire to stay.

"I'd like you to stay because..." He hesitated and took a breath. "Because when I think of a life without you in it, I can't breathe, I can't think. I need you, Saint. You're in my head, my veins, you're in my heart. If that's love, then I feel it. I can't do this without you, or without Jayden. I need you both. But I know it's a lot to ask. I know you hate it here, and fuck, I know you and Storm will try and kill each other. Maybe I'm wrong, and it's all over, and if it is, then we'll ride off into the sunset together, fuck the world and the Brotherhood. But I can't leave just yet." He turned his head and gazed into Saint's eyes. "Will you stay?"

It wasn't going to be easy. Saint eyed the Atlas compound through the falling rain and felt its restraints try to tighten around him. But in truth, he couldn't walk away without Octavius. His heart would never allow it. And Jay wanted to go to college, put down roots, have a life. Saint would do anything for the pair of them, even give up his final ride into the sunset. Besides, what good was a happily ever after if he couldn't share it with the men he loved?

"We'll figure it out," Jay said, echoing Saint's earlier words.

"What did Storm say?" Saint asked. "You asked him if I can stay?"

"He said to keep you on a tight leash."

"That asshole."

"But he didn't say no. Because he knows he needs you. They all do. The others didn't stop your fight, and they could have. If Storm had ordered them to recapture you, they wouldn't have obeyed. Things have changed. *They've* changed. They care, they care about a lot of things. This is not the Brotherhood you knew."

"You know that for certain?" His little wolf's eyes glowed with certainty, and perhaps a touch of silver sparkling in their Brotherhood blue. Maybe he should believe him. He already believed *in* him.

"Yeah, I do. And Storm will come around."

Saint snorted. "Maybe I'll stay, just to see that."

"You will?" Octavius's eyebrows lifted in surprise.

"I'm here for you. Always. I'll fight nyks for you, topple gods, change the world for you. But don't ask me to do it for the Brotherhood. They do not deserve either of us."

Octavius grinned and leaned in. "Good enough." He laid a kiss onto Saint's lips. "And if anyone hurts you, I'll break their minds wide open."

Saint grinned into the kiss and encircled his arm around Octavius, drawing him close, intending to keep him close. "My fierce Little Wolf."

CHAPTER 42

ctavius

THE CAGE HAD BEEN BUILT into the Atlas compound blast crater far below ground level and stood several stories high. Too big to hold a nyk, it had to be for something *other*.

Octavius stood on the extended walkway that acted like a bridge to the middle of the cage wall. Next to the cage, he was a small thing, insignificant. And he didn't much like that feeling.

Whatever Mikalis's reasons for building it, he hoped it wasn't needed.

But feared the worst.

Nothing had changed inside him. The impending sense of dread hadn't waned. He still felt as though a delicate balance was about to tip off a ledge, as though they were all about to fall. They'd stopped Raiden, Mikalis was gone, and Nyx—or whatever that creature had been—appeared to have vanished. But he wasn't alone in fearing this wasn't over. The Brotherhood was on its knees, here and across the world. Atlas was as much dust as the nyks they'd killed during the New York uprising. And the world now knew monsters were real.

He had Saint, and Jayden, but it didn't feel like a happy ending. It felt like the beginning of something far worse than had come before. It felt as though whatever came next, the Brotherhood would need to be stronger, better, harder, and they'd need their godtouched alongside them to have any chance of surviving.

What have you done.

Octavius withdrew a crumpled note from his pocket, found by Zaine in the office Mikalis had been using here, and read the words again.

History is written by the winners

Nothing else, no date, no explanation, just those six words.

He grasped the safety rail and stared at the enormous metal and glass cage.

There was one fear that stuck in his mind, a fear that haunted him whenever he closed his eyes.

When it came to Mikalis, he feared he'd made a terrible mistake.

EREBUS AND HIS SISTER, NYX. DARKNESS AND NIGHT.
FROM THEIR UNION, TIME AND ORDER WERE BORN, TAMING
CHAOS BETWEEN THEM. BUT EREBUS SOUGHT MORE, ALWAYS
MORE, ALWAYS HUNGRY. HE TRIED TO CONSUME NYX, TRIED TO
KILL THE GREAT GODDESS. TO PROTECT HERSELF, THE
BOUNDLESS GODDESS STOLE FRAGMENTS OF EREBUS'S DARKNESS
AND MOLDED THEM INTO TWO ETERNAL WARRIORS. TWO FIRSTS,
AND WITH THEM AT HER SIDE, AND USING EREBUS'S OWN POWER
AGAINST HIM, SHE OVERPOWERED HER BROTHER, SEALING HIM AWAY
BETWEEN WORLDS, BEHIND DAWN'S FIRST LIGHT AND THE DYING NIGHT.

THE FIRSTS BEGAN THE NYKTELIOS. THEY BOWED ONLY TO NYX.
THEIR LIVES, AND THE LIVES OF THEIR PROGENY, SERVE THE GODDESS.
BUT ONE AMONG HER CHILDREN THEM SOUGHT TO TOPPLE HER REIGN,
AND TO FREE HER ETERNAL ENEMY EREBUS. THE TRAITOR CLAIMED
HE ONLY WISHED TO SAVE HER AND GAVE HER A SINGLE BLACK ROSE
AS A GIFT. WHILE DISTRACTED BY THE ROSE, THE TRAITOR TURNED
NYX'S OWN CREATIONS AGAINST HER... AND NYX WAS DRIVEN
INTO THE EDGES OF REALITY, BEHIND THE VEIL OF SHADOWS,
TRAPPED BEHIND DUSKLIGHT AND THE DYING DAY.

AND THERE EREBUS AND NYX REMAIN, LOCKED AT OPPOSITE ENDS
OF TIME, IMPRISONED BEHIND THE TWILIGHTS OF DUSK AND DAWN.

UNTIL THE SUN RISES NO MORE.

ALSO BY ARIANA NASH

Sign up to Ariana's newsletter so you don't miss all the news.

www.ariananashbooks.com

***

Shadows of London

(Five book urban fantasy series)

A sexy assassin, a billionaire boss with secrets, and magic bubbling up through the streets of London. All in a days work for artifact agent, John "Dom" Domenici.

Start the Shadows of London series with Twisted Pretty Things

***

Silk & Steel Series

(Complete four book dark fantasy series)

Elf assassin Eroan, falls for the dragon prince Lysander, in this heart-shattering star-crossed lovers tale.

"(Silk & Steel) will appeal to fans of CS Pacat's Captive Prince and Jex Lane's Beautiful Monsters." *R. A. Steffan, author of The Last Vampire.*

"A few pages in and I'm already hooked." *- Jex Lane, author of Beautiful Monsters.*

"The characters yank, twist, and shatter your heartstrings." -

Start the adventure with Silk & Steel, Silk & Steel #1

❦

Primal Sin

(Complete trilogy)

Angels and demons fight for love over London's battle-scarred streets.

Start the sinfully dark journey today, with **Primal Sin #1**

ABOUT THE AUTHOR

Born to wolves, Rainbow Award winner Ariana Nash only ventures from the Cornish moors when the moon is fat and the night alive with myths and legends. She captures those myths in glass jars and returning home, weaves them into stories filled with forbidden desires, fantasy realms, and wicked delights.

Sign up to her newsletter and get a free ebook here: https://www.subscribepage.com/silk-steel

Printed in the USA
CPSIA information can be obtained
at www.ICGtesting.com
LVHW042100261023
762248LV00031B/339/J